AFLP

Willis, Karen
River With No Bridge

Happy Reading!

8-18

This Large Print Book carries the
Seal of Approval of N.A.V.H.

RIVER WITH NO BRIDGE

KAREN WILLS

WHEELER PUBLISHING

A part of Gale, a Cengage Company

Farmington Hills, Mich • San Francisco • New York • Waterville, Maine
Meriden, Conn • Mason, Ohio • Chicago

Copyright © 2017 by Karen Wills.
Wheeler Publishing, a part of Gale, a Cengage Company.

Wheeler Publishing Large Print Western.
The text of this Large Print edition is unabridged.
Other aspects of the book may vary from the original edition.
Set in 16 pt. Plantin.

LIBRARY OF CONGRESS CIP DATA ON FILE.
CATALOGUING IN PUBLICATION FOR THIS BOOK
IS AVAILABLE FROM THE LIBRARY OF CONGRESS

ISBN-13: 978-1-4328-5309-9 (softcover)

Published in 2018 by arrangement with Karen Wills

Printed in Mexico
1 2 3 4 5 6 7 22 21 20 19 18

To my mother Evelyn Wills,
who gave me so much,
including the idea that
grew into this book.

CHAPTER ONE

Boston, February 1882

Nora Flanagan shivered as she strode from the Parker House Hotel's staff entrance into the winter night. In minutes her shoe leather and stockings were soaked through, coat and maid's uniform darkened wet at the hems, and she still faced a two-mile trudge to her tenement. Her worn heel skidded on treacherous ice, and she grabbed a stranglehold on a lamppost. An image of Paddy, her father, slipping under the horses' hooves leapt unbidden. Would icy streets always bring that memory?

Holding on, she lifted her face into the swirling snowfall that muffled the light. It would purify the city for a few hours before surrendering it back to dingy gray. Nora missed white flakes blanketing the Wicklow Hills of her childhood. She summoned memories of Ireland as she released her grip and walked on through the heavy flakes.

As though conjured by her footsteps crunching on fresh snow, a figure emerged from the alleyway ahead. Gaunt to the point of spectral, the woman carried a bundle that might be an unnaturally still baby. Dressed in rags, she spoke Gaelic in a thin, urgent voice, holding out a dirty hand, sores visible on her arm below a ragged sleeve. Nora froze.

A ghost from the Great Hunger? No, only another Irish woman crushed by circumstances.

Fear and pity competed in Nora's mind. Thugs hid behind such beggars, murder and assault common on these streets. Just last week a girl from Nora's tenement had been violated, beaten, and left for dead. Ready to crack skulls before falling victim to such a fate, Nora gripped Paddy's twelve-inch blackthorn shillelagh tucked in the special pocket she'd sewn. She should have stepped into the street even at the risk of being run down like Paddy, but memories of her da's broken body stopped her.

"Could you come out of the shadows, please?" She forced her voice to be firm. The woman, perhaps Nora's own age of eighteen, took a step forward, alone.

"I'll leave you a coin. Don't pick it up until I pass." Nora bent to set a dime on the streetlamp's plinth — who knew what disease the girl carried — before she caught her breath. What would Paddy Flanagan remark seeing her treat this poor unfortunate so? Despite his weakness for drink he always shared a kind word with the fallen and downtrodden, and he'd taught her to do the same regardless how tight money might be for them or how unappealing the destitute. "No. Let me hand it to you. I wish it could be more." She dropped the coin into the claw-like hand.

In response to the soft, Gaelic, "God bless you," Nora crossed herself and hurried on.

Thoughts of Paddy continued. Once when she was just a little red-haired snippet of a girl they'd come upon a magpie dragging an injured wing. Paddy had pulled the wagon to a stop, climbed down, picked up the bird, and fashioned a splint. She remembered his words, "Every feathered creature needs strong wings. They're like our dreams that carry us above our everyday woes. We'll have this good luck charm soaring into the clouds before we know it." They'd kept it until he pronounced it able to fly again. Nora wished she could've done the same for that hollow-eyed beggar girl.

A gleaming carriage careened around the corner. The driver lashed his sleek black horses with a great black whip, their hooves thundering. Nora heard the animals' hoarse breathing as she shrank back.

"Murderers! Arrogant robber baron!" She wailed after it barreled past. This could be the very Boston Brahmin whose carriage ran Paddy down on the cobbled street. Some callous rich man wanting his warm bath and clean sheets after sating his appetites in Boston's sordid North End. Pity any heedless creature wandering into his path.

Light-headed, Nora squared her shoulders, shuddered, and walked at a brisker pace. She'd gone too long without eating, but couldn't spend money for more than her one meal at night. She would go hungry before becoming like that desperate street girl. Nora still had work and a place to sleep, wash, and dress, dreary as her life might be. That wretched woman stood only a section below Nora on America's ladder that she'd dreamed of ascending, but in reality the rungs proved so precarious, so slippery.

Paddy had died with no money and worse, they owed rent. The collector had been by and given her a short extension, but he'd also eyed Nora up and down in a nasty way. Paddy'd been a drinker, but no man

14

would've dared leer at his daughter while he lived. Now she must navigate a social wilderness inhabited by predators ready to pounce on an orphaned immigrant girl.

At last Nora reached her tenement, climbed its porch steps, and entered the dim hallway. She grimaced. Gray, humped forms squeaked and scuttled along the cracked, uneven floor. Five by her count. Rats leaving their filthy droppings. Children went barefoot here. No wonder so many sickened and died. She'd stopped trying to learn their names, but she remembered bewildered eyes in grimy faces. Innocence deserved so much better.

She knew it irrational to fear rodents would run up her skirt with their twitching noses, but she always imagined their claws catching at her stockings, their teeth biting at her knees and thighs. She put her work-reddened hand to her mouth, fighting the urge to retch. The devils skittered on the stairwell. They must be in the very walls of this place, them and the roaches.

She stomped and braced to go forward, clomping heavily, watching to make sure none sat on the railing. What a disgusting sight to come home to. Vermin. They needed St. Patrick to lure them off as he'd done the snakes. Her neighbors here needed decent housing, medical help, even clothes. It all came down to needing better than slave wages.

A muscular orange cat leaped from a corner and seized a rat half its size. The victim's legs scrabbled at the air in futility as its tormentor carried it off. "Good for you, old tabby," Nora muttered. "Save the children." Cats grew fat in the North End.

Smells of cabbage, fish, and nameless stews mingled with odors of cramped and overcrowded rooms. The stench of poverty. Sounds of little ones' wheedling, whining voices, and quarrelling couples surrounded her as she climbed four stories to her thin-walled flat. Inside, the only light shone from the moon through the window.

Nora hung her coat on a nail, unbuttoned and removed her wet shoes, and slipped off her stockings. She put on a pair of worn slippers and padded to the window, undoing her collar and releasing her long red hair.

The moon hovered, a glowing cloud in the snowy sky. Nora pulled a threadbare shawl over her shoulders and warmed leftover stew on her hot plate, enough for a bowl containing a piece of meat with the cabbage. Trying not to fixate on the skeletal beggar or the black horses, she dragged a chair so she could eat before the window with the moon, at least, for company. The stew warmed her weary body, but she ached with missing Paddy always joking and telling stories across from her. She set the bowl aside. "I have nothing and nobody," she whispered in the emptiness. "What am I to do? What happened to America?"

Silence lived inside her flat while human life hummed in adjoining rooms where neighbors lived crowded, contentious lives, loving and bickering. She heated water, sponge-bathed, and climbed into an old nightgown. For some reason, tonight she prayed to St. Christopher for . . . what? She had no plans for further journeys, but she prayed to the patron saint of travelers anyway. She yearned to find a way out of all this. She'd thought adventure and respectability and freedom from want would all be hers when she left Ireland. Now she prayed for something, anything better than this solitary life of toil and degrading poverty. "St. Christopher, please give me a chance," she prayed. "I've come far, but this life is so hard. I'll better myself. I'll work to better myself, if you'll please give me one chance."

Next morning, Nora collided hard with her blank slate of a future. Cradling a stack of monogrammed linens against the dampened bosom of her uniform, sniffing the comfort of their hot, clean smell, she half ran through billowing steam in the laundry. Head down so, she rushed past burdened workers hauling tubs that sloshed with the menace of scalding water. Dulled by grief, she performed her tasks like an automaton.

Tade Larkin stood alone in the slanting light below the high window.

She crashed into him.

Stepping back she recognized him at once for one of the black Irish, a stocky blue-eyed man with the curling, thick hair that earned them their name. A burlap bundle rested at his feet. He grinned at her, and she found herself smiling in return at the open admiration in his blue eyes. She hadn't smiled since Paddy's death, but there was such a clean, open approval in this man's face. Their contact had been brief, but with something electric in it.

"May I help you, sir?" she bobbed a maid's curtsey, her heart inexplicably thumping against the shiny linens, a blush betraying her attempt at nonchalance.

"Would you be helping me all the way to Butte, America?" he asked, mock-beseeching. "No, the fact of it is, I'm looking for my aunt, Agnes Larkin. I'm Tade

Larkin, come over the water from County Cork."

"Nora Flanagan, Boston. Aggie finished her shift and went home."

He frowned and picked up his bundle, muscles straining against his jacket. She noticed his big hands. Since her tinker's childhood, Nora had relied on her survivor's instincts. They'd been asleep, but now reawakened. Could this man be a result of her prayers to St. Christopher? Could he be the start of a journey to something exciting? Better? Meeting him shook her from her dull sadness. How could she prevent his walking away, this clear-eyed man who looked at her with respect, not like so many who assumed an Irish hotel maid came with the room, to be used and left behind?

Nora cast back to his first words. "Butte? Where the miners go? It's really in Montana Territory in the West, isn't it?" So many questions. She'd barely spoken since losing her father. Now it seemed important to manage a whole conversation. She tried to slow her breathless prattle. "I have an old family friend there. She writes me from time to time."

"It is in Montana. They say the Irish get steady work in Butte and a fair wage, too, bringing out the ore. Sure, some of the men

19

from Cork are nearly there already — headed west straightway off the ship."

"What's the news from Ireland?" Her voice trembled. Her brother Seamus joined the rebellion so young, just a boy really, yet he died like a man when the British caught and hanged him. The steamy air turned stifling. She willed sorrow over Seamus to recede into the other griefs lingering in her heart's shadows.

If Tade noticed her distress, he didn't let on. "Let me buy you dinner when you're off work and I'll tell you. You can answer my questions about America."

Nora hesitated. She'd been so lonely, but wouldn't a social event during mourning show disrespect? Of course, her da wouldn't care for any outward show of grief. He hadn't cared about being respectable when she scolded him for drinking, had he? She winced, feeling guilty. Paddy's indulgence had mortified her often enough, but he never stopped encouraging her to pursue her dreams.

After the shattering news of Seamus's death, Paddy insisted, "We living owe it to the dead to make the most of our remaining days." Paddy loved life. Intuition and those words urged Nora to accept this invitation. She studied her shoes, then gave

Tade Larkin a level gaze. "Yes, but it has to be a decent restaurant, mind. No din of drinking songs with our talk."

"It will be your choice entirely." He stepped back, solid as one of those lovely male statues in the museum she sneaked off to see when she heard people describe them. She'd blushed as she admitted doing so in her first confession afterward.

For the next two hours, Nora moved in a daze as she dusted ornate armoires, changed the linen scarves on dressers, and made up high four-poster beds. She hadn't spent much time thinking of any man in particular, although her red hair and green eyes drew glances and unwanted propositions. A drunken guest once cornered her in his room. Luckily, his ice-eyed wife interrupted, tapping his shoulder. Life in Boston's tenements and this maid's job taught lessons no good Catholic girl in the old country would expect to learn.

Tade Larkin seemed both familiar and exciting. When she saw him, an image emerged of Ireland's green Wicklow Hills and foam-flecked strands, worlds within worlds where she'd once inhaled salty breezes from faraway American shores. She'd dreamed into clouds that flowered over the sea of some different life, one with challenges, but dignity, too. After four years in Boston's overcrowded North End, she'd all but given up. The Irish seemed destined for endless losses. But this manly Tade Larkin had a future. Even a melancholy Irish maid could see that.

Her shift over at last, she joined him by the servant's entrance. She'd have preferred they meet in the lobby under the chandelier radiating light lovely as rainbows, but the prissy manager would fire her on the spot if he caught her there. Tade offered his arm. She lifted her chin and slipped hers through the crook of his elbow, aware of his warmth. She was on her own time now and as good as any of the fine folk whose rooms she cleaned. Better than some by the look of their cast-off litter.

Nora had never been to the restaurant she chose, but always imagined it would be lovely, with candlelit tables and all. She'd never imagined herself there with a man as handsome as the one she sat across from now. As often happened in a port city, the restaurant stayed open all night, its dinner menu changing to breakfast offerings once dawn came round. Patrons took their time.

They ordered seafood stew served with

crusty bread. Nora wondered if Tade was as hungry as she, but both kept their manners, paying much more attention to each other than to the savory food. Over the scent of fresh bread, Nora told Tade how she came to Boston, crossing the ocean alone at fourteen to join her father, her life as a maid in the grand hotel, the prejudice that sometimes met her and those like her.

"I always loved books, even to hold them in my hands. They mean other worlds, ways to learn what a person needs to get on in life. I tried to get work in a bookshop. I dressed up in my finest and went to offer myself for the job. I was that nervous I didn't notice the sign in the window, 'No Irish Need Apply.' The toffee-nosed owner nearly pushed me out of the place. I'll never forget it." She felt her pale skin redden. Had telling that story been a mistake? He mustn't think her bitter or resentful.

"In Butte, it's 'Irish Should Apply.' " Tade tapped the tablecloth beside his plate for emphasis, making the candle's bright flame wobble.

"Well, this Butte, I hear the money's good, but it's a dirty town." *Now why had she said that?*

"Show me a miners' town that isn't. At least the Irish earn a living there."

"The men do well enough to buy their own houses, the hard workers at any rate. They send money back to their families, too." Nora struggled to remember everything she knew of the Montana city. She'd never suspected knowledge of it would be crucial. She had to keep Tade Larkin's interest. His earnest blue eyes interested her. "Would you believe my da told me the mines shut down on St. Patrick's Day?"

"I'm told they have churches as well, with Irish priests," Tade said. "Not like our troubles in Erin with the Fathers hiding in ditches and teaching school behind hedges, always in fear."

He changed the subject. "Do you live with your da?"

"You mean Paddy Flanagan that was." Sensitive to the slights of those who'd scorned her tinker family, Nora decided being honest was worth risking the truth. "I might as well tell you he loved his whiskey, and it killed him." She took a sip of tea that tasted bitter. "Da slipped and fell in the street outside our flat. He got run over by a rich man's speeding carriage. The wheels broke his neck. Whoever drove over him just kept going, leaving him in the gutter, broken so. As though he were not even a man, just trash."

her as she fought for breath in a storm-
roiled sea.

CHAPTER TWO

As winter dawdled into spring, Nora not only grieved for her rapscallion father, but obsessed over Tade Larkin. Could he be all he seemed? He still wanted her to come, didn't he? For six weeks she heard nothing. Had something happened to him? Had he forgotten her? Met another girl? She sifted through memories of their conversation. Had she told too much? Not every respectable man, even one with little education, would look twice at a tinker's brat. Why had she let raw hope slip back into her life?

She'd all but given up when his letter arrived. Nora recognized Rose Murphy's round handwriting, but the words were Tade's. Riveted, she read that he had a job. He assured her that maid positions awaited young women at Butte establishments like the Hotel de Mineral and the Centennial, boardinghouses, and the few lace-curtained Irish homes.

30

Nora grimaced. It seemed there would always be people who wanted the likes of Nora Flanagan to clean up after them. Would it just be more of the same, only in the rough frontier?

Was her attraction to Tade Larkin drawing her into something even worse than the North End?

But Rose ended with a few lines of her own. "He's a fine fellow, Nora. A blind man could see how high he places you. Respectful and smitten, for certain. Patrick and I would love for you to come and stay with us and our four girls. What a grand time we could have. Come on. Join us here in Butte. Oh, it's so very sorry we are about Paddy. He was a sweet man."

Nora wrote back that she'd love to see Rose, and praised Tade for his hard work. She was so pleased for him. She asked questions about the journey, and admitted trying to save for the fare.

In his next letter, Tade sent money. "I don't go to the pub with the boys so much," he wrote. "There's more for a man to aim at than draining his glass. I want a house and a family in it. We're both alone, Nora. I don't mean to rush you. I just wish you'd come see the place for yourself. See me again, too, before you forget my ugly mug.

I'll never forget your green eyes. If you find the place and me to your liking, perhaps we could consider marriage." Yes, she thought, this man who lit up her heart might also enable her to break poverty's shackles and achieve her dreams.

Nora fingered the money, sitting up late, analyzing her life. If he'd lied about the pub, Rose would have warned her. Drudgery at the hotel for slave wages paled against vivid images of traveling west to be with this handsome, decent man. In these weeks since she met Tade Larkin, two more children had died in her tenement. She'd also been aware of the defeated faces of unmarried maids ten years her senior still eking out an existence toiling at the Parker House.

And hadn't she already taken one great risk in sailing to America? If Boston wasn't the destiny she'd dreamed of, perhaps in Butte she could find freedom from want and prejudice. Tade appeared like the brass ring on the merry-go-round at the park. You only got to go around so many times. His blue, honest eyes, his warm smile, his hopes for her. A house of their own. She answered in a firm hand. She would start her journey in May, a good time to travel.

She'd nearly stopped dreaming of bettering herself. It hurt to start again, but the pain reminded her she still lived, still had a life before her. This differed from the heart-stopping moments when she missed her father.

Perhaps the name of this pain was love.

Nora wore her mourning coat from the moment she boarded the first of several confusing spur lines in Boston. Seated in the hot passenger car, she perspired in misery, suspicious that she even "glowed" not so much like a genteel lady as a lantern. Her waist itched from sweat caught under her belt, drying, dampening again. She squirmed against the tufted wool upholstery. One loose button had poked her in the back since she changed to the Union Pacific in Chicago.

Her round-topped trunk swayed in the baggage compartment. Her worn satchel slumped against her feet. When Nora sailed from Ireland, missing those left behind battered her like cold Atlantic waves. Despite grimy rigors of travel, fusty, jostling crowds in depots, and shaky moments over this reckless thrust into America's West, Nora told herself she'd made the right decision. There were Irish in Butte, America. Tade Larkin with his gentle voice and big sheltering frame wanted her to come. But she'd started the trip with little money, and that went so fast. She would be penniless by Butte.

She adjusted her window shade. Through dust-specked glass, she gazed at forested foothills seamed by tumbling rivers. Scenery had become mountainous, its mystery both compelling and frightening as the train surged north. She'd only eaten in the dining cars twice. She could feel her stomach rumble. Thank heavens the noise of wheels on tracks drowned out others hearing it.

At Shoshone, Idaho, passengers disembarked and rode carriages to view Shoshone Falls, the Niagara of the West. Nora drank in breaths of air that almost fizzed like champagne. She heard the water's thunder before she alighted to walk toward the falls, captivated at once by its savage beauty. She stopped, transfixed, taken aback by a sense of intimacy that she couldn't distinguish as strictly physical or spiritual. If nature were a goddess, like in the Greek stories the priest had taught them, then this would surely be her very pounding heart.

Foam rose into spray and then mist that chilled surrounding air. A rainbow arced above all that relentless roar. Nora had never been anywhere so pure, elemental, and untouchable. The great falls and the airy, light-filled prism rising from its base became a glorious sign for her journey, lifting her out of weariness and gnawing hunger.

Comforted, staring wide-eyed into the tumult, she offered a quick prayer of relief and thanks, crossing herself discretely with a travel-smudged glove.

After her train switched back east toward Butte, man-made structures announced civilization at longer intervals until they became rare sights against the darkening backdrop of wilderness.

How vast America was, how various her people. All sorts boarded and disembarked. Nora made a solitary game of pegging fellow passengers by occupation. She judged one man with an expensive suit and elegant silver-flecked sideburns, fixated on a small black book, to be a banker. Another in a thick wool jacket, trousers tucked into boots, had to be a railroad worker heading home, a miner like Tade, or maybe a logger. A pockmarked young fellow in an ill-fitting suit and thick glasses, she judged a school-teacher. A blowsy woman who'd struck up a noisy conversation with a cowboy wouldn't be respectable, saloon work or worse her lot.

Nora avoided eye contact with any. Late-afternoon sun sagged behind the summit of an unknown mountain. Another friendless end to another friendless day. She nibbled on a bun purchased at one of the water stops. It would be her last food before Butte. Finishing it, drumming her fingers on the armrest, she dared peek at the dapper neighbor across from her as he rattled his newspaper. Its masthead read, *The Butte Miner,* May 14, 1882.

He'd boarded at Shoshone. This one's long, tapered fingers had never gripped pick or shovel. Besides, he sported a meticulously etched mustache. Odd.

Catching her glance, he smiled and offered his paper. She sat forward, flustered.

He spoke anyway. "Fate has seen fit to throw us together as strangers in a strange land. Let's not stay that way. I'm Bat Moriarty, late of Boise, Coeur d'Alene, and Shoshone. I do travel."

"Nora Flanagan." Nora managed a prim smile, then turned her profile to him to discourage conversation. She'd had the full impact of his dark good looks, though. An Irish name, dark hair, brown eyes. Some Spanish blood, she guessed. Sailors in his family history.

"Nora Flanagan? Let me guess." Bat ran

tic raspberries that made Nora laugh in spite of her fatigue. They set off on foot, passing a lumber company, outbuildings, feed stores, the occasional log cabin, and taller buildings along a dirt roadway. Rose pointed out the imposing Star livery on the corner of Galena and Main. Rose's little Annie began to insist they should go in there. Rose objected, but the child stamped her foot. "I promised Tade. I promised to make you."

"But it's all but in the middle of Chinatown." Rose frowned. "What on earth? Well, all right."

They passed into a neighborhood where a few Chinese men moved about. Nora tried not to stare at their dress of loose baggy trousers, shirts of silk or cotton buttoned from neck to hem, and floppy, heelless slippers. They covered their heads with high binder hats or tight silk skullcaps, the hair beneath in braided queues. The stores were log cabins with picture-like writing on the fronts. Pungent odors wafted into the street, reminding Nora of her hunger gnawing to near nausea.

Rose sniffed. "Noodle parlors, herb shops, laundries. They're all right, but not the gambling and opium dens. And what do you think? They keep women as slaves. They sell them." Rose nodded toward the only two-story structure. "That's the Joss house. They practice their heathen religion upstairs. Their political gangs, the tongs, meet on the main floor. Pay them no mind."

At the livery, they learned to their delight that Tade had paid for a wagon to carry them all the way to Dublin Gulch. Nora looked back at the Chinese neighborhood. She'd expected none but Irish in Butte. Rose explained there were also Cornish, Finns, and Welsh come to be miners.

When the road ran out, they walked up the hill. Hard-packed dirt surrounded scattered, one-story houses gray from smoke. But Rose said she and Patrick paid timely on their little mortgaged home, filling it with noisy daughters.

Rose glowed with pride as she showed her friend through the dark entryway-kitchen, small parlor, and two bedrooms. A privy stood in back. No trees grew in Dublin Gulch. Exhausted, starving, and overtaken with longing for the green of Ireland, Nora blinked against unexpected tears.

"Nora, what is it?" Rose touched her arm.

"Oh, it's nothing. You've a sweet home, Rose. I just need a bite to eat."

"Heaven forgive me," Rose stated. "You must be famished!"

delight. She did what she'd wanted to do since meeting him, and ran her fingers through the tangle of his black hair.

At the table Patrick told dramatic and funny stories about Butte life. After Tade's reluctant departure, all hurried to bed. Nora lay awake on the lumpy couch, unable to shake the sensation of train wheels rolling under her. She stretched, releasing the ache of travel in her hips, playing the evening over and over, a song with an escalating tempo. Tade was poor yet, and she poorer still. Too soon to think of marriage. And this Butte, just a rung up from a mining camp. She turned over, unyielding bumps pressing into her shoulder. She must find work.

Later in the hushed house, she heard the rhythmic creak of bedsprings supporting Rose and Patrick's lovemaking. She'd learned that sound as a hotel maid. Making another baby, Nora thought. Wasn't their little shotgun house so cramped already? Dear Rose handled it all with harried grace. The warmth and love of family would make it worthwhile. Nora felt stronger, less bereft, here with people who cared about this tinker's orphan.

CHAPTER THREE

Morning started early. Helping dress the children and tidy up after breakfast, Nora tried not to recoil when Rose threw their slops outside. She'd not seen such disposing of waste since childhood. Dublin Gulch already stank from rotting meat, vegetable scraps, sewage and fumes from nearby smelters. Rose saw her expression and shrugged. "Where else can we put it?"

Nora remembered losses to illness in unsanitary tenements. She hoped it wouldn't happen here.

Later that morning, Nora started on foot to the Centennial Hotel on the corner of Main and Granite. She first saw the false front identifying it. A terrace ran across the second story. She sighed. No chandelier would grace this place. She stepped inside a lobby filled with men smoking cigars and reading the *Butte Miner.* Through an adjoining door to the left, she noted a high-ceilinged dining room. Nora approached a man in a gray silk vest, manning the desk with an alert, proprietary air. He studied her through thick, round glasses.

Why, Nora asked herself, do these desk-minding boys always resemble each other? Like dogs guarding their masters' gates.

"May I help you, miss?"

"I would like to speak to the manager about employment. Is he in?" Nora felt her confidence slump under the clerk's stare. He gestured with a knobby wrist for her to follow.

Frank Flynn stood as they made introductions. Behind his desk, rocks sat from floor to ceiling in glass cases, a mineral collection Nora would learn was the manager's passion. Perusing Nora's references, he said, "We just lost a girl to matrimony, so we can benefit each other."

"I'm used to working in a good hotel." Nora tried to convey faith in her own competence without sounding smug. She needed this job, a rung up that slippery ladder.

"But you're not used to working in one where all the help is Irish and many speak Gaelic." Flynn had a boyish smile.

"Oh, I understand Irish," Nora said,

"although I don't speak it except for a little."

"You'll be paid twenty-five cents a day. I believe we'll assign you to housekeeping and kitchen work. Will that suit?"

With a flash of joy, Nora let her tension melt. "Indeed, sir. I'm happy for the job."

He spoke to the clerk. In moments a young blonde woman in a maid's uniform appeared.

"Bridget, this is Nora Flanagan come to work with us," the manager announced. "Nora, meet Bridget Kennedy. Help Nora find a uniform. She's on straightaway, the lucky girl."

They started in the lobby, a room of pine and horsehair furniture. After the dining room and kitchen the two looked into the attached saloon, its burnished oak bar lined with glittering bottles, a mirror above it. A few men with creased faces nursed beer or whiskey even in the morning. Nora noticed a poker game in progress and chuckled. Bat Moriarty sat at the table, the mystery of his soft hands solved.

Bridget's blue eyes widened. "Why are you staring at Bat Moriarty? Don't tell me the man has managed to turn your head when you only just arrived yesterday."

"I met him on the train. Now I see why he made fun of miners. The rascal's a gambler." He sat half-turned from her, cards in his hands. It was a quiet game, but something one of the other players said amused him. His laugh sounded smooth and deep, like a stone under water. She judged it a poor second to Tade's open and frequent shout of cloudless delight.

"He's a black-hearted charmer with the ladies so," Bridget whispered.

"Is that something you'd be knowing from experience?" Nora teased.

Bridget shook her head. "Not I. I keep company with a steady man from the mines, but another girl left here with her heart broken in little pieces right along with her reputation. Bat Moriarty had been giving her attention at the same time he kept Cat Posey busy."

"Who's Cat Posey?"

"No one for us or any other decent woman to speak of. She's one of the girls at Erin's Joys. It's the only bawdy house in Butte with Gaelic-speaking girls. Bat Moriarty gambles there, and they say he's thick as honey with Cat Posey."

Nora shuddered. "What a way for the Irish to show themselves. As if we didn't have a hard enough time making ourselves respectable."

"Aye, true enough. Let me show you a

room or two." Bridget leading, they climbed the staircase to a shadowed corridor. Nora had an impression of men crowded into close quarters, not too clean by the sour smell of the hall.

They ended with the basement where a changing room sat next to the laundry. Nora noted the baths and toilets, all dark and stuffy, and made a face. "It's none too fresh down here, is it?"

"It's what we have. There's an icehouse and storage buildings out back. The best air and cleanest rooms are in the saloons, but you wouldn't want to work in one of them, Nora."

In her new uniform, a black dress and white apron like Bridget's, Nora started in changing bedding and setting out clean towels. The sheets and linens, along with the clothes of some of the men, gave off smoky puffs.

"It's silicate dust," Tade explained that night. "It's not good for us. Seems like all the men get 'rocks on the chest' sooner or later, some of the women as well. There's many buried from the consumption, but we need the steady work, don't we?"

Nora shuddered. Why were the lower classes always exposed to the horrors that await those who shovel, remove, and inhale the worst the earth can give? Anger flashed through her. "Oh, yes. We from Erin always need steady work. That we do." Consumption had claimed her mother. They could make a living in Butte, but the mines held menace seen and unseen.

And steady work it turned out to be. Nora reported to the kitchen before daylight, her hands red and damp by noon when she started on rooms. The work tired her, but camaraderie among the maids brought fun to cleaning even the messes hard-living miners left behind.

Bat Moriarty became a subject of discussions. Two maids claimed he repulsed them, while one confessed she dreamed of him in ways that made her blush. One afternoon Nora opened a door believing the room unoccupied. She stooped to smooth a wrinkle in the carpet. When she raised her eyes, she returned Bat Moriarty's bemused gaze.

The gambler poured water from a pitcher to a bowl. His shirt lay on the bed along with his vest, shoulder holster, and pistol. Water glistened on his bare chest as he turned back to her. "Sweet Jesus, girl. You look like you've seen a ghost. It's only a man with his shirt off."

"I mistook the room to be empty — I'll just leave these towels." Nora averted her eyes.

"Wait. It's Nora Flanagan from the train, isn't it? Don't run off. I'll put my shirt on so we'll be quite beyond reproach."

"I've work to do. I mustn't lollygag." Nora felt like an idiot.

"Work can wait. I didn't know you hired on here. How are you finding Butte, America?" He smiled, white teeth startling under the slope of his dark mustache.

Nora tried to keep from glancing at his chest, smooth and hairless, but lean and powerful, too. She'd never seen Tade so. She needed to escape this impropriety. What the girls giggled over in the kitchen about Bat and the notorious Cat Posey rose to mind. "I find it a dirty city as you said, but it seems a fine start for the Irish in America." She hated her voice for shaking.

He stepped toward her. "You're a lovely addition to the place, Nora. Don't be thinking it more than it is, though. I told you the Irish have paved these streets with their bones. An Irishman knows how to dig, and that's what he does here. But look about you at the blind and those missing limbs." He buttoned his shirt. "Don't you have a sweetheart? A man from Cork, was it?"

"Aye, a good, careful worker. He takes pride in what he does, and I take pride in it as well."

Bat laughed that melodious, insinuating sound. "As opposed to being a gambler. You're too good for the likes of me. I can see that. Your man is lucky in his woman, at least." Without warning, he stepped forward, took one of her hands, and touched it to his lips.

His lips felt soft below the fringe of mustache. Nora caught the scent of musky pomade. She pulled away, lips parted in surprise, then whisked out the door. She felt mortified — an awareness that brought its own chagrin — because her hand was rough, and her fingers smelled of onions.

Even worse, Mr. Flynn strode toward her. He frowned, unusual for his pleasant countenance. "What's wrong, Nora? You look pale. Has anyone bothered you?" He kept strict rules about guests observing propriety with the maids.

"Oh, no. It was my fault. I thought a room to be empty, and it was not, for certain."

Flynn laughed. "Always knock, young lady. These brutes are healthy men, after all."

Nora nodded. So they were. Healthy men after all.

■ ■ ■ ■

That evening talk turned to the coming community picnic, when even the mines would be shut down. "It's a great occasion," Rose explained. "There'll be bars, a lunch counter, athletic contests, and a dance hall, all set up for a few thousand of us. The money — 35 cents a ticket — goes for a free Ireland."

"What a lovely idea," Nora said. "But I wonder if I'll get the day off. In Boston, a maid would be fired for the impertinence of asking."

Tade laughed. "Flynn's no tyrant. Just say, 'Mr. Flynn, I'm wondering if I might have time off for the picnic. My friends that have been so kind, they've asked to take me.' Stand respectful before him. You won't have to elaborate."

Nora pictured her boss leaning back, frowning, then bestowing one of his infectious smiles. What he actually said next day was, "All our guests will be there anyway. We'll get old Fritz and a couple Chinamen to keep the place going and we'll all be off."

On the day of the picnic Rose and Nora were up by first light. Both wore white shirtwaists with lace yokes and pleated oval bosoms. Nora fastened her hair at the nape of her neck and topped it with a straw hat trimmed in a cotton print that matched her green skirt.

She glanced in the mirror. A pinched, wan excuse for a face stared back. I'm growing pale, she thought with dismay. How many weeks since she'd moved through clean air and sunshine? She squeezed her cheeks, creating a temporary blush that failed as a substitute for health's ripe glow. Would Tade notice her brightness fading? She frowned. If ever she dared depend on a man, it must be Tade Larkin. Hadn't she come across the country counting on that very thing? He'd never abandon her. She thought back to the worn-out single maids at the Parker House. Had they still held out hope for a better life? Their faces said not.

Light-hearted workers and families rode in horse-drawn bench wagons. Ascending from the yellow smoke and ceaseless industrial noise, they progressed toward a sky that turned a darker blue the higher they went. Nora all but gawked at the multi-shaded forests of the foothills. Bright mountain water rippled over mauve and aqua rocks. The sun warmed her upturned face. When a vivid mountain bluebird sailed overhead, she joined the Murphy girls clapping and cheering.

The wagon creaked to a stop at last. A stream of people sauntered past striped tents, makeshift booths, and a long, crowded lunch counter. The breeze carried the scents of meat cooking, pies baking, and fresh bread served by overworked but smiling women.

Tade stepped from under its awning. Nora waved, but willed herself to wait for him to come to her. He took her hand, saying, "I'm playing in the Gaelic Football League this afternoon. Will you come and cheer me on?"

"Football? Is it bashed and bloody you'll be?" Nora felt a stab of impatience. Why did men love such games? Hadn't they learned that life is fragile enough without unnecessary risks? "I'll come, but I'll shut my eyes."

"I promise I'll come out of it alive. And I'll make you proud."

Rose and Nora picked a quiet patch under huge ponderosas to spread a blanket. Rose rested her broad back against a pine trunk's rough bark. She played with Tillie, a fat, perpetually astonished baby, who took her first staggering steps on the uneven forest floor. Tillie frowned as she concentrated on her high-legged walk, straddling nothing but air.

Tade extended his hand to Nora. Wandering among the crowds, they stopped to watch the drill contest. Two giants stood on a raised platform, a block of granite in front of them. "Watch these boys." Tade spoke with reverence. "There's none can hold a candle to them."

Indeed, when the competition started Nora understood. While one brought down the double jack, the other held and turned the steel drill after each blow. In fifteen minutes the team had drilled a hole forty-five inches deep in granite. The crowd's approving roar shook the ground, vibrating the soles of Nora's feet until they itched.

At the knife-throwing contest, Nora nearly stumbled in surprise. Bat Moriarty waited his turn to throw a bone-handled knife.

"Well, if it isn't Bat Moriarty, the gambler." Tade bent to speak in Nora's ear. "I've met him in the saloon the few times I've gone there. He's one to avoid. We won't let the likes of him in the Ancient Order of Hibernians."

Bat turned, rolling snow-white shirtsleeves above forearms with small wrists, but muscles well defined toward the elbows. His frock coat and vest were thrown over a nearby chair. He still wore his bowler, tipped far back. When he noticed Nora, he flashed his white-toothed smile and approached with movements slightly less intense than a prowl.

"Miss Flanagan, you've escaped the city that's paved with the bones of Irishmen, if only for a day. Is it still to your liking?"

Nora kept her arm through Tade's. He covered it with his square, callused hand, and Nora thought it good and forthright compared to the smooth, tapering fingers of the knife-wielding gambler. "I like it well enough," she answered, then explained to Tade how she and the gambler had met.

"I'm surprised to see you in a contest such as this one, Moriarty," Tade interjected. He straightened, and Nora could swear her sweetheart puffed out his chest like a rooster.

"A man needs to know how to protect himself when sensitive situations arise. Cat Posey came at me with her knife two nights ago. I didn't kill Cat," Bat said, his grin wicked, "but I pinned her to the bar by her skirts. I see it's time to start. Excuse me."

As Nora and Tade turned to walk on, a rush of chill breeze stirred the tops of the pines. Nora shivered at their sound of a thousand sighs. Open talk of Cat Posey annoyed her. All combined, it seemed a harbinger of bad weather within and without. A white banner of cloud hooked on one snag like a flag of surrender.

She calmed as they waited in a long line for mugs of lemonade and meatloaf sandwiches to carry back to share with the others. The Murphy girls gathered wildflowers, black-eyed Susans, violets, and treacherous, thorny wild roses while Nora and Tade settled on the ground.

"It's a different world, entirely," Nora murmured, drawing in air laced with tangy pine. Another breeze lifted the blanket's corner and swirled pine needles up from the forest floor. She squinted and brushed at her face.

After they'd eaten, Tade urged, "Come walk just a bit more with me." They crossed a shallow stream, balancing on flat rocks. More wildflowers riffled on its banks. Bulky clouds shouldered into the bright sky.

"Sure and it's beautiful. Nothing like that loud jungle of a place below," Nora said.

"Butte is a booming city." Tade enfolded her hands in his as though praying. "A man can marry there and raise children and keep them fed, clothed, and educated. And that's what I want. It would be sweet to me if you would be the wife I dream of. I love you. Ever since you near knocked me over in Boston."

"Tade." Nora breathed a prayer of thanks that he'd finally asked, that she'd been right to come, that she had won the heart of such a fine man, that she had someone of her own. She touched his square jaw and said, "When I'm with you I feel as much at home as I did in Ireland. Of course, I'll marry you. There's hardly been a doubt about that, now has there?"

Tade gathered her to him, and they kissed. When his breathing quickened, she moved to look at him. "Let's tell Rose and Patrick now, sweetheart. The rest must wait."

For a moment she wished they could stay forever in this meadow that felt like a sanctuary. But then, she thought, we would be poor and hungry. No more of that. Not for us.

Patrick and Rose hugged the engaged pair with boisterous congratulations.

Patrick thumped Tade on the back. "Grand news, but it's time for the game. We'll leave the women to talk of less important matters." The two men left together, laughing.

Nora and Rose spoke of housing and

clothes and the life of married women. And the wedding. "The only decent thing I own is this shirtwaist. I can't afford a new dress," Nora said.

Rose shook the blanket-tablecloth in a fierce billow. "Let's talk to Molly Boyle, a fine seamstress. She might know of something to be done. I saw her here today."

Walking to the game, Nora carried solid little Tillie, the Murphy daughters following behind like ducklings. The littlest started to cry as more dirt and needles swirled into their faces, the wind stronger and colder. "There's Molly," Rose said, pointing at an angular, severe-faced woman. Rose introduced Nora, and they spoke about her need for a wedding dress as the wind flattened and whipped their skirts.

"I tell you, I believe I can help," Molly raised her voice to be heard above the soughing pines. "I ordered navy corduroy for a Welshmen who planned on going home dressed like a toff. But he went home in a coffin, leaving me with the goods. It's a soft material. I can let you have it on the cheap if you don't mind the story."

Nora did mind the story. The chill wind invading her engagement day along with this tale of the unlucky Welshman combined to flatten her spirits. Joyous as she'd felt, omens now conjured the despairing, helpless gloom that she'd hoped Tade's proposal had banished forever.

"Patrick and I will help as our gift," Rose said, interrupting Nora's somber thoughts. It was a generous offer and after all, the Welshman hadn't touched the cloth. Rose and Molly waited.

Foolishness, Nora chided herself. I mustn't take a cool breeze and another's bad luck as some dark portent. She accepted, forcing a smile and pushing away thoughts of the Welshman.

Nora, Rose, and the girls, fidgeting with eagerness to see their father and Tade play, found seats on makeshift benches, snuggling together for warmth as the game began.

The Gaelic football teams were divided by mines. It was an old game, dating in Ireland back to the sixteenth century. Nora hadn't seen it played in Boston. Now she remembered its exuberant violence. Tade and the others crashed into one another with sickening thuds. Nora clutched her handkerchief and cried out as a giant on the other side tackled Tade and both came up with bloodied noses. Her gentle Tade blackened another man's eye in the battle to get the ball, the *lithroid croise,* in the proper place. Nora squeezed her eyes shut, but the grunts, snaps, and shouts of players and onlookers sounded all the louder. She peeked again.

Tade moved gracefully for a man so big, and in spite of alarm for his well-being and shock at the unharnessed aggression, Nora felt a thrill of pride and desire. Tade looked every bit the Irish hero with his black hair and muscular body. The fearful wind died down during the game, and Nora relaxed into the fun.

A chill wind meant nothing. She must learn to truly believe in the future as Tade did.

Tade's team won and celebrated with mugs of stout, cigars cocked between split lips below swollen black eyes. At the evening's dance the blind fiddler stopped his reel. "We've just been informed that Nora Flanagan and Tade Larkin are engaged. Let's have the sweethearts lead this waltz." He tucked the fiddle under his chin and began the tender melody.

Nora's heart filled. She'd found a wonderful man, a fortress. She had something real to make her proud. People surrounded them, friends who'd made something of themselves, happy for their happiness. White stars hung overhead as Nora floated in Tade's arms. She remembered how on that first evening in Butte, she feared she'd taken too great a risk. Foolish. Because she'd come to be with this man she loved, she faced no risk at all, did she?

Long into the night they listened to impassioned speeches for Irish independence. Political rhetoric filled every gathering of Butte. When stars washed into the graying dawn sky, parents wrapped blankets around sleeping children flushed from sun and fresh air and tucked them into wagons.

Nora pillowed her head on Tade's shoulder. Their wagon lurched in uneven ruts while it bore them down to the sulfurous smoke and wrenching noise of Butte, America.

■ ■ ■ ■

On her August wedding day, Nora awakened on the horsehair couch, stretched, flung her arms out and thought how she'd never awaken alone again, or in someone else's parlor. The shrill blasts wouldn't summon Tade Larkin this day. This day belonged to the two of them. Mrs. Tade Larkin. The tinker's child come up in the world.

Nora Larkin. Future proud mother to a brood of Larkin sons and daughters. The thought of the change that would take place this night brought only a little fear. Guests of Boston's grand Parker House often emerged from their rooms looking downright smug, altogether pleased with whatever had gone on before they dressed to go out. Tade, gentle loving man. She flung the covers off and put her virginal feet on the floor. After tonight she would wake every morning to Tade's blue eyes gazing into hers.

She spent the morning bathing and putting up her hair. In late afternoon she dressed in the navy and lace wedding gown. She joined Rose and the girls who hushed, for once shy and impressed. Rose would tell her later that her daughters played "Nora's Wedding" for months afterward.

■ ■ ■ ■

At St. Patrick's church, the Irish community turned out in its finery. Tade, his expression solemn, wore a black suit. He'd slicked back his unruly hair. Nora wore hers upswept with little tendrils falling to the lace collar.

As she stood poised on Patrick's arm, inhaling the scent of flowers and candle flame, for one terrible moment the packed church felt indifferent, empty. Smiling faces craned toward her, but all day she'd been trying not to pine for family gone before or left behind. To steady herself, Nora used an old ploy from childhood and imagined her mother, whom she missed most of all, smiling down to sooth and reassure her.

The organist commenced. Nora nodded to Patrick to begin their walk toward the altar. Tade Larkin held out his hand for hers long before she could reach him. At the aisle's end, she detached herself from Patrick and placed her hand in Tade's. He was her family now.

Kneeling before the priest, they recited their vows. Nora heard Rose sniffle and wondered why people cry at weddings. All she felt as Tade slipped the ring on her finger was joy. They kissed with the priest's permission and turned to face the room filled with smiling faces.

The wedding dance in Hibernia Hall became a raucous celebration. Shuffles, slides, and stomps vibrated the floor. The blind fiddler who'd announced their engagement led the band with even the crinkled lids around his milky eyes joined in his smile. A tenor sang. Rose and Patrick managed a sedate waltz or two despite Rose's pregnant condition, which gave her the appearance of a frigate, its sails billowing.

Nora grew giddy as Tade swung her in looping circles. Men cut in, and all but once Tade relinquished his bride without hesitation. On that occasion they turned and looked into the fathomless dark pools of Bat Moriarty's eyes.

"Moriarty. Are you daft?" Tade bristled. "What man would let his wife dance with the likes of you?"

Bat's eyes glittered, narrowed, then widened again so quickly Nora almost missed the shift. For the first time she wondered if he might truly be dangerous. "This is America, Larkin. Why don't you let your wife speak for herself?"

"I'm the husband. I speak for us both."

Nora giggled at hearing the word *wife* applied to herself and Tade calling himself the husband. Did he imagine she couldn't make her own decisions? Still a bit light-headed, she gave his arm a gentle prod. "Dear, don't be silly. What would Mr. Moriarty do to me? Sure and he told me all about this country on the train coming out, and I still arrived in one piece."

Tade's fierce look softened. "All right, but it will be this once and not again."

Bat's white teeth gleamed as he gave Tade a wolfish smile. The long deft fingers of his left hand nearly encircled Nora's waist. It already felt unnatural to be touched by hands not rough enough to catch on the soft material there.

"You are beautiful, Mrs. Larkin. This blue becomes you much more than black."

"Well, I've Tade to thank for making all this happen. We bought ourselves a house, you know." Nora didn't care if that sounded proud.

"And soon you'll have it full to the rafters with little red- and black-haired Larkins."

"And have you never wished to fill a house with babies, Mr. Moriarty?"

"If they could have been with the right woman, Nora, if they could have been . . ." For one instant he dropped the customary mocking smile. Was that self-pity, or was he teasing her?

"Mr. Moriarty, I would bore a man like you, and well you know it. Sure and you're only flirting because I'm unavailable. I didn't fascinate you one little bit on the train."

"You did fascinate me," he protested, the devilish smile returning. "Every minute."

The music stopped. Tade appeared, reclaiming Nora. They danced again until without warning he lifted Nora into his arms and whirled her around and around.

"Say good night to the Larkins," he cried. "We're off to our own home." With that he carried Nora out the door, all the way to their house, over the threshold, and into their bedroom.

The coverlet had been turned down. Soon, the blue wedding dress settled on a chair, as did the corset, pantaloons, shoes, and stockings. Tade undressed as Nora lay warm and watching. When he approached in the flickering light of one candle, she reached for him. He brushed her with his body, so massive yet seeming weightless as he took such care not to hurt her. She tightened her hold, pulling him down to lie full length on her, this man who had called to her all her life. He touched, kissed, caressed her until she felt surrounded, as if water flowed around her and she were floating in his protective, possessing arms. Then mists over green hills swirled and hovered over a sea — such a sea as she had never known. Nora's cries were muffled against her husband's shoulder until the sea quieted and the mists dissolved.

Her voyage had been long, but she'd found her safe harbor. The candle sputtered and went out.

CHAPTER FIVE

Nora and Tade developed the endearments and games of contented lovers. Nora's life became a routine of housework, never quite giving in to the smoke and grime, going to the market, and taking part in church matters with other married women. She didn't miss the Centennial, but did miss Bridget and the other maids' irreverent joking. Butte's single and married women moved in separate circles.

They created a space in their lives each evening that she'd never forget. Tade seldom stopped for a pint with the others and took loud ribbing for it, but he tromped straight from the Neversweat to his Nora. She prepared his bath every night. It took a long time to heat water and fill the tub, but she loved his enjoyment of it. Tade would come in, kiss her, and take off clothes filthy from the mine. She poured the last kettle of steaming water into the galvanized tub and rolled up her sleeves to scrub her husband's back, bringing a ruddy glow to the pale skin over his hard muscles as he groaned in pleasure.

She doted on the male smell of him and his big body, sculpted by labor and powerful from good health. As she dribbled soapy water along his shoulders, he told stories of Cork. More than once her stroking and their laughter ended in whoops and a great thrashing of water, most spilled on the floor, and Nora carried into bed, clothes dampened by her husband's chest and thighs.

At stores she mingled with German, Italian, and Cornish miners' wives. The differences intrigued her, but conversations never lasted long. There were Cornish mines and Irish mines and the groups kept their distance. One exception was the Cornish and Irish wives' exchange of recipes. Tade expressed delight over his first taste of a Cornish pasty from his lunch pail.

"We're all just Butte Hill folks, after all," Nora replied. "We all just want the same in the end, don't we? To prosper in America. I don't see such great differences among us."

A year after her wedding, Nora went to the market one day with Rose. Chinese sold tomatoes, lettuce, cabbage, and potatoes, some in baskets hung from yokes across the sellers' shoulders.

"Sure and I thought their kind only chopped wood," Nora said.

"French Canadians chased them out of that business. The Canucks took their axes to them. Patrick says some wound up minus their heads. But the clever devils found something new. Growing vegetables. Well, anything that keeps them out of the mines."

Nora approached a stall. Something about the tall vendor made her peer up at him. She saw recognition in his eyes and dropped the plump tomato she'd chosen, hating herself for blushing.

Rose gaped, casting a sharp look at the seller who busied himself rearranging produce. "Nora, what in blazes? Did that Celestial say something to you?"

"No, not a thing. I just felt strange for a moment." Nora bent to pick up the tomato.

"You'd not be expecting a little one without telling your closest friend?"

Nora rolled her eyes to halt Rose's questioning. Such things weren't to be spoken of in public.

But a few days later the dizziness returned as she lifted water from the stove for Tade's bath. Then a second monthly failed to arrive. The nausea that replaced it convinced her. She told Tade first, then broke the news to a gleeful Rose. The Larkins would become parents in April 1884.

The Ancient Order of Hibernians planned their New Year's Eve Ball as usual. Nora, too bulky by then to dance, but still not showing so much that a loose jacket and ample shawl couldn't camouflage her condition, sat alone observing the unencumbered and nimble. Tade had gone out to have a cigar and a whiskey with Patrick. Rose remained at home, hostage to a colicky baby.

The sound of breaking glass outside pierced the hum of voices. Roused from dreamy thoughts of changes the little one would bring, Nora turned toward the door to see boys and men kicking a curled form on the ground. Tade and Patrick stood beyond the circle, watching, wincing in physical sympathy at each thud of a boot on the man's body. A pistol's discharge echoed off clapboard buildings. The men froze in its reverberation.

Nora, hands at her midsection as if to protect the child, heard the sheriff's voice.

"All right, you boys don't want to murder this Chinee. Let his friend take him home. They've learned the lesson."

The sole Chinese person Nora could

recognize stepped into the circle of red-faced men to lift the crumpled figure. By the fan of light from the doorway, Nora saw the tall man eye each of the attackers, holding the look just short of the length of time they'd consider a challenge. At last he turned, carrying his friend who bled from one ear. The men muttered as he strode away with the wounded fellow in his arms as if he were weightless.

"The Chinaman has a hard life in the American West, but he stays." Bat Moriarty appeared at Nora's side. "Think what it must be like where he came from." He offered her a punch cup. His nails looked very clean.

"Yes." Nora accepted the cup. "I've seen that man. He pops up everywhere. He's taller than the others, isn't he? He's . . . different." Nora shuddered at the violence she'd witnessed. Her mouth had gone dry, and the cup shook in her hand.

"His father was a Scot missionary. Jim Li speaks English, but stays with his own kind. He grew up in China. Poor Devil, he's an educated man with nothing to do but smoke opium and raise vegetables." Bat sat down beside her.

"Do they really smoke opium?"

"They do. They gamble as well and still

work like mules. Quite an interesting people."

"What might you be doing here?" The baby kicked. "Isn't there something more interesting for you on New Year's Eve?"

"Nothing interests me more than conversing with a beautiful lady, Mrs. Larkin. And how are you finding life as a married woman?"

"Altogether to my liking. We're going to have a family, you know." Nora shifted again. Indelicate, she knew. A real lady wouldn't have alluded to her condition.

"Tade's got luck on his side. Pity he doesn't gamble," Bat said, obviously not bothered by Nora's frank revelation.

Nora shot him an angry glance. "Tade is the sort of man who raises the Irish in others' eyes. He's no fancy man."

Bat grinned. "A fancy man, am I? Mrs. Larkin, I'm as simple as you'll ever see. I like my freedom, beautiful women, a good poker game, fine food, and drink. Where's the harm in such a life? Do you know how many Irish have been killed or maimed slaving in the mines for three dollars and fifty cents a day? There are different ways to be simple."

Nora rose. "You'll have to excuse me, Mr. Moriarty. Something has just given me the

hands and went to the kitchen.

A weary Father O'Toole sat, his elbows on the oilcloth-covered table.

"Father." Nora let the habit of manners carry her. "Have some tea. You look done in." She ran a hand over Helen's hair as her daughter sat in her high chair poking in distaste at a biscuit.

"Ah . . . thank you. I've more to visit this night, so I can't stay long. You look to be standing up well to this bitter day."

She knew he was being kind, but accepted the words. "I don't know for how long, Father. How is Patrick Murphy faring?" Nora realized that she'd given no thought to Rose's husband since learning of her own tragedy.

"He'll live, but he's lost his sight, and it can't be brought back. The Ancient Order of Hibernians will help with some of the medical bills and finding him a political post of some sort. The family will survive. Rose is strong."

"Well," Nora couldn't stop the bitterness in her voice, "She still has her husband. I'd give anything to have Tade back, blind or broken in whatever way." She lifted Helen and the high chair's legs scraped along the floor, the noise no less harsh than Nora's own voice. Helen squirmed from her mother's arms and ran to find Bridget.

"I know, my dear. It's your sorrow that the Lord willed otherwise. Do you have savings?" He didn't look hopeful.

Nora shook her head. "No, Father. I'm not sure we can keep the house. Even if I were to take in a boarder, we've got to eat and make the payments as well. I can do laundry perhaps."

"The Chinese have the laundries mostly. The brothers will help all they can, you may be sure."

Father O'Toole told Nora that the five dead would have a joint funeral Mass after separate wakes at the men's homes. Only two bachelor brothers would be sent off from Hibernia Hall.

"It's where our wedding dance was, Father," Nora said, a catch in her voice.

"I know, child, I know. Let's pray now and I'll be leaving to see the others."

Nora obediently crossed herself and lowered her head during Father O'Toole's words. She dutifully said "Amen," but cold anger against the God who snatched Tade away gnawed at her heart.

Helen, rubbing her eyes, wandered back into the kitchen as Nora closed the door after watching Father O'Toole depart. His narrow, black-clad shoulders stooped in weariness and sorrow as he walked toward the next grieving household. She knew this was not the first time he'd given what comfort he could to widows and families. The clergyman had served his parish here for years. No wonder his hair stood out in wild white shocks.

"Where's Da?" Helen asked, looking up. "When will Da come?"

"Ach, my treasure," Nora cuddled Helen in her lap. "Your Da has gone to be with the saints. He's watching over us with the angels for as long as we live." She said the words, but the earlier rebellion crept back to mock them.

"When will Da come home?" Helen frowned.

"He won't be home, Helen. We'll keep him in our hearts, but he won't be coming home."

"Yes. Da will come home today," Helen insisted. Her face puckered. "He has to play with me. I want Da to put me to bed. I want Da! I want Da to read to me!"

Nora hugged Helen and remembered how it was when her mother died. That awful abandonment that no one could help. She reached for the memory of one thing that had been of comfort. "When you go to bed at night, remember his dear face. He'll be with you then. Now, let's wash you up and tuck you in."

Helen shook her head in defiance and sobbed, tears clumping her thick eyelashes.

"I'll do it," Bridget said. "You should eat, too."

"I can't. I'll just sit here awhile. You've been that kind, but I'm able to manage things now. Thank you. Thank Mr. Moriarty as well." She embraced Bridget, who reluctantly put on her coat. Before she slipped out the door, Nora caught her rolling her eyes, no doubt still mortified at the memory of her stumbled speech about the wretched coffin lid. Bridget had always been a good friend. Of course, there could be no hiding from knowledge of the awful burns, no matter what they did with the coffin lid. Still, she wouldn't want others to see her handsome Tade as he must now be.

When she'd rocked and soothed her exhausted daughter into sleep, Nora sat in the kitchen until time for the whistles. She saw Tade's practice notebook on the shelf and reached for it, crying again over his strong script. She changed into her nightgown and spent the first night without Tade beside her since their wedding, resisting the urge to carry Helen in to sleep with her, but placing the notebook on his pillow.

She'd have to get used to this emptiness that stretched before her like an airless, charred tunnel.

In the morning, the funereal, draped wagon pulled up and two broad-shouldered, beefy-faced undertaker's sons unloaded Tade's coffin and brought it in. Bridget and other women from St. Patrick's and the neighborhood arrived with plates of bread, rolls, thick slices of ham, cakes, and apple pies. Husbands saw to it that poteen was in good store to loosen the men's tongues in the evening for the praising of the dear departed.

They started coming in the late afternoon. Nora had put on the worn, high-necked mourning dress from her days after Paddy's death. It felt loose. In six years she'd grown thinner than that girl of eighteen. Not like Rose, who gained a little permanent plumpness with each new daughter. Nora would never have that. No chance of any more children as came so easily to Rose and her Patrick.

No more of Tade Larkin's babies.

Nora shook her aching head. How foolish to the point of madness to envy Rose and Patrick with him blind as a chunk of coal and them barely getting by as it was. Still, she would have liked to have borne Tade a son. A big high-spirited boy with blue eyes and tangled black hair. The tears came again. After wiping her eyes, Nora stepped into the living area. The sideboard stood laden with food. Extra wooden chairs, borrowed from neighbors, filled kitchen and sitting room, what wasn't taken up by the coffin.

A tiny, bent old woman clutching a corncob pipe came in and spoke a few words in Gaelic to Bridget. Bridget walked to Nora and whispered, "It's Guennola the Keener. She never misses a wake. We'll give her a little poteen to get her started, and she'll render us her fine keen in the old language. You'll swear we were in Ireland."

Nora nodded. She could hear the volume of men's voices rising in the kitchen, talking of Tade with tongues loosened by poteen. Tade's strength, how much rock he could take out of the mines in a day, how he had won matches of the Gaelic Football for his boys at the Neversweat. How smooth he ran, like a racehorse, big as he was. With pride, Nora heard the sorrowful respect in their voices.

Women came to embrace and sit with her as tears flowed. Old Guennola wailed in a wild voice, an unearthly lamentation protesting all the unbearable Celtic losses suffered since before the shaping of words to mourn them. At times more than one woman joined in the keening. Nora herself, minding the old words, began to rock, first moving her lips, then joining in, communal sorrow enfolding her. She remembered her mother's wake back in Connemara. Behind closed eyes, she pictured the emerald green of the mist-enshrouded shores of Connemara just as she'd sometimes seen it while lost in Tade's arms.

The wake went on for three days and three nights. Helen cried at first, then slept sprawled in restless dreaming or whining wakefulness on her mother's lap until Bridget insisted on carrying the child with her to the Centennial. The community of miners made the rounds of all the victims' homes, never leaving one without representatives of their supporting presence at any time. Even Rose took time to come from Patrick's bedside. On the afternoon of the third day, the horse-drawn undertaker's wagon arrived again and the burly sons, looking tired and overheated, had drinks in the kitchen before carrying Tade's coffin out of his little home forever.

Nora had no tears left, but the removal of Tade's body felt almost as hard as those first shattering moments at the Neversweat. She hid her desperation and fear, saying and doing everything expected of her. Still, enraged rebellion drummed in her pulse. How could God take a good man like Tade, leaving Helen fatherless and Nora without her beloved husband?

On the appointed day, Dublin Gulch swelled with mourners who walked behind five wagons, each with a similar burden draped in black crepe. At St. Patrick's Catholic Church, Father O'Toole said five funeral Masses. Dan Harrington, a sweet-voiced tenor, sang "The Minstrel Boy." The song resonated in Nora's forlorn heart. She'd never listen to it again. After the funeral, the five wagons followed by mourners on foot went to St. Patrick's Cemetery.

Nora clutched Helen's hand until the little girl started to pull down and drag her feet. She stooped to pick up her daughter without once taking her eyes from Tade's coffin. At the graveyard more words were said and Tade Larkin's remains, along with all the dreams his Nora could imagine, were lowered into the ground and buried, deep and forever in the rocky soil of Butte, America.

Nora carried Helen home, the child asleep on her shoulder by the time she pushed

back arched against him.

"It is right. It's the only thing that is."

Nora sought for a reason to stop until Cat Posey occurred to her. "Stop it. I'm not Cat Posey. You can't just take me as you wish."

"Cat is nothing, an old friend. We haven't been together except for a drink at Erin's Joys for months. She sleeps with one of the other girls for that kind of pleasure." In answer to Nora's startled stare, he explained, "It's the way some of them can stand the life."

"What a country you travel in when you leave my house at night, Bat Moriarty."

"It's a country rich with many pleasures. But none could compare with nights of love with you, Nora." He ran languid fingers through her tumbling hair and dropped a kiss on her shoulder.

"I have a child and a reputation. I can't be what you want to bring me to." She did not speak the next thought. I'm a good Catholic girl. What if there's a child?

He answered her fears. "Then we'll marry. I crave you. I have since we met on that train and I first laid eyes on you in that ridiculous black coat. Little Nora. Always in mourning. Let me make you happy. Helen sleeps peacefully in another home tonight. Let's not waste this gift of time."

His hand slipped to her breast, caressing it, and with the other he tilted her face toward his to kiss. When he released her, caught between dreams and the irresistible memory of lovemaking, Nora took his hand as if pulled by gravity to lead him to her old room. They undressed, stopping for caresses, for lingering kisses. It felt so good to be touched, to be filled by a man again.

The smelters of the Neversweat billowed poisonous clouds the color of pearl in the moonlight, clouds that drifted skyward to disperse in tatters high above the turbulent city. The stars sustained their cold impassive vigil over the great delights and follies of humanity.

CHAPTER EIGHT

Nora spent a sleepless night after Bat, sated and content, spooned against her. She tried not to move for fear of disturbing him. It had never felt that way with Tade. She finally dozed, to wake at dawn gazing on the profile of her lover distant and disregarding her in sleep.

"Forgive me, Tade," she whispered. "But my life continues. It seems it must."

She thought how censorious Father O'Toole would be. But watching Bat Moriarty open his eyes, she couldn't sustain regret. As before, he had that capacity to seem fresh and unrumpled, even coming out of sleep. He pulled her to him and Nora for the first time experienced lovemaking in daylight.

After a delicious time of drifting in sensual pleasure, she raised her head, tangled gold-red curls falling over Bat's smooth chest. "I must bring Helen home," she said. "Sure and Rose will know what we've been up to when she sees me."

"Everyone should gaze on you," Bat said, his voice muffled as he nuzzled her throat. "You are a wonder."

Bat left to see what he'd missed in the way of games. Nora picked up scattered clothes from the night before, put on an everyday housedress, and left for Rose and Patrick's. The exhilaration born of sensual pleasure dimmed as she approached their door. But the dreaded reproaches didn't come. Rose's attention focused on feeding her brood and Helen.

Wanting to stay, Helen ran and hid under the older girls' bed. Their laughter encouraged her, but Nora coaxed her away with the promise of a real tea party, for once glad of the Murphys' everlasting commotion.

Nora went into her home expecting somehow that life would have changed, but Bat's door stayed closed, only silence from the other side. No sign of last night remained. Nora had the promised tea party with Helen.

As Nora went about baking and sewing, lapping anxiety churned to waves of guilt. She said the rosary while Helen napped. Bat's door opened after their supper. He walked through the house, dashing with that dangerous edge. He chucked Helen under the chin and turned. "Oh, Mrs. Larkin. There seems to be something amiss in my room. May I see you for a moment?"

Nora followed Bat, who took her in his arms. He cupped her breast, and then moved his hand lower. She didn't resist or respond. So Bat had no doubt she was his for the taking from now on. Without speaking he released her, tipped his hat, waved to Helen who lifted her favorite doll's arm in a floppy farewell, and was gone.

Next morning Nora didn't hear Bat come in. His door remained closed. She put the house in order and saw to Helen's needs. At the market several Chinese sold red tomatoes, bright carrots, and varied greens. The vendors in their distinctive clothes, hats, and speaking their own language all looked familiar. But Jim Li, the one whose name she knew, wasn't among them. At his former stall, she heard a dissatisfied Welsh woman berate the girl trying to serve her. "I can't understand you. Where's the one who used to be here? The big one who speaks English? I want to deal with him."

"Jim Li gone Helena. Jim Li gone." Small as a child before the broad Welsh housewife, the Chinese girl bowed.

Nora shrugged. Just as well. She wondered that Jim Li had stayed in Butte as long as he had. She'd heard that Helena had a large Chinese community.

Back home she baked cinnamon rolls and bread as Helen took scraps and formed them into letters and numbers, then sprinkled them with cinnamon and sugar. Nora dreamed in spite of herself as she kneaded a pillow of bread dough, that Bat might break his routine and have dinner with them. He'd spoken of marriage to make things proper. Then she thought of the gambling. Distracted, she remembered his kiss. She shook her head. It must come right somehow.

He didn't emerge. Finally, she knocked on his door. No response. She turned the knob and pushed. The bed hadn't been slept in. He hadn't come home at all that morning. Odd. She hoped he was well, but she could hardly go to the saloon and ask.

Nora read nursery rhymes with Helen. Helen favored the line, "Gentlemen come every day, to see what my fine hen doth lay." Nora found it unnerving. They prayed, then Nora tucked the sleepyhead in, relieved of the need to pretend calm. Helen had an only child's way of focusing on her mother's moods, so Nora tried to keep fears and sadness at bay.

She sighed and sat to darn stockings, the ticking clock and constant hum and shift whistles from the mines the only sounds.

At midnight she went to bed, lying awake listening to Helen's soft, rhythmic breathing. Was Bat with Cat Posey? He'd told her they were just friends. In the early-morning hours she said a rosary, dressed, and sat at the table, hands folded on its scratched surface. She resolutely faced the door. Tade had never caused her a minute's worry. She thought of how he used to come home straightway from work. Tears stung her eyes.

Bat didn't come.

Helen woke up. Shoulders burning from the tension of her vigil, Nora mechanically washed and dressed her daughter, then prepared oatmeal. By midmorning the narrow house began to close in. She imagined having to stand, arms straight out, hands pressing the walls back to keep them from crushing her and Helen. "Come on, my treasure." She shoved Helen's arms into a sweater. "We'll go see Aunt Rose."

Helen brightened. "Aunt Rose!" she crowed. "We're going to visit my Aunt Rose Murphy and all my Murphy friends."

They found Rose scrubbing laundry over

a tub behind her house, mostly little girls' worn knickers made from flour sacks. She brushed disheveled hair out of her eyes and greeted Nora with urgent gloating. "Well, did you hear the news about your fancy lodger?"

Nora's heart jolted. "I've heard nothing about anyone. What is it?" Helen let go of her mother's hand and scampered off to join the girls.

"It appeared in the *Miner.* Here, I'll show you." Rose dried her hands on her streaked apron and motioned Nora inside.

"Just think," Rose said, opening the paper to personal notices. Nora's hands shook. She read where Rose's finger left a damp smudge as Rose read aloud, "The wife and children of Bat Moriarty seek any information regarding his whereabouts. He is rumored to be in Montana. Contact Deirdre Moriarty c/o General Delivery, Saginaw, Michigan. Modest reward offered for good information." Nora took the paper, reread it, then folded and laid it on the table before she faced Rose. Any words had drained out of her head.

"Is he at your house now?" Rose asked.

Nora struggled to be matter of fact. "Not for over a day. I wonder if he knows." She lowered her eyes again to the newsprint.

"I'll wager so. Might be planning a quick escape, the scoundrel. Is he paid up in his rent?"

"Not quite, Rose," Nora said, rising from the table. Her voice shook in spite of her. "Not quite paid up."

"I wonder how Cat Posey will take it. I guess the likes of that upstairs girl wouldn't mind knowing her fancy man engaged in adultery." Rose couldn't help having a bit of malicious fun with the scandal.

Nora winced, but said nothing knowing how the Dublin Gulch housewives like Rose despised Irish prostitutes. What would they think of her now? Making a quick good-bye, she took Helen home, and as she passed through her kitchen's yeasty fragrance toward their bedroom she noticed Bat's door ajar. He must have come back to explain! She flung it open. Empty wardrobe doors gaped. She pulled drawers out of the little dresser. Empty.

The gambler she'd given her honor to for one night of passion had fled without a word. Nora sat on the bed, emptiness all around her. Then, with a growl, she tore the bedclothes off, yanking sheets and blankets to the floor. She grabbed them up and set about doing laundry, heating the water to nearly scalding before she rammed the bedclothes into it. She scrubbed the room after that, on her knees, wiping every trace of Bat Moriarty from her home.

Helen watched her mother with a sensitive child's awareness that this was not a time to make trouble. She asked no questions, although if Nora had noticed, the questions were in her daughter's eyes. Nora only muttered wild, strange words into the armoire as she scoured its inside.

Helen finally had to ask. "Did Bat die?"

Nora finally turned to her daughter's frightened face. "Oh, my treasure," she said, the rage replaced by remorse that she'd caused Helen to look so stricken. "He had to leave, Helen. He has a family back in Michigan. That's a state far away."

"But, I wanted him here. With us."

Nora gathered Helen to her. "Oh, so did I," she murmured into her child's sweet-scented hair. "Oh, so did I."

In the evening, her hands raw from hot water and harsh soap, Nora remade the bed and moved her things back in. Whatever the loss of money, she would never again take in a lodger. At least the comfort existed that no one knew about her fall. She would have to tell one soul, good Father O'Toole. He would hear her confession. Afterward Nora would put that foolish night behind her. She willed herself not to think of Bat's touch or the delicious abandonment to lovemaking after the lonely drought of widowhood.

When the Sunday *Butte Miner* appeared on the newsstand, Nora read more shocking information. Cat Posey lay dead from a morphine overdose. A friend returning from a night's work to the room they shared found her, dead for some hours. Her friend stated the deceased had become despondent after being deserted by a man she believed would one day marry her.

So Bat Moriarty had talked marriage to a prostitute, the same ruse that toppled Nora into his arms. She shuddered and reached for the rosary beads, but her hand hesitated, and she left them untouched. She'd brought herself to the level of pathetic Cat Posey, a shameful joke.

She gritted her teeth. He wouldn't be the death of her, not of Tade Larkin's widow and Helen's mother. She picked up the beads and pressed them against her burning forehead. Then she slipped them back into her pocket and looked around her neglected kitchen. Time to tidy up. At least things could be made right on the outside.

Overwhelmed by weariness in the weeks

that followed, Nora thought it due to a heavy workload and bitter remorse. When she missed her time of the month, she felt the first sense that dark wings spread across the sky, whirring in pursuit, catching up to her.

Soon other signs showed themselves. Nora's heart plunged with the certainty that her single passionate night with Bat Moriarty, a man who'd abandoned one family and broken the heart of a tough Butte prostitute, couldn't be washed away after all. She thought ruefully of all the times with Tade when no more children had come, and now this. Fear of the future, of shame, of the loss of respect this would bring, of a return to worse poverty, tore at her.

Sitting at the table, head in hands, she yearned to unburden herself to Rose, but balked at the thought. Even in anguish, she hated to admit Patrick had been right. She felt shamed enough without acknowledging she'd scorned wise advice. Patrick's warning words tolled in her memory like funeral bells. She'd ignored the oracle and now must live out her fate.

Later that night in the darkened kitchen, Nora stood at the window, glaring toward the life-thieving mines, anger vying with desperation. What should she do? Finally at first light, stiff from spending hours in a chair, she stood and made coffee. She must leave Butte, America, the place she'd thought her lifelong home. She'd believed this little house would signify dignity and freedom from want. Now through folly she'd tossed away what little she'd kept after losing Tade. Bat could walk off. She'd forgotten that a woman's curse is always to pay — like Eve who ate of the forbidden apple.

As soon as she could comb Helen's tangled gold hair and help her dress, she took her delighted daughter to Rose's. Leaving Helen playing jump rope with the Murphy girls, Nora proceeded on to the Centennial, telling Rose she planned to ask about hiring on there.

Bridget answered Nora's knock on the manager's door. Even in her distress, Nora admired her friend for advancing so.

"What brings you back to the Centennial?" Bridget asked, pulling Nora into the office. "Is it a job you're needing? As you see, I'm assistant manager at least for now, so in a position to help. I heard about Moriarty disappearing after the missing person notice." She talked as she helped Nora slip off her old mourning coat.

"You always get right to the heart of a matter, but you didn't hear all there is," Nora said. She stopped, the tears welling up, this time with relief that she could finally share her dilemma with another woman.

"Sit down here. Tell me what's wrong." Bridget sat beside Nora on the office couch.

Nora burst into the first racking sobs she'd allowed herself, then raised her eyes and said it aloud. "I became one of Bat Moriarty's conquests. Now I'm going to have a baby."

Bridget paused only a moment, one hand raised to her mouth, before she reached out to take Nora into her arms and rock her. "Faith, dear, don't be hard on yourself. It can't be good for the little one. A baby is a good thing. Michael and I pray for one every day and try to help it come into being every night. Our sorrow is that we aren't blessed."

"Is this a good thing?" Now that she had someone to talk to, Nora rushed on with downcast eyes. "I even thought for an hour about ridding myself of this one. I know there are those who know the ways. But the church says that's a mortal sin. I'll have the child, only not in Butte. I have to take Helen and leave. I was hoping you and Michael might want the house. I'll let it go for little enough. I've a mind to go to Helena until the baby is born." Nora sniffled into the handkerchief Bridget offered. "I can probably get work in a city that big until the baby comes. I'll lie about when Tade died and pretend it's his."

"Michael and I've been saving to buy a house. I work here all day and then live here all night. Believe me, it grows tiresome. I'd like to quit this job as well. Michael could walk to his mine, the Exile of Erin, from your house. I'll talk with him."

"Thank you, Bridget. You'll not tell anyone about me, will you?" Nora lowered her eyes, fingering the couch's leather armrest. "I thought about renting the house and coming back with some story, but people figure such things out sooner or later."

"Only Michael, and I'll swear him to secrecy," Bridget answered, patting her hand. "But won't you be seeing Father O'Toole before you go? It might be hard, but you'd feel better after."

"I can't put it off any longer. It will be easier now I've told you."

"I can help you with the Helena move as well. I've an old friend there who owns a boardinghouse. Let me give you her address and I'll send her a note before you leave. She's a kind soul. Now as to the babe, don't be too harsh with yourself. You know you aren't the first and you won't be the last to wind up so. Michael would hate me for telling, but he was started sooner than he should have been. It's made no difference to him now, has it?"

It remained for Nora to tell Rose. It wouldn't be right to just leave her dearest friend without telling why. Nora found her removing biscuits from the oven in the Murphy kitchen. Helen and two of the Murphy girls had settled to play with dolls on the floor. Rose brushed a streak of flour from her shiny cheek and scrutinized Nora.

"Sit down. You look as tired as I am. I wish you didn't have to work so hard."

Nora eyed the children. "I need to speak to you. Alone."

Rose's smile turned wary. Nora hated to visit more trouble on her friend who had endured so much. "Well then. Let's walk outside. These girls can watch each other for a bit."

They wandered by the railroad tracks. Shabbily dressed women and boys scouted near the rails for lumps of coal to take home for fuel, a dismal scene in the October landscape. Nora shivered and began straightaway with just the shameful facts. "I sinned with Bat Moriarty the night of the benefit dance. I'm going to have his baby. Would you believe it, all that time with Tade and only Helen when we wanted more so badly? Now Bat's gone, and I have to leave, too."

"Oh, Nora." Rose looked ready to weep. "Where will you go? Stay here. Stay in your house with us nearby. Your home . . ."

"I'm selling to Bridget and Michael, and I'll buy train tickets to Helena. I'll find work there for as long as I can, and then I'll have the house money for right after." Nora strove to sound strong and certain, no matter that fear and regret had driven her for weeks.

"Have you spoken to Father?" Rose gripped Nora's arm.

"I went to confession this morning. He hardly had to tell me not to do this sort of business again, now did he?"

Rose dabbed at her eyes with roughened fingers as they walked, trying to convince Nora to stay in Butte. Nora's decision stood. The town had given her its best and its worst, and she didn't want the shame of staying on.

"How we'll miss you and Helen," Rose said, engulfing Nora in a tight embrace.

Nora held Rose tightly. "We'll miss you

more. Promise not to tell why we left."

"I promise." Rose used the end of her shawl to wipe her eyes. "We'll say you had a family emergency."

"Good," Nora said with a wry smile. "In a way it's even true, isn't it?"

CHAPTER NINE

October 1888

Six years after her journey west from Boston a much-altered Nora Larkin boarded a passenger car of the Helena, Boulder, and Butte Railway line. This time her inquisitive daughter bounced on the seat beside her, the child's every question beginning with why, what, when. Nora had packed the same round-topped trunk, wore the same black coat, but it now signified deceit. Others would believe she wore it for mourning Tade, none aware that Bat Moriarty's baby grew under the heavy wool.

No, she was not the same naive girl. Her astute instincts had failed. She'd given herself to a tawdry gambler just to taste the sweet fruit of desire again. Tade had ignited passion in her and she'd missed it enough to give herself to Bat Moriarty. The price of sin was death according to St. Paul. The girl she'd been hadn't just changed, Nora thought. She'd died.

Helen cried a little as they waved good-bye to the Murphy brood as the train pulled away. She eyed Nora with a flicker of hope. "I don't want to go anymore, Mama. Let's stay."

When she repeated it louder, a couple across the aisle peered over, annoyed. What would those judgmental strangers think if they knew my whole story, Nora wondered. Yes, she'd taken a man's hand and led him to her bed, she'd removed her clothes with slow pleasure, she'd pressed his hands against her breasts. That night planted a child in her womb. As Butte vanished and the air outside cleared, she forced aside another truth, that she wished this unborn baby gone.

Helen tugged at her sleeve. "I'm Helen going to Helena." Helen had seen her sadness and tried to be cheerful now for the adventure ahead. Nora put her arm around Helen's shoulders, so delicate they reminded her of a little bird's bones. To engage Helen she pointed out deer feeding on tender grass near the rails. Helen would soon be hungry, and the old fear of want crept into Nora's heart. Food cost money, and since Tade's death money melted like ice blocks in summer. She wondered if her well-dressed fellow passengers ever noticed the silent poor who struggled against hunger and sought any decent means to shelter their children.

Nora patted the inside pocket where she'd buttoned the cash left from Bridget's down payment. Somehow I'll get us through, she mentally chanted with the wheels below. Somehow I'll get us through.

They reached Helena at dusk. Homesickness struck Nora as passengers stepped down and embraced friends and families. No one greeted her and her tired daughter. The station bustled with confident strangers. Clutching Helen's hand, Nora arranged to have their luggage delivered to Mrs. Leary's boardinghouse.

She paid the ten-cent fare to ride in a gaily painted horse-drawn trolley. Helen revived and pointed as they passed raucous saloons, silent lumberyards, heaped boulders and gravel, abandoned mine shafts, and ditches. Helena lacked Butte's ruthless ugliness, but Nora wondered if she were destined to live in scarred mining towns forever. Perhaps it would be less dreary in daylight.

The trolley descended to the end of the line in downtown Helena. After asking directions of the conductor, Nora and

Helen stepped off and walked past buildings of varied architectural designs. Nora's feet hurt. The inside of her left shoe pinched in at the ankle. The blister would be troublesome.

The air chilled. She pulled Helen up a steep street with the hand not gripping her satchel. Helen reacted by going limp. "Carry me, Mama." Nora sympathized with her exhausted child. Helen had looked at books, watched out the window, chattered with her, but it was time for a little girl with dark circles under bewildered eyes to be in bed.

She felt a rush of blood that signified anxiety striking her on this unfamiliar street. The bad thoughts came. What if I can't care for us? What if this Mrs. Leary isn't as Bridget said? What if I can't find work? What if one of us gets sick? With an effort, she reined in approaching panic. She had to be strong for Helen. Helen meant everything.

"Carry me, Mama."

"No, my treasure," Nora repeated in a soothing sing-song. "Take a few more steps. It can't be far." Exchanging that litany, they moved on to a street where Nora made out pleasant homes, grassy yards, poplar trees, and shrubbery. She checked addresses posted on gates, stopping at a tall white house with a broad front porch. They limped up the steps and Nora rang the bell. A slender, handsome woman with graying blonde hair twisted in a knot on her head answered.

"I'm Mrs. Larkin," Nora said. "My daughter and I are to rent a room here." She nodded at Helen, who rubbed her eyes.

"Yes, my dear, come in, come in. Why, this child looks half sick." The woman glanced at Nora's green skirt inside the open coat. "I expected to see you in full mourning. I'm Mrs. Leary."

"Oh, I felt it best to save my money for when the baby arrives. Tade would understand if I couldn't buy black clothes. Your house is so lovely." She meant it. Flowered wallpaper covered the high-ceilinged hall, which led into a parlor on one side and a dining room on the other. Oak stairs rose to the second story.

"You must be worn to a frazzle," Mrs. Leary said. "Let me show you your room." Their landlady picked Helen up as the child swayed on her feet. "What a sweet little girl. She must miss her father."

"We both miss him," Nora said, grasping the rounded top of the newel post, feeling suddenly light-headed. She inhaled to clear her thoughts. One had to appear healthy to make the right impression, no matter how hunger attacked. She followed Mrs. Leary up the steep staircase.

The high-ceilinged room held a big four-poster bed next to tall windows draped in blue brocade overlooking the quiet street below. A cot sat next to the bed, made up with a blue crocheted coverlet for Helen.

Nora sank into a willow rocker in the corner. "It's lovely. Just lovely." An evening breeze ruffled white lace curtains, and Nora drew in a breath of the crisp fall air. Perhaps by some miracle of providence, they would be all right. She shuddered at the thought of the strange streets she'd just navigated. Little divided the three in this room from those with no place to sleep but alleys. Once more, she felt grateful for the money from her house sale. Yet how money flew from her grasp.

"Come down for lamb stew. It's still on the stove," Mrs. Leary said as she pulled off Helen's coat and scuffed shoes. "We'll just put this little one down. She's asleep as it is. We'll feed her when she wakes."

"Sure and I'm almost asleep myself," Nora murmured.

"You need the nourishment to be strong, dear."

Nora gratefully surrendered to her landlady's maternal attentions. In the course of their conversation Mrs. Leary agreed to take care of Helen for a small sum while Nora worked. Nora explained that she would hide the fact of expecting Tade's second child as long as she could to keep working. Mrs. Leary summoned a cautious smile, but accepted the plan.

As Nora nestled later into her soft bed in that airy room, she felt an almost forgotten sense of hope and fell asleep feeling better than she had in weeks.

Next morning, standing before the hawk-nosed manager of the Mineral Springs Hotel as he perused her references, Nora knew this would be a different kettle of fish from the Centennial. This four-story hotel had no dark and dingy corridors. Brass gleamed and windows admitted shafts of late fall light. But none of the staff smiled. She'd watched this man stride through the lobby, stopping to bestow effusive greetings on well-dressed guests. Now she saw that his warmth only extended to those whose money benefited him. She mustn't invite his ready disdain. She stood straight, pulling her stomach in, although her condition hadn't become obvious yet.

"Are you in good health? You look peaky."

He peered over his glasses.

"I am in good health. I suffered a recent loss. I —"

"No need for explanations. We'll try you in housekeeping. We're strict with you Irish maids. Be here by 6:30 a.m. You work until 5:00 p.m. with a twenty-minute lunch break. If late once or caught shirking, you'll be fired. Is that clear?"

"Altogether clear, sir." Nora's heart stretched between relief at being hired and sorrow at the hours away from Helen.

Nora watched for mail from Bridget, but when it arrived it brought catastrophy. Mr. Flynn had departed to start another business and the new manager disapproved of a woman as his assistant. He fired Bridget. Michael, in turn, had suffered a broken leg in a partial cave-in. It would be months before they could send money. Nora gripped the letter and forced herself to breathe. She finally set it down and wrote back that, of course, they must stay in the house. She would manage. Wasn't it always the poor, she thought, most apt to help other desperate souls? Her father had taught her that.

Thanksgiving arrived. Nora and Helen spent it with Mrs. Leary. After a turkey dinner, they decorated a small tree in the parlor. Helen was delighted to set out Mrs. Leary's creche. She handled each piece with delicate reverence while the women drank cider and talked of Ireland. Mrs. Leary had never been there and reveled in Nora's stories and descriptions. Nora avoided speaking of oppression and violence. Battles and arson made poor holiday fare. Reality too often crushed romantics and their ideals. She'd learned that lesson well.

That peaceful, gracious day would remain in Nora's memory as a green island of peace in a gray sea of despair. Neither woman knew that a financial calamity would force Mrs. Leary to give up her home and worse would be visited on the young mother seated across from her.

Four weeks later the strangling angel of children came swooping over the mountains to descend on the city. The angel whom some called diphtheria did not discriminate, but visited homes great and small that sheltered little sons and daughters. Eventually the angel entered the haven of Mrs. Leary's boardinghouse and seized all that was left of what Nora cherished. The angel grasped without mercy until Helen's breath ceased.

Helen's burial plot in the unkempt paupers'

section of the cemetery lay between two other little mounds. Their twisted, faded headboards bore inscriptions weathered to unreadable. A local priest spoke rote words above the gaping hole that received Helen's casket, paid for by the county for those with nothing. Driving snow mixed with freezing rain, but Nora didn't feel it pelt her. She'd given up trying to hide her condition. Her rounded stomach thrust open the unbuttoned mourning coat flapping at her sides. After the somber priest departed, she stood, head bowed, staring at the lowered casket. She closed her eyes and listened to the silent gravedigger shovel hard clods back into the grave. She opened her eyes when she heard the ragged fellow's voice. "I'm sorry for the loss of your child, missus, but you best get home before you catch a fatal chill."

For the first time she looked at the older man, his patched clothes and cracked boots. Like her, forgotten by all, another of the wretched poor.

"God reward you for your kindness," Nora replied. "But I need more time alone with her."

She didn't add that if God existed at all He was probably indifferent at best, vengeful and punitive at worst.

The man doffed his cap and moved off.

After he departed she bowed her head, staring at the lumpy mound of earth that covered Helen.

After a quarter of an hour, sifting through memories that included Helen and Tade, heads together learning to read and write words that would lift them up in America, Nora raised her head and clenched her fists. "No, not like this. Never like this," she declared to her desolate surroundings and the driving snow. "Not for Helen. No unmarked grave for Tade Larkin's daughter. We didn't come for this."

Nora marched with clumsy steps out of the cemetery and down the rutted road. She'd stupidly dreamed that Helen might one day take her first communion at a church she'd noticed under construction. Slabs of white building stone waited on the snowpacked site's ground for spring.

Well, she intended to put one to good use.

Becoming canny, she noted surrounding weather turning to true storm. Increasing whiteouts might hide her. She entered the church grounds and bent over several flat building stones, some small and useless, some too big to move. One, about a foot and a half by one foot, she could budge by forcing it over on its corners. Lifting and shoving, Nora pushed the stone inches at a time. Sweat dampened her unwashed hair even in the cold. Her hands reddened. She grunted as she turned the rough block over, then over again. A pair of coarsely dressed men walked past, holding their caps against the wind. She heard their sneering laughter before the blinding snow swept their images away. Did they laugh at her? Small matter as long as they asked no questions.

She noticed with dismay that another, more attentive man stood across the street watching. She stopped her clumsy struggling and straightened to face whatever accusation awaited her. The figure stood tall and straight in a black frock coat and wide-brimmed hat. But when he turned in profile for a moment, Nora discerned the telltale queue.

Jim Li stared at her again, his expression unreadable.

A swirl of snow whipped up between them, then died away. Nora started, then glared as she remembered the river, the vegetable stand, the New Year's Eve when his friend had been beaten. A flash of anger struck her that the tall Chinese would show up even here to catch her in this desperate hour of thievery.

Panting, she raised her voice. "You're

right. I am stealing this damn stone. Yes. You can turn me in or you can help, but I wish you'd give up watching. I'm not your day's entertainment."

He spoke above the frigid gusts. "You are Mrs. Larkin from Butte. We have met, in a way, before. You won't move that stone far. They'll catch you." Li's expression didn't change, but his voice, enunciating the English words in what any Irish would think might belong to a fine tenor, carried sympathy.

Nora's head dropped. "It's for Helen. I lost my child to the diphtheria, and I'll not leave her to lie in that grave without a decent headstone." Sweat froze on her and she began to tremble. The white ground of the building site swam before her as she stumbled.

Jim Li crossed the road in long strides and cupped her elbow. She looked into his kind face with its brown eyes, more rounded than other Chinese she'd seen. She dried her own with rough palms. "You always come up on me when I'm breaking the rules," she said, sitting down on the stone as though it were a chair in someone's parlor. She felt weak and sick. She couldn't even manage this one thing for Helen. And now this misfit Chinaman hovered over her.

"Your charming daughter caught diphtheria?"

Nora broke under his sympathetic tone. She struggled to speak through heavy sobs. "The doctor was useless, but he said something I keep remembering. He called diphtheria 'the strangling angel of children.' Could an angel do such evil? I stayed with my beautiful girl and prayed and bathed her poor hot body, but she went anyway. I thought she was over the worst, and then sometime in the night she just stopped breathing. Her little heart had been strained so, the doctor said. I'd only fallen asleep for a few hours right beside her. I should have stayed awake, shouldn't I? I know I should."

Jim Li only said, "Honor me, Mrs. Larkin. Let me help you."

Nora pushed herself up awkwardly.

His eyes swept across her swollen belly. He bent and lifted the stone easily to his shoulder. "Tell me where you wish to carry this marker."

"Bless you," Nora sighed. "Bring it along to the graveyard. To the paupers' corner." She shuddered, remembering the rough men's laughter as they strode past her.

They walked in the blowing cold without speaking. Icy snow pebbles stung their faces. None of the few scurrying pedestrians they met commented as Jim followed Nora by two or three strides as if hired for a job. At the cemetery, he set the stone down at the head of Helen's grave and waited while Nora disappeared to the caretaker's rough shed. Planks flapped in the wind. Earlier she'd noticed a loosened window. Now she returned with a chisel and hammer. "I'll take them back when we're done here."

For the next hour, Jim Li pounded blocky letters that formed 'Helen Larkin' into the stone. Nora knelt on the bumpy frozen ground as she stroked Helen's grave, whispering to her daughter. Misery overwhelmed her. She wished herself in that ground, too. "Let me have a sign," she prayed. "Let me know she's with her father."

The indifferent snow offered no solace.

Jim Li stood, the headstone ready. Nora pushed herself up as he positioned Helen's marker to rise higher than any nearby.

Aching with cold and fatigue, Nora shivered in the twilight. She wiped her eyes and turned to the silent man waiting behind her. "Thank you."

He gave a slight bow. "It has been my honor. You look unwell, Mrs. Larkin."

"I look like a woman who's going to have a baby, Mr. Li." She made a wry face.

He paused, studying the finished marker,

159

before asking, "Do you have money?"

The abrasive wind pushed against Nora. Her eyes stung. Was the man going to ask for pay now? "None. The last of it went to the doctor. Not that he made any difference."

"Do you have work?"

"The Hotel de Mineral fired me when I stayed home to care for Helen. Who would hire a woman so big with child as I am now? I can't hide it anymore." She spat out the bitter words.

"Someone I know. How badly do you want work?" His tone remained mild.

"I have no money. I need to eat for this one I'm carrying. Otherwise, I wouldn't care a pin about anything." She sighed. "I have to move. My landlady lost all her savings to a bank failure. She has to go live with her son and I have to be out for the new owners. It's all a dog's breakfast. What kind of work?"

"Housekeeping." He gathered the tools he'd used.

"Housekeeping for a family?" Nora felt a twinge of interest.

"No. Housekeeping in a place where working girls live."

"Working girls! Man, are you talking about prostitutes?" She almost laughed. Did even Jim Li think she'd fallen so low? Was all her struggle to end in this? Disrepute? Degradation?

"It is the place where they live, not where they work. The housekeeper runs it like a boardinghouse, keeps the girls from fighting, drinking, sees to their health. The pay is good. No one asks questions."

Nora looked at him, her eyes narrowed. "You know, don't you? It was you in the alley watching as Bat Moriarty and I left Hibernia Hall that night."

"Yes. I wished I could have warned you away from him. I learned about him through those who worked in the saloons. He came from a prosperous Southern family before the South seceded. As a young boy he knew losses of money, family, lands. That turned him into a cynical, heartless man known to gamble on anything, on other peoples' lives if it suits him."

As the two left the cemetery, Nora looked back reluctant to leave, but satisfied that Helen's white stone marked the spot she would revisit. She stopped along the way to drop the borrowed tools through the caretaker's window. "Others tried to warn me," she said, walking back to Jim. "I didn't listen. I wouldn't have listened to you. I was lonely. I'm paying for my selfish foolery.

Perhaps Helen would still be alive . . ." She lowered her head.

"There is no way to know." His voice gentle, he added, "Butte held dangers of disease just as Helena does."

Nora, not consoled, asked, "How is it you know of this house? Do you work there?"

"I clean, help cook, do laundry. I mend broken things."

Nora shook from the cold, the wind tugging at her clothes. The world blurred through her tears. "Well, I doubt you can mend broken lives. I'm that desperate. I don't approve of such women, but I need to feed this child in me. I don't care if I live or die, but I never seem to die. Others do. Perhaps this baby will survive. I owe the one I've started the chance to live at least. Not that this child might not curse me for it some day." The idea of a curse pierced her. Was she to wander the earth like Cain in the Bible? Despised by all decent people? Never at rest?

Jim nodded. "You'll want to gather your things, Mrs. Larkin. I will walk with you to carry what you want to bring."

Nora tottered along beside Jim Li on feet so cold they'd lost all feeling. He waited at the boardinghouse's back porch while she packed. She paused for one last look at the room where Helen had died. Here she'd allowed herself to feel a thread of hope for her child. God had crushed that cruel illusion. She remained the tinker's brat after all, just another poor Irish git trying to feed herself after losing everything and everyone.

She said good-bye to the new owner, a reserved, bookish man clearly relieved to see the back of the hapless widow. No friend remained to wish Nora farewell. Yet this Chinese was kind. She might surprise herself and live through the next months.

She dragged the trunk. Its every bump down the stairs jarred like a warning, but she could no longer stay. What choice did she have? Once she hauled her trunk outside, Jim Li picked it up. Nora frowned in distrust. "Why are you helping me? I called you a name once."

"I am helping you because you need help. I do not think you would call me that name again."

"No, Mr. Li, I would not." The solemn look they shared seemed to seal a pact.

The two walked without speaking further for blocks before Jim stopped. "Mrs. Larkin, I misled you. The house we are about to enter is a brothel. But your job would be as a matron to the girls."

Horror and disappointment gripped Nora.

In worse trouble than ever, she covered her eyes. She couldn't return to the boarding-house after the new owner's open relief when she, the penniless, ghostly, bereaved widow and expectant mother, departed. "Why didn't you tell me this before?" She cried in anguish. "I can't go in there."

"Do you have a choice? Your duties are as I described them. You act as go-between with the girls and the madam, Lillie McGraw. She is tough and crude, but fair. You will preside over the kitchen, the servants, make sure furniture is not broken. It won't be as hard as being a washer-woman. The pay is better than maid work."

"But why did you wait to tell me?"

"You would not have come, and it is the wisest course. Did your Jesus not sit down with such women? Is that not in your Christian Bible? Who is more worshiped here in America than your Christ?"

"Sure and he turned water into wine, too, but I don't suppose I could manage that." Her voice broke with despair. "Well, it's true he didn't care what others thought of him. But these people — I'm afraid of them."

He smiled. "The ones who worship or the working girls?"

"Now that you ask, I'm not so certain. The high and mighties were disapproving of me taking Bat in for my lodger."

"You would be living with girls from poor families, most often visited by lonely working men. Just come and see." He continued to hold the big trunk on his shoulder. Her weariness as convincing as Jim Li's words, Nora nodded.

They walked up the steps to the heavy closed door of what appeared to be a large, ordinary house with a roseate glow from a lamp in a front window. Inside, tufted red wallpaper lined the entry lit by two soft sconces. Nora had the nightmarish sense of walking into a mouth that would swallow her whole.

CHAPTER TEN

Jim set down the trunk and left Nora to her raw fears. The interior was at least blessedly warm. She caught the surprising scent of fresh baked bread, and that triggered hunger gnawing into her exhaustion. Jim returned and bowed her into the offices of a woman seated behind a heavy desk.

Lillie McGraw, large-boned with coarse hands, wore an elaborate burgundy silk walking suit. She had a cunning, broad face and green cat's eyes that scrutinized Nora for a long moment, pausing at her bulging midsection and shabby mourning coat.

"Can you keep a house?"

Nora summoned what dignity she could. Her instinct for survival asserted itself with that one fragment of her history. "I've kept my own and with a lodger. I also worked in large hotels. I could manage a place this size well enough, I believe."

"Do you think you're above us?" The

166

woman lit a cheroot, one eye closed against its rising smoke.

Nora shrugged. "I just stole a marker for my child's grave. I'm not above anyone."

"Well, we'll try you out. Have that worthless Chinaman take your bags upstairs." Nora saw Jim Li's face stiffen into a carved mask. He bowed and picked up the trunk. "I can't abide the Celestials, but this one works hard and cheap, and he and the girls keep a distance from each other."

Nora winced. Apparently even the lowest of the low cast around for someone worse off to scorn. Why were people so cruel? The two ruffians who laughed at her were far below Jim Li with his unexpected rescue of a bereaved mother, but only she viewed things that way.

Lillie's gravelly voice snapped her back. "My old housekeeper Gert will show you the ropes. When is your kid due to enter this world of sin?"

"In about five months."

"Planning to leave us then?"

Frowning, Nora dropped her eyes to study the figured carpet. "I don't know what I'll do then."

"With yourself or the baby?"

Nora shrugged. She had no answers. She hadn't thought past the birth, just wanting to escape Butte and start anew with Helen and the newborn. For a fact, she felt nothing but resentment for this child she carried. She couldn't help the thought that haunted her. Why couldn't that cold, neglectful God have taken the gambler's unknown, unborn child and spared Helen? She turned to follow Jim Li. There was only so much even Lillie McGraw had a right to ask or know. "Thank you," she said with a forced smile. "I'll earn my keep."

Jim set down the trunk. "Gert Hensley is in the kitchen." He bowed and left Nora alone in her room.

Her new quarters were light and clean, with a wardrobe, wash stand, and double bed. Framed pictures of pale ladies draped in scarves that didn't cover everything reminded her where she was. Nora sank down on the creaky bed with one thought. So this is what I've come to. She felt lightheaded. Disoriented. But she had no choice. Unreal as it seemed, thanks to Jim Li she had work to do that would feed her. She removed her coat, washed her chapped face, fixed her hair, and with a deep breath started down the hall with its red carpet and wallpaper.

Visible through a half-open door, a thin

Why didn't they focus on the scantily clad girls? She swore off forever from any doings between men and herself.

She learned to speak in a commanding voice to restore order when altercations broke out. Lillie addressed her in the tones of a businesswoman who didn't intend to get close to the help. In many ways, she reminded Nora of the observant manager of the Parker House Hotel in Boston, at least until she opened her mouth. Nora worked not to flinch at Lillie's language.

One night she observed a different Lillie McGraw. From the hallway, Nora heard Josephine scream, a man yell, and then sounds of splintering wood and breaking glass. Jim rushed past her followed by Lillie. They opened the door and Nora, close behind, saw that Josephine lay against the wall, blood running from her nose and mouth. The red-faced man's fists were still raised. The brothel owner didn't wait for Jim, but grabbed the customer by his collar, swinging him against the wall. When he squared off at Lillie, she whipped a knife out so fast Nora hardly saw the movement, only the slash of red from the man's ear to his nose.

"Son of a bitch," Lillie shouted. "You can fuck my girls if you pay the price, but you play no fucking games with me. Take him out," she ordered Jim, who handed the bleeding drunk a towel and his pants and marched him away.

"Take care of our girl," Lillie ordered Nora, swishing the knife in the washbowl and drying it on the sheets before slipping it back into her pocket. "Put her to bed, and sit with her awhile."

As Nora washed Josephine's face and straightened the bedclothes, she remembered how swift Lillie had been. If a man ever attacked her, she'd want her gruff employer on the premises. Lillie looked after her own. Not a bad trait, for certain.

By May Nora began obsessing over the approaching birth. She had decisions to make. Everything had changed since Butte.

One rainy night, alone with Jim Li in the kitchen, she ventured, "I have to admit the job you tricked me into has worked out well." She lay down the pencil she used to make a list of kitchen supplies and food at the table, and straightened. Her back bothered her, especially that evening. "These girls have been good to keep house for. Easier than guests at the hotels. I didn't realize they're just poor ignorant souls in a man's world. With no education and no family it could happen to any creature. I'd never have thought it, but I like them better than the society women I used to clean up after. These don't pretend to be anything but what they are."

Jim continued unloading the wood he'd brought in for the stove, then turned and studied her. "Your baby will be born soon, Mrs. Larkin. What will you do then?"

Nora rubbed her eyes. "I'm thinking this isn't the place to raise a child, even if Lillie would agree to it."

"In my country it is not so unusual to place a child in a good home if circumstances show it to be best."

Nora looked hard into Jim's eyes, then lowered hers. "God forgive me, I don't love this child, and I didn't love this child's father. I don't feel toward this one as I did Helen. I've no prospects. What if it's a boy? What will he do with no father to teach him?" She stood up heavily and moved to the window.

"What would be best for you and the child?" Jim studied her.

Nora took in a long breath. "My baby must go to a decent family, not be given up to strangers. I have to know this one will be loved. My friends Bridget and Michael Doyle in Butte haven't been blessed yet. I know Bridget would make a loving home for any baby. Michael should be working again by now. I'd write a note turning the house over to them to make sure they'll always have property through their ups and downs as the child grows up."

She paced the length of the kitchen. "If I decide to give the little newcomer up, would you take it to them? I'll write a letter promising never to interfere. They'll have the house free and clear for raising my baby. Rose and Patrick Murphy will be the only people who might guess where the child came from, and they won't tell. If Bridget won't agree, bring the baby back, but I know she will. She wants a little one that much." Nora took in a shaky breath and directed her gaze at Jim Li. "Would you do this for me?"

He answered without hesitation. "Yes, Mrs. Larkin."

Nora nodded. She thought, how fast we who are desperate make decisions! My heart has broken, but I can save this child. "Mr. Li, they don't treat you as they should here. No one does anywhere. You've come to my rescue twice. If you want to use my Christian name, it's Nora."

Jim Li bowed. "Jim is my American name." His smile turned wry. "You might say my Christian name, although I am what you would call a heathen."

Nora ran a linen napkin through her fingers. "I had a brother back in Ireland, rest his soul. I can't help but think if he were here, Seamus would act toward me as you have."

"I am honored. Ah, but I do have a motive, Nora. You have seen and remarked on how it is for the Chinese, how we — I — am treated. People are different with you. Doors open for you whatever your circumstance. You still need my help, and I need to walk through the doors behind you before they slam shut."

Nora dropped the napkin in astonishment. "You want what exactly?"

He smiled. "I want us to be partners, an alliance. I am not certain yet in what precise way, but we can help each other in work, in business."

He'd ambushed her again. She'd only just settled the fate of Bat Moriarty's baby. She could hardly think of making another decision so soon. She still hovered around that decision. How far have I fallen to give away my child? Will I be able to? Of course, I will. I have to.

She brushed a shaky hand across her eyes. "Let me consider this. I'll need to know more and think longer. All I've wanted, all my life, is just a home and family of my own and to escape this poverty, this being looked down on like trash. Right now, I have to check on the customers."

Nora moved down the hall to the saloon. At the doorway, she started. A man she knew at once sat at the poker table. She recognized the shape of his head, the line of his cheekbone turned three-quarters away from her. A diamond ring glinted as if lit from within on one of his long, tapering fingers as he shuffled the deck and laughed at another player's remark, the sound like water over hard, smooth stones.

Nora backed into the hallway against a wall that seemed to bend. The memory of their night of passion and its aftermath struck. She remembered the desire those hands brought to life, then the betrayal. Anger slashed like a knife. Fifteen minutes later Josephine found her gasping, folded over. She supported Nora up the stairs to her room. "Send Jim Li for the doctor," Nora begged. "Please. It has to be Jim Li."

Lillie took over Nora's duties, protesting in loud, profane resentment that Nora could hear echoing down the hall even as she labored. Hours later, Lillie visited Nora's room where the doctor worked as his patient groaned and endured. Lillie returned to her business matters.

Giving birth to Helen had been uncomplicated. But this child, born of foolishness and disgrace, fought her, fought to avoid the world, fought his fatherless entry into it. Nora struggled. There was too much blood, too much. At last, torn and shattered, she felt her body split, rip, and empty. The curt doctor, whiskey on his breath, tended to the afterbirth.

Washed and in clean sheets thanks to Josephine, Nora finally reached for her son. Josephine placed a sweetly puzzled, puckered, frowning baby boy with pale, downy hair into her arms. Invaded by an unexpected rush of love, Nora stroked him and rubbed her cheek over his soft scalp. "Well, for certain you'd make anyone proud," she whispered.

The jaded doctor, weary and gruff, but fortified by Lillie's gratuitous gift of three shots of whiskey, spoke to her before leaving. "This birth was difficult. Your boy's a fighter or he wouldn't have made it. You won't ever be the same, young woman. I hope you'll be relieved at what I have to tell you. There can be no more babies. Too much damage to your nether regions. You can live a normal life, but no more babies."

Nora stared at him, both stunned and relieved. No more children. None of the joy of giving life, but none of the unbearable anguish of loss either. She realized she'd not once thought about her own future. She'd not thought of men, except to be finished with them. She hadn't thought beyond this child going to Bridget. She'd been intent on getting through his birth and settling him elsewhere.

"Now there's the matter of my bill," the doctor announced after cleaning and putting away his medical instruments.

Nora sighed. She gestured to her old satchel in the darkened corner. "See if what's there will cover it."

After rummaging through its meager contents, he sneered. "No."

Lillie stopped in the doorway. She studied the baby for a few moments in a detached, almost meditative way, then appraised the doctor holding the few bills from Nora's satchel. "Come on with me, you heartless bastard of a sawbones. This girl doesn't have enough to cover your damned remittance, but that looks like most of it. You can take the rest out in trade if you can still get it up. Hell, I'll even give you more of Lillie McGraw's fine Scotch. From my private

Stay in Helena. Leave word with Lillie where you'll be."

Jim Li disappeared, swooping gracefully away even with the baby wrapped in a full-size blanket from Nora's bed.

"Where I'll be," Nora murmured, closing her eyes against the apocalyptic scene.

After the roof collapsed in an explosion of smoke and sparks, Lillie approached and sat down, legs crossed at the ankles under her sooty skirts. The excitement all but over, she leaned back on her elbows, impassive, watching her house smolder. "I'll rebuild the damned whorehouse," she said matter-of-factly. "In the meantime, I have to make money." To Nora's unresponsive silence she added, "Don't sulk. I'll put you up in one of my other houses, but you understand things can't go on like that forever." Then her voice dropped. "I saw you send the kid with the Celestial. I did that once. Gave one up. It's the right thing."

One of the men began complaining that he wanted his money back or a poke, one or the other. "Oh hell, will you listen to that horny animal over there." Lillie tilted her head, surrounded by wild tufts of undone hair. "Shut up, you mindless piece of meat," she yelled. "You can see us at my other establishment, the Purple Palace, in two hours. I won't forget a face as ugly as yours. You can have what you paid for there. All of you can." She clambered to her feet and left Nora lying on the ground, watching fire reduce the big old house to charred ruins.

CHAPTER ELEVEN

Jim stopped in an alleyway to rebundle the baby. A cat yowled and the infant jerked his hands and legs in tiny spasms. He needed food for Nora's son, perhaps goat's milk or sheep's milk. He made his way south to an area still riddled with patches of dirty snow where Chinese work gangs and prostitutes lived. Even with Nora's note, he could find real safety only in Chinatown. No one questioned him, and the baby slept. When he reached Wood and Main Streets, he knew the residences would be those of Chinese from Canton. Jim didn't speak their dialect with perfection, but well enough.

He took long strides, hurrying to the home of Joe Sun where four men lived with a prostitute named Mai Wing. Jim knocked on its red door. Mai opened it, eyes widening in her broad Mongolian features when she saw the baby. She took him from Jim with the confidence, he guessed, of a large family's oldest daughter. Usually a Chinese woman living as Mai did would be submissive, but galvanized by the baby's arrival she ordered one of the men to get bottles, nipples, goat's milk, and nappies from a neighborhood merchant even if he had to wake him.

While Mai prepared the flat glass bottles and goat's milk, giving the baby his first food, Jim bargained with Sun for a horse and tack. Negotiations concluded, Jim tied a calico sling around his neck, the baby cocooned in it against his chest, and started out of Helena. Walking the horse, he tucked his queue into the black slouch hat pulled low over his eyes. No one stopped him or looked at him. He rode south, blending into the vast, lonely night.

After a few hours, the baby stirred. "Little one, she did not give you a name, did she?" Jim asked in Chinese. "It is not my place to do so, except on this journey."

A shooting star soared across their path. "Ah. Did you see? I should call you Taipai, the evening star. In my country there are important stories about the evening star." The baby quieted at the sound of Jim's voice. "You like the name Taipai? I like it, too. None of these white ghosts have knowledge of my country. Now that you have a name from it, I should tell you about my life there."

The baby sighed. One open eye peeked at Jim from the sling.

"I will tell you my story since your mother's and my wanderings have brought us here together. It is a story about change. Life changes all the time, you know. We remake ourselves to its demands." Accompanied by the soft thud of his horse's hooves and its occasional blowing and snorting, Jim Li, for the first time, told his whole history to another human being in America.

Traveling between Butte and Helena through the starry night, Jim murmured to the baby slumbering on his chest. He recounted what his aunt White Plum had related to him.

Jim Li was born the son of a Scottish Presbyterian minister. He'd pondered his father's character enough to guess at how his own unlikely conception came about. Jim imagined that Douglas James McIntosh chose to become a missionary out of Christian duty mixed with a compelling hunger for adventure. McIntosh found Sian, in the Chungnan Mountains, a place of leopards, bears, wild pigs, monkeys, and intrigue. He discovered a place steeped in the ancient ways of Taoist and Buddhist nuns and monks.

Douglas McIntosh would certainly have heard with bemused interest of two brothers who, protesting the behavior of the founder of a ruling dynasty, attempted to subsist on a diet of doe's milk and ferns. They starved. Unimpressed, Douglas McIntosh continued his lifelong diet of hearty porridge for breakfast. However, his needs transcended porridge.

A wealthy Chinese merchant, well traveled and fluent in English, invited Reverend McIntosh to his home. There he met the man's two daughters, both graceful and delicate as lilies. The older, Moon Jade, also conversed in English.

The attraction between Moon Jade and Reverend McIntosh became a life-or-death pull for body, mind, and soul. Moon Jade chanted her sutras, fasted, but found that her thoughts still strayed to the missionary. McIntosh prayed and doused his head in pitchers of ice water that made little horns of his curly hair. Guilt and desire kept him awake in the nights. His clothes hung loose on his tormented frame.

They finally surrendered to their passion on the seventh day of the seventh month.

Reverend McIntosh did not know, as Moon Jade did, that this was Lover's Night in China. Moon Jade met Douglas McIntosh in an apricot orchard. Perfume from ripe fruit and the floral slope of her slender neck pulled the young minister to the earth, then to a place at the earth's pulsing center. Afterward, she told him this was the Chinese night for lovers.

McIntosh rose wiser only in carnal knowledge. Guilt and shame rippled through the grass and stole into him. Two days later, according to Jim's aunt, McIntosh numbed Moon Jade with a stumbling, remorseful tirade. "You bewitched me. I came here to save souls, not lose my own. What did you make me do, witch? Never again. It's a sin, I gave in to your wiles. Never again, you scheming heathen." He left Moon Jade bewildered as to why he found passion so fearful.

He never returned to her. After much thought and meditation, at the appointed time Moon Jade shaved her head, the shimmering hair that had brushed the backs of her knees cascading to the floor. She put away her silk and brocades to wear the robes of a Buddhist nun. When she learned she was with child, she asked and received permission to remain in the convent until the birth, at which time she would give her baby to White Plum.

Moon Jade's son arrived in March. Ice crystals still hung in the air and hoar frost softened bony branches. White Plum, by then married, retrieved her nephew from the convent. There was no pretense. Jim Li knew his origins from childhood. He knew his father had departed for America, and his mother had become a religious recluse, a hermit living in a nearly inaccessible place in the Chungnan Mountains.

Jim Li glanced down at his sleeping audience, then continued. As a boy he grew surrounded by tasteful luxury in Sian, taught by gifted tutors, even an American from New York City.

He also learned about shamans, those masters of the ecstatic state. In it, they could leave their bodies, pass through a series of heavens, and communicate with spirits, seeking and gaining knowledge for the welfare of their communities. Shamans defended and aided their society, but lived apart from it. Jim identified both his hermit mother and his reverend father with shamans. He took as a given that one day he would find his parents, study their wisdom, and then become a monk himself, perhaps even a hermit. To that end, he studied until fluent in English.

At fifteen, Jim became a novice Buddhist monk. His aunt's husband died, and her sons clearly wished him to leave her care to them. After three Spartan years of temple life, rising early, reading the sutras, working in the kitchen and garden, and meditating, he left to find Moon Jade. Perhaps he would become her disciple. The abbot told him she lived on the far side of Taipaishan, the highest of the Chungnan Mountains. She lived above forests of chinaberry, birch, and fir, near the top where blue pine and azalea grew. Laypeople brought her food in exchange for her wisdom. White Plum paid for the upkeep of her sister's stone hut and for new clothes once a year.

Jim spoke aloud to his charge. "I traveled alone and unarmed." The gelding blew and Jim spoke a bit louder over the plod of its hooves. "I remembered the writings of Chia Liu, another climber, 'Here the world's illusions come to an end.' It was then that I learned to revere and require mountains. I believed Chia Liu's words to be correct, but I have since learned it is really here in America that illusions end. I have not found my father, but I have found bigotry, hate, and violence. I stay among my people, seeing how they are despised by the white ghosts. I will find a way to escape this poverty and disrespect.

"Your beautiful mother has much to learn, but I will teach her if she permits me. She will learn to trust her instincts that already tell her people's worth is not measured by their wealth or even their beliefs. She, too, must find a place where the world's illusions come to an end. It is possible that we will do that together. That is my hope."

Jim sighed, the fire and Nora's giving birth taking their toll. The baby stirred and whimpered, seeming to want more of the soothing sound of Jim's narrative. "I shall continue to explain myself to you. Let's see, I began the search for my mother.

"My path from a shrine where people prayed for rain followed a stream through the forest, gradually ascending higher and narrower until all was lost in curtains of hanging vines. I crossed ravines on fallen trees. In all, I walked ninety *gongli,* what the English call kilometers, to reach the summit of Taipaishan.

"There I met an ancient nun. She told me Moon Jade had not arrived for a gathering of hermits. My mother had been ill, spitting up blood.

"I could only stare at the calm woman. She prepared for the coming hermits and did not seem concerned about Moon Jade. I left determined to see my mother as soon as possible. I scaled a steep promontory so lofty that I heard thunder roll in the gorges beneath me. A rainbow arced across my difficult path. My sweat left dark handprints on the rocks to which I clung. A whirlwind of leaves flew toward me, veering away at the last moment. I thought I saw a flash of green. Perhaps I caught a glimpse of Maunu, she who escaped from the Emperer's court and was taught by a shaman. Hunters sometimes see her or hear her zither. I felt certain I did catch the sound."

Nora's son made a small mew. "Yes," Jim said to the quizzical little face. "Mist shifted and the ledge widened. I continued until I came to a cold, dark pool in the upper reaches of the mountain. A woman's voice called my name. I scrambled up a rocky incline, thinking it must be my mother, so eager to see her I forgot all fear. To my surprise, I reached a promontory where a small platform looked out on the purple Chungnan Range in all its plunging light and color. I turned toward a hut behind the platform. A young nun, her head shaved, knelt in her robes before the porcelain-like corpse of a tiny woman whose skin, like her robes, appeared frozen, shiny and stiff."

Jim stopped his story as the horse continued its measured pace. " 'Moon Jade told me you would come. Now she is dead,' the young disciple told me. 'Your mother went to the pool alone when I was practicing, becoming one with the Tao. I heard your mother coughing,' she continued. 'But that was not unusual. When I finished, I returned to the pool. She lay in the black water, a ribbon of red blood floating from her mouth. I carried her back, but she is gone.'

"I knelt before Moon Jade's opalescent figure, she whose love for the Reverend Douglas James McIntosh had rendered only the son she could not keep any more than Nora could keep you.

"Her face was aristocratic and delicate even in age and death, the brows like little bird wings. I bowed until my forehead rested on her folded hands. My tears covered them. I felt living fingers touch my neck. The disciple spoke, 'Do not grieve. Your mother knew you would come and told me words to give you. These words are the essence of the life that you must live if disorder is not to overtake you. These words are goodwill, compassion, joy, detachment. Wisdom will bring compassion. Detachment will come when you accept the natural order of things. Joy will come from suffering. She told me other things as well. Now we will bury her. Then I will stay, and you will travel far to seek your father."

Jim patted Nora's baby, looking into his soft eyes. "So you see, Taipai, the woman preparing for the gathering of hermits had only been detached. She had accepted the natural order of things." The baby's eyes drooped, and Jim fell into a reverie, remembering.

He spoke again. "I awoke when morning stars dissolved one by one into a peach and salmon dawn, and walked to the door to look again upon my mother. Her small form lay there, its tiny feet bound when she was a small girl. So, I realized, she had been crippled.

"I did not want a tiger or wild pig to drag her away. We carried Moon Jade a few feet farther from her platform and dug a grave, which we covered with dirt and stones. 'She is well,' the nun said. 'Your mother has become one of the immortals.'

"I knew then that my mother had succeeded in her quest to return to the Tao, the heavenly nothingness from which we come. Not all reach immortality. 'Will she ever appear to me?' I asked her."

" 'I don't know. Will you search for the man McIntosh?' She seemed to know my answer, and smiled.

"That is when I decided to travel to America. I came for my past and I stay for my future."

The baby, lulled by Jim's story, jerked fully awake when he stopped speaking. Its thin cry spoke of some problem. Jim felt its full nappy and turned the horse. A rim of light lit the mountains on the far side of the river. Before him stretched a level valley floor, no other travelers heard or seen.

He dismounted in the dawn and built a small fire, then changed the baby. Hidden in the cottonwood stands, he heated goat's milk. Taipai nursed in contentment. After burping his charge, Jim stretched a blanket on the ground, unsaddled and hobbled the horse, then lay with Taipai between him and the fire. Both slept. Jim kept one hand curled around Bat Moriarty's ring in his pocket. It seemed to radiate heat. Mingling with early spring water songs, in his dreams he heard the sounds of a zither.

Under cover of darkness, Jim traveled another night and slept another day, stopping only to tend to Taipai. Finally, at dusk, he rode through thin snow patches down a long hill to Butte. The town seemed more hellish and demented than ever. He found the home of Su-Chen, the prostitute whose quarters he once shared. She gazed at him from her musty cot, heavy-lidded in an opium stupor, a crusted sore on her upper lip. She stared without interest at the baby and rolled over with her back to them, not having spoken a word.

Jim saw to the baby, slept for a few hours, then heated water and bathed his charge, putting a clean nappy on him. The newborn's bottom had turned red and peeling, but he didn't cry. Jim fed him, then studied him for a long moment. He touched a finger to the baby's nose in a farewell pat. Finally, he put him back in the sling and set off for Dublin Gulch.

In the grimy predawn, comforting lights brightened a few windows, Bridget and Michael's among them. Jim Li walked to the door and knocked. Michael answered in his union suit, Bridget peering around him, tumbling blonde hair soft on her shoulders.

"A Chink. What the hell?" Michael's tone showed he intended intimidation.

Jim Li bowed, his eyes slits. He spoke in Chinese, "Pig-nosed devil, you have a son." He held out Nora's notes, careful not to touch Michael's thick fingers. As Michael and Bridget read, they looked in joyous wonder first at each other, then at the wriggling lump in Jim's sling.

Bridget stepped around her husband. "Jim Li, I know you speak English. Please let me have this baby."

Jim removed Taipai from the sling.

"Does he have a name?" Michael asked.

"No," Jim answered, bowing. "That will be for his mother and father to decide."

Bridget stepped forward and took the sleepy baby from Jim. "He has a little rash," Jim said. "From the journey."

"We'll fix it. You want some tickee for this?" Michael rubbed his fingers together.

Without a word, Jim took off the sling, dropping it on the ground. He bowed again and backed away, not turning until he could barely see them, his hands balled into fists in his pockets. He'd lost detachment over giving Taipai to such a father. He forced himself to relax his hands, reminded himself to breathe slowly. It was done. Detachment.

At his old lodging, Jim merely glanced at the opium pipe Su-Chen offered him. The air hung sweet with the smell. He gestured no and settled into sleep on a woven mat. When he awoke hours later, Su-Chen's cot was empty. Could she be seeking customers? What man would go with a woman so clearly blighted, who would pass disease on to any who entered her? As good a time as any to leave.

He wrapped a bit of cooked pork in newspaper, added a sack of rice, and rammed both into his duffel bag. He left money for the food, flung the duffel over his shoulder, and left. He'd never touched Su-Chen or spoken to her, mindful of the open sores on her body, the stench of early decay.

Jim traveled again at night, less afraid of trouble since he'd delivered Taipai. However, Bat Moriarty's ring still rode with him, this time hidden deep in the rice bag. The Silver Bow River burbled of spring breakup, but the sound depressed Jim. He thought of drownings and of water spirits pulling mortals down to their deaths. Owls swooped through the cottonwoods, great gray shadows that could be dire messengers from beyond this world. At least night protected him from white ghosts and their violence.

Jim Li took stock. Nora couldn't stay in Helena without eventually becoming a prostitute. She would do well in that profession, he reflected matter-of-factly. Then he turned from that thought, remembering her direct gaze. When Nora Larkin saw him, she saw a human being, not a subspecies Chinee. They could help each other. He would show her the ring and make plans.

They needed to disappear for awhile, let Nora recover from giving birth and both be out of sight of any who might remember Bat's ring with its glittering, captivating facets and want it for themselves.

Jim entered Helena wondering what he would find. Lillie's house lay in ruins. Iron bedsteads and blackened mattresses littered the charred foundation. The place smelled evil. He saw no one. He rode on to the Purple Palace, the stone structure on the hill that now would have to serve as Lillie's main house, and for the moment, place of all business. Jim dismounted and tied the horse to the hitching post before knocking at the back door.

"Jim Li." A short, stocky girl with frizzy black hair opened it.

"Is Nora Larkin here?" he asked.

"She is in body, but we've been taking bets on where her spirit is. You hand over the kid?"

Jim nodded.

"What the hell. Maybe if you tell her, it will cut through the fog. It's worth a try."

Jim kept his duffel bag slung over his shoulder as he followed the girl down the flowered carpet of the hall, her hips rolling inside her thin chemise. She led him to the last room.

Jim stepped inside. Nora lay on the double bed in a nightgown open at the collar. Lines of dirt streaked her neck below her white face. The girls had brushed her hair, but it needed washing. Her eyes were black holes in a skull. The girl shook her head and left, closing the door hard behind her.

In the dim light Nora kept silent, although she seemed awake. Jim lowered his duffel bag to the floor where it thudded on the carpet. Nora's eyes slid to him.

"Did they take him?" she whispered.

"Yes. They were full of joy. They will love him."

"Sure and they would be." She turned her head to the wall. Jim could barely make out her next words, "Anyone would love him."

Jim saw that he had to reach her quickly. "Nora." He sat on the foot of the bed, his voice soft. "When the house was burning, I took something from Bat Moriarty's body. I took his diamond ring. I believe we can both make a fresh start from it. He owed you that much."

"I remember it, and I want nothing of that devil's," Nora said, her eyes meeting Jim's, tears glistening at the corners.

"Nora, where we came from, both you and I, what could bring security and dignity? What did we want more than anything?

What did people kill and fight for?"

"Why land, for certain. The land meant everything. But would one ring, even one so alluring, bring enough?" She closed her eyes from the effort of talking.

"Not here. But let me finish the story for you that I started telling Taipai on our journey."

"Who?"

"Your son. I named him just for our journey. It means Evening Star."

"I have no son. I thank you for taking him, but we'll not speak of him again. I can't bear it. If I think of him, I'll go mad. It's enough that I can't stop wondering if I should have kept him. My last child. But then, I know he's better off with Bridget and Michael. He must be." Tears trickled into her hair. She wiped them with the backs of her hands, seeming to forget Jim's presence.

He took one of her hands, squeezing it in desperation. It was bold of him, the first time they touched in such a way. Still, the fit of their hands felt right. Anything to bring her back. "Let me tell you. Let me tell you what I've seen in my past."

"Get on with it, then." She pulled her hand away, not unaware after all, just indifferent.

Jim hesitated, unused to this hard bitterness in Nora. "My mother became a hermit in China. I searched for her, but she had become one of the immortals. I decided then to search for my father. My aunt, White Plum, told me I would find him in western America or Canada. She gave me money for my passage and entry into this country."

Nora's eyes showed no glimmer of interest.

Jim continued, "My cousin helped me book passage on a ship to America. He had contacts who could smuggle me in. After a long voyage, my ship docked in Vancouver. Following instructions, I found a man who agreed to take me and another to Fort MacLeod in Alberta.

"For a prearranged price, a Chinese café owner there kept me and two others from Canton. Two white men in great hairy coats pulled up in a wagon. They were drunk and disrespectful, but for $250 apiece they agreed to smuggle us into America. When we started, they covered us with a tarp on the floor of the wagon among sacks of supplies. The smell of oats nearly suffocated us.

"Even at night in the moonlight, I saw looking out from the tarp we were in a land approaching the magnificence of the Chungnan Range in China. We rested one day, and on the next one of the men hid us in a little cabin deeper into the forest than the larger one he lived in near a lake. Two days later, he dressed us as hunters and we traveled again by horse. I wore a buckskin jacket and goat hide chaps. I imagined I must look very western.

"Often on that journey, I heard wolves howling and elk bugling. I watched a grizzly bear and saw a sea of elk. We crossed meadows and creeks and traveled through a high pass. We followed the North Fork of the Flathead River on horseback. We dropped down to a place at the lower end of a lake, Lake McDonald. I have seen nothing more beautiful, even in China. Then we went on to a town in the valley."

"Why do you tell me all this? I can't follow you," Nora rasped.

"Nora. There is land to be had on the North Fork of the Flathead River. We could become business partners. We could raise cattle, hunt, trap, fish, garden, and survive with few people to interfere. As a white woman, you could someday claim the land. I can provide in strength what we need to get started. It's a place where your soul can come back to you. We could help each other and present ourselves as mistress and servant. The mountains are far from these troubles you have had. It would be a place to start over. A place with no illusions."

"Land." Nora tested the word on her tongue. A memory of green fields and garden plots penetrated her blank grief. "Could we grow vegetables?"

"Yes. Vegetables and flowers. Will you agree?"

She sighed. "Well, I can't stay on here, I suppose. One place is the same as another. But you'll be working with a ghost, my friend. The life has fair drained out of me."

"Just put land in your name, Nora. Life will fill you again. We will do it."

An interval of silence followed. Jim told her he would return and left to make inquiries about selling the ring.

CHAPTER TWELVE

After Jim left, Nora considered his idea. She struggled out of bed and tottered to the wash basin, shocked at her haggard reflection in the dresser mirror. "Jesus, Mary, and Joseph," she muttered, splashing water so cold that color flushed her bloodless cheeks and throat. She staggered like a person on the rolling deck of a ship. She thought of the sea, then the Wicklow Mountains. She recalled her brother fishing in his little boat. All as scattered and lost as her own children.

But Jim Li had talked of land. Nora thought she'd become a dry, empty husk. But a thin string still vibrated. Land. Land gave life. It created home. Whatever this wild country Jim talked of was, it had to be better than lying down and dying in a house of prostitution. Nora pulled the nightgown over her head. She still ached, but that and her bleeding would end. She braided her hair in back with awkward fingers and dressed. She rolled up her sleeves and opened the shutters, looking down on the city.

Somewhere down there her only friend was making dangerous inquiries about the sale of a stolen diamond ring. The poor often had to bend the law. The fact of it was, she thought, survival knows no law. Nora squared her shoulders. Well, then. If she must go on, she'd do it right. When it came to bargaining, the Irish could still show the world a thing or two — especially where land was involved.

Nora started down the hallway, aware of doors creaking open as the girls verified that Nora Larkin walked among them once again. Lillie responded in a gruff voice to her tap on the door, but Nora entered without fear. She felt quite sure she would never feel fear, along with many other emotions, again.

"Lillie, I have a thing I need to sell. I don't know where to take it."

Lillie's eyes narrowed as she looked up from her ledger. She exhaled through her nose. "What the hell kind of a thing?"

"It's a piece of jewelry, a family heirloom that my husband brought from Ireland." For a moment Nora wondered if Lillie would demand some sort of payment for her stay at the Palace. She avoided looking into her employer's narrowed eyes.

"Take it to Sean Kehoe's bank. Ask for Kehoe himself. He'll buy it with his own cash."

"Thanks, Lillie." Nora decided to offer Lillie something after all. "I'll pay you for my keep as soon as I have the money." Nora turned and rested her hand on the door knob, a wash of exhaustion passing over her.

"Are you heading out?" Lillie asked, putting down her pen and stretching.

"I believe I'll take Jim Li as a servant and go toward Flathead country. I hear it's beautiful."

"Watch out for mountain men. If you see Beartracks Benton or Pete Dumont, you greet them for Lillie McGraw. You're stealing my Celestial, huh?"

"There's more to him than you ever saw." Nora added, "I thank you for the help you've given me." Lillie stared at her for a moment, then nodded and returned to the neat columns in her books. Nora closed the door behind her.

Nora met Jim on Main Street. Passersby stared at the intense, gaunt woman and the tall Chinese man bending to listen to her.

After a moment, Jim threw his duffel bag to the boardwalk and squatted beside it, hands searching inside until he pulled out the gleaming ring. They walked to the bank where Jim stood in one corner as Nora sought a meeting with the president.

The teller, thinning hair pomaded, glared at Jim, then knocked on a door, its black letters announcing it to be the bank president's inner sanctum. The teller went in. When he reappeared, he motioned for only Nora to enter.

Bulky, canny-eyed Sean Kehoe stood and extended his hand. A long oak desk, varnished nearly to black, separated them. Nora leaned forward to take his soft fingers. "Nora Larkin," he said. "I knew a man named Tade Larkin back in County Cork it was. A good man. Good miner."

"He was my husband." Nora's smile was, for a moment, unforced.

"You don't say. Was, you say?"

"My husband died in an explosion at the Neversweat in Butte." Nora paused for a moment, trying to control her voice. "Tade died in the fire. His best friend was blinded. Others died or were hurt as well."

"I heard of that one." Kehoe shook his head, and gestured to one of the leather chairs in front of his desk before sitting back down. "There's no denying the mines are treacherous. Are there little ones left behind as well? Have the boys taken care of you?"

"We have no little ones left," Nora answered. "Our daughter died of diphtheria in the epidemic here."

Collins nodded. "I'm sorry to hear of your misfortunes, Mrs. Larkin. You've had your share. Now, how can I be of service?"

Nora hesitated. She hadn't bargained on Sean Kehoe knowing Tade. He'd never believe such a large, compelling ring had been worn or even owned by a working man. She inhaled. "A man who knew us wanted to help and gave me a valuable ring, but made me promise not to tell where it came from. He said there were those who'd think the worst. There was nothing improper going on, I assure you." She kept her eyes direct on her listener's even as she hated the need to lie and her ability to do it so easily. "So, I find myself needing to sell the ring. A friend told me you might transact business of this very nature."

Sean Kehoe raised his eyebrows. Nora would figure out later that he only made such private purchases from whores and gamblers. He extended his hand. "Let me see it, my dear." His tone had altered slightly, become more familiar. Nora felt a frisson of unease.

Kehoe took a jeweler's glass from a small drawer in his desk, put it to his eye, and inspected the well-set jewel. He ran through figures under his breath. She guessed that he was thinking a young widow wouldn't know its value. Still, men had always admired her looks, and she was the widow of a man from County Cork. She detected a surge of pity in the banker's voice. "I'll give you $1,500 for the ring."

"I'm thinking I need $2,000," Nora said, depending on his previous note of sympathy.

Kehoe laughed. "My dear woman, it's a compelling object. I'm not sure why, but it is. However, you must see I'm being generous."

Nora leaned forward. "Mr. Kehoe, I've lost everything. I'm going up to the Flathead River area to homestead. I need money. I believe the ring to be of high value."

"Maybe not so high as you think when you can't say the name of its source." His mouth hardened.

Nora kept her gaze steady on Kehoe's shrewd eyes. "How about $1,800, then?"

"$1,750 and there's an end of it." He put papers from the desk in his drawer and tapped his finger on the blotter before him.

"You've bought yourself a most attractive

ring, Mr. Kehoe. May good fortune follow it." Nora mustered a shaky smile.

Kehoe reached to a safe beside his desk, twirled the combination, opened it, and counted out the bills. "It's a great deal of cash for a woman alone to handle and protect."

"I'll travel with a trustworthy Chinese in my employ, so I'm not all that alone," Nora replied. She stuffed the money into her satchel and stood, finally able to be truthful. "I'm that grateful to you for your kindness. It's good to meet someone who knew Tade."

Kehoe stood and extended his hand again. "A fine man. A real loss. Stop and see us if you ever get back from the country of the Flathead. You may not want to return, though. They say it's a hard life, but close to paradise."

"Well, I wouldn't mind seeing paradise," Nora said with a catch in her voice. "Nearly all the people I love are there."

Back in the lobby, she nodded to Jim Li, who followed her out to the corner where she turned. "Sean Kehoe paid me $1,750. We have our stake."

Jim bowed. "Very impressive. Your bargaining power is in robust health. Now we

214

need to get a wagon and supplies. We'll make a list."

They walked up to the Palace, settling in the kitchen, heads together to the cook's consternation. The first need was for a wagon and horses. Horses were going for about $100 apiece. They could get a wagon used, but even so, over a quarter of the ring money, as Nora thought of it, would be gone. They decided to make the whole trip by wagon, no train fares and shipping costs for them.

Then they penned a long list: axes, a hammer, knives, nails, a hatchet, cooking pans, a tin wash bowl, dippers, buckets, silverware, plates, and two tarps for each to sleep under on the journey. For domestic comfort once there, they added needles, thread, material, and scissors. For the garden they needed carrot and cabbage seeds, apple tree seedlings, onion sets, seed potatoes, rhubarb roots, a rake, a hoe, a shovel, a pitchfork, barrels. Finally, they wrote down mousetraps, an 1873 Winchester rifle, and an 1873 Remington Whitmore shotgun, plenty of ammunition, lanterns, baling twine, a crosscut saw, rope, matches, wash tubs, a cook stove, and over one hundred traps. Clothes included heavy shoes and jackets, heavy skirts and trousers, then blankets. They would also buy flour and sugar, coffee beans and a coffee grinder, salt and pepper, and dried apples.

One week after the ring's sale, Jim Li drove the loaded wagon up to the Purple Palace. Before Nora climbed up to the seat, she paid Lillie in full — $1.00 per day for her keep while ill and useless. The two women said an awkward goodbye, both aware that Nora never really belonged in Lillie's house. Nora remembered that Lillie, too, had given up a child, but if anything it made her question herself. She really wasn't above any of the upstairs girls.

The girls in Lillie's employ waved Nora and Jim on their way with a mixture of head-shaking at the risky venture and envy at Nora's pluck. The man at her side seemed to have no place in their estimates of her chance for success.

Sean Kehoe pulled back the lace curtain from an upper-story window and spoke to the naked, pouting girl on the bed behind him. "She'll make it. She's like me. She does what she has to do, and she finds the ones who can help her do it. A true daughter of the Emerald Isle." At that he dropped the curtain, along with his musings on the Widow Larkin, and resumed his pursuit of

until after we'd done what brought the baby. I'd taken him for a lodger in Butte. I should have known better, him a gambler and all. Anyway, he took off when he learned his missus placed personal ads in the paper looking for him. They had children."

Father Shaw sat forward, bushy eyebrows almost meeting as he concentrated. "Let me see, child. You stole a marker with the help of a Chinese man. This same Chinese found you your job at a bawdy house, and then he stole a ring off your married lover's dead hand so you could leave for the North Country together? You and this Chinaman?"

"The Chinaman is a friend only, Father. We look out for each other. You know how they treat them here. He's half white anyhow. His father's a Presbyterian missionary."

Father Shaw smiled for the first time. "Ah, Presbyterian, is it? Well, that would explain a great deal about the boy, would it not?"

Nora, who hadn't seen humor in anything for weeks, gave the lattice a sharp look. "Well, I'm sure that might be it. But he's a good man. He did everything to help me survive. I believe he's a survivor, Father, and there's something to be said for that, isn't there?"

Father Shaw's face grew solemn. "Yes, but

221

to survive as a good Catholic you must examine what you've done. Where is your baby?"

"I gave him up to friends not blessed in their marriage. I didn't love his father, and I had no means to care for him. Well, I didn't know then about the ring, but it's for the best. He'll have a good, normal life with Bridget and Michael. Two married parents. Good Catholics. Perhaps they'll take in others, or perhaps have more born to them." Nora's voice wavered and dropped. "My life now seems so uncertain. The doctor told me I can never have another child. . . ."

"I'm sure you chose well for your son's future, and I'm sorry you'll have no chance of more," Father Shaw said. "But there are others involved. Your fancy man had children and a wife he abandoned. His property is rightfully theirs. Your moral duty is to see that the proceeds from the ring are restored to that family. How much was it worth?"

"Well, Father, $1,750, but most is gone for supplies. Anyway, by our agreement, half belongs to my partner."

"No, my daughter. It all belongs to the man's wife and children. You've no claim on it. Your child has other parents now. You must see that that family's rights are respected. Assure me that you will reimburse

222

the family for the ring. There can be no absolution otherwise."

Nora reflected. "It will take time. I'll pay them when the day comes that I can."

"For your penance say the rosary and make a good act of contrition, and do not let your Chinese friend lead you into any more schemes."

Father Shaw blessed her. He slid the little door shut, and Nora walked through the cathedral's rich stillness into the glare of day.

Jim helped her into the wagon, giving her a concerned glance.

Nora felt relieved that she'd unburdened herself, but troubled over the money. She had to return it some day. She studied the dark figure of her companion, his queue tucked into his slouch hat as he made final entries in his notebook.

He finally smiled. "Did the confession strengthen you?"

Nora stared at him. Jim astonished her with his knowledge of religions. How did he know? "It did, but Father says I must give all the money from the ring to Bat Moriarty's widow, Dierdre, and their babies. I never saw the facts of it that way. Do you think we sinned, Jim?"

"I think fate placed the dead man's ring

in our reach. In time, I believe you will have the money to pay over to Dierdre Moriarty and her children with interest if you still feel the obligation. This morning, we have a journey to start."

CHAPTER THIRTEEN

As they moved through Helena, Nora broke a long silence. "Jim, if you want to stop pretending you're my servant, we can. Perhaps the world up north will be ready to accept two ragtag loose-end partners such as ourselves. Sure and it's as likely as them believing a tinker's daughter from Ireland has an elegant manservant such as yourself."

Jim shook his head. "Not yet. People on the trail might behave like animals. There are many ways to kill a man and hide him in the wilderness. They also might not respect you. I don't believe it wise to take chances, at least until we settle."

"All right." Nora wondered at how he could accept the necessity with such composure, as though it were the normal order of things. Perhaps for him it was. Her tinker family made a show of holding their heads up, pretending insults from the so-called respectable folk didn't hurt, even though, of course, they did.

Nora's visit with Father Shaw had cost time. They'd only passed through the outskirts of Helena by late morning, gaining elevation as the day warmed while their horses strained to haul the wagon. Nora took the reins, glad of her work gloves, as Jim got down to push as needed or walk beside the horses. At early evening, they stopped in a flat area by the road.

Almost shy, they made their first camp, finding what they needed to cook, not yet in a routine of the trail. They ate in front of a small fire, alone in the vast dark. Later under her tarp, Nora curled in her bedroll feeling vulnerable without walls around her. She slept fitfully, listening to unfamiliar sounds, even though Jim slept on the other side of the wagon, rifle at hand. During periods of wakefulness, her thoughts turned to questions. What if Tade and I had left the bitter smoke of Butte after we had Helen? What if the three of us had ventured west to find our land? Would they still be with me? Now I'm alone with this Chinese man. Longing for what might have been stung her until dawn.

Next morning meant more of the same, the climb up the pass grueling for humans and horses. As Mullan Road ascended, the panorama to their left spread as a great sea of mountain ranges like frozen waves rising and dipping to the horizon. To the right, more forested giants rose beside them. The limitless sky rendered them small and insignificant, a strangely soothing sensation after the strife of Helena when everything Nora did seemed so important.

Except for the rare cabin, they saw no signs of human habitation. Redtail hawks screamed, plunging from bright blue airiness for prey.

Nora gazed in wonder. She hadn't realized how massive the Rocky Mountain range would be. As the horses' work grew harder and the grade steeper, she and Jim alternated climbing down to walk. They stopped often to rest Wink and Cotton. She didn't mind being on foot, the breeze cool against her sun-warmed face, the tang of early-summer grass pleasing after winter's vacuum.

Next morning they arrived at Mullan Pass, which seemed the apogee of the world. They rested the lathered horses. Even there, though, Nora mourned her losses — Tade and Helen — the world such a big place — her relinquished son so small and far away. She didn't speak of it to Jim. What could she say? Silence had become their third companion.

They descended into a rich valley sprinkled with pine and cottonwood groves lining a creek. Jim gathered firewood, and they dined on biscuits, beans, dried apples, and coffee. Neither spoke much, both tired but comfortable, growing used to every evening's work. It almost seemed Jim was her servant as she said good night, leaving him to check the horses. Before Nora sank into exhausted slumber, she heard him moving about, keeping guard. She awoke once and peered out. Jim slept on the wagon bed, rifle crooked in his arm. They would reach their land without loss of supplies, of that she felt certain. She backed under her tarp and fell asleep cocooned in her bedroll.

Following the second night west of the pass, they traveled to Elliston. An old hostel there would offer a bed, but the sound of drunken laughter warned them off.

"Inebriated men might not accept me even as your servant," Jim said. They spent the night back in the trees that stood like sentinels, although Nora knew that only Jim stood between her and unspeakable dangers.

With dawn their fears lifted like departing owls as Nora and Jim moved toward Avon, a stage station. There she saw the wisdom of his determination to be her servant. The my father. 'We have heard of a Presbyterian missionary in Demersville. It might be Douglas McIntosh,' the older brother told me. The younger said the Reverend has a wife. He did not know about children. Of course, they would be grown, don't you think?"

After Missoula, the wagon bumped through country full of boulders, thick forests, and torrential streams. Because its wheels slid hard into old ruts, Nora preferred to walk. Still grieving, she found some comfort in the splendor around her and Jim's alert watchfulness over her and their possessions. At evening Jim gathered water and firewood, and as often as not, washed their few dishes. She thanked him, but didn't offer to do more. Left alone, she took needed time to think of all that had happened, of her lost husband and children.

After five sunny days and cold nights, they left the variegated shadows of high pines for the flowering expanse of the Jocko Valley. The Flathead Indian Agency presented sudden, squared angles of civilization.

"Perhaps we should construct ourselves an agency. It looks so grand," Nora said, awed by the settlement with its own mill, smithy, main house, outbuildings, orchards, and huge garden.

The agent and his wife had a reputation for providing warm hospitality to all passing through, regardless of status or color. As Jim and Nora pulled up to the two-story white house, several well-dressed children spilled out to greet them. A tall blonde woman wearing spotless summer white and a welcoming smile followed the boys and girls.

"Welcome, weary travelers." Her smile embraced them both. "I'm Fiona Bond, and we'd like you to join us for dinner and stay the night."

Nora glanced at Jim.

"This time, we will be safe," he said. He climbed down from the wagon and bowed. "It would be our honor. I am Jim Li. This is Mrs. Larkin."

Nora followed Fiona Bond into the gracious interior. The sight of horsehair furniture, elegant tasseled lampshades, and bookshelves flanking the massive hearth drew her admiring sigh. Mrs. Bond showed the two to rooms where they could wash away the travel dust and shake out fresh clothes.

They joined her and the children at dinner. Nora sat at the center of one side of the table, winged by four red-haired Bond shiver. A fenced cemetery greeted them. But behind that, the mission buildings clustered before the graceful sweeping curtain of the Mission Mountains.

Jim only clucked to the horses, leaving the disturbing cemetery behind on the curving road. Jim guided Wink and Cotton to the far side of a little church, beside the log cabin serving as residence for the Sisters of Providence.

The Reverend Mother Alenthe, small, neat and welcoming, stepped out of the cabin holding both hands out to Nora. "Well, we have guests. Welcome. Young man, the Fathers will see to you. My child, you follow me." She showed Nora to a cot in the two-room shelter for nuns, its white walls relieved by colors of a painting of the Virgin.

That night they ate in the school dining room. Nora felt a bit disconcerted at the sight of tables of serious Indian children, hair combed and dressed in trousers and plain pinafores. It occurred to her that their parents must miss them. She pushed away the memory of a soft, fragrant head, of small hands clutching her own.

Jim piqued the children's curiosity more than Nora did. Dark, solemn eyes focused on him. Nora admired his unself-conscious ability to keep dining as though they ate alone on the trail. She found herself scrutinizing him with a flicker of bewilderment similar to the one of several nights before that had unsettled her so.

After dinner and visiting she lay in her narrow bed, breathing cold mountain air and trying to lie still. She wondered at herself. Could she be discovering feelings for Jim Li? She didn't feel matched and easy as she had with Tade, or excited over forbidden fruit as she had with Bat. She found Jim Li . . . intriguing.

The more she puzzled, the more uncertain she felt. She twisted on the cot, holding her breath, hoping her restlessness wouldn't disturb the gentle women who were the first to mother her since Mrs. Leary. The Virgin's gaze from the wall held a touch of rebuke. Nora closed her eyes and resolved to think only of the trail ahead. That promised challenge aplenty.

Chapter Fourteen

After four hard days of travel, Jim pulled Wink and Cotton to a stop as they topped a ridge overlooking an astonishing body of sunlit blue water strewn with a few pine-covered islands. White peaks of the graceful Mission Mountains rose to its east.

"Flathead Lake," Jim announced. "As big as a sea."

"It shines as bright as one," Nora said, standing to stretch and appreciate the glorious revelation. "Jim, you've guided us to a place stolen from paradise."

"We must take care," Jim cautioned. "There may be spirits in such water."

Nora laughed, then remembered his mother had drowned. Still, the land before them held such fruitful promise. In all America nothing could be more beautiful.

The horses descended to the lake and plodded past Lambert's Landing where they would proceed by ferry the next day. Its few rough-hewn log buildings, a large one in the center, comprised the only settlement to be seen. They continued five more miles to the ranch where the man who played his fiddle at the Bond home lived with his Nez Perce wife and their daughter. He'd invited Jim and Nora to stay at his ranch when they came through.

"We'll be comfortable here," Jim said.

Wiry Dave Polson and his family welcomed them. Hosts and guests ate venison stew at a table outside as the mountaintops glowed pink with what Dave called alpenglow. They visited and watched the lake's blue water tint to cherry, lavender, then indigo. Wrapped in her shawl, Nora sighed in surprising contentment. She helped with dishes, then returned to stay outside with Jim for awhile after the Polsons excused themselves to tuck their shy daughter in. It felt comfortable for Nora and Jim to be alone now with no real need to sort out or analyze who and what they were, the pair of them.

Nora reminded herself there were worse traits than mystery.

Next morning they bid farewell to the Polsons, then arranged to take the wagon on a big, flat-bottomed ferry from Lambert's

Landing across the Flathead River. Nora leaned against its wooden railing, enjoying the sight of transparent rippling water and mountains rising toward a cloud-strewn sky. Jim sat rigid on the wagon seat, clutching the reins with whitened knuckles. His jaw clenched until they reached the west bank. When he climbed down, he turned away from the lake and inhaled.

So, Nora thought, climbing down without his help, Jim Li truly does fear water.

"Can you not swim?" she asked. When he shook his head, she smiled. "I'll teach you one day. You'll enjoy it." Jim only offered a hand to help her climb back on the wagon.

This next stretch, the ten-day leg to Demersville, proved rough going. The wagon lurched over mud that spattered them, rocks that jolted, and a rutted road that threatened the wheels. They passed rustic habitations along the shore, but chose inconspicuous campsites. Still, the company of Flathead Lake in all its moods, from mirror-like calm to foam-flecked waves, and the sight of occasional Kootenai villages fascinated the two. Nora walked often, muscles stronger as the past year's physical ravages receded.

The sojourners stopped at the lake's north end, five miles from the bustling town of

Demersville. Steamboats stopped there in season, making it a hub of activity. They made camp in customary near silence, cooking beans, salt pork, and biscuits over the fire. While Nora watched their supper, Jim scoured the area for kindling. Stirring the thoroughly cooked beans, Nora fretted that he was taking his time about it. She disliked having Jim out of sight, although she couldn't have said which one of them she worried about more. When he returned with several fresh trout, they cooked and ate them, Nora in secret relief that he'd returned to her unharmed.

Later, he asked, "Would you stroll down to the lake? We can keep the campfire in sight. I'll carry the rifle."

Nora looked up from gazing into the low flames. "I don't mind. Sure and we could walk across the water on a trail of moonlight." She stood, adjusting her shawl against the night air. They meandered to where water lapped and whispered like shifting campfire logs. They reached a piece of blowdown, swirled by nature into a seat for two. As they watched, the white disc of a full moon levitated into the spangled sky.

Jim began, "We are the best of friends, and you have always honored me by acknowledging me as a worthy person. You must never feel alone or afraid. I pledge this to you with my life."

"Yes, we are." Nora smoothed her skirt. "The best of friends. I've been blessed before with Rose and Bridget, but never with anyone better than you." Rising trout occasionally dimpled the lake's placid surface.

"Those islands could be lily pads," Jim mused.

"I imagined they could be fishing boats, returning to shore loaded with the day's catch," Nora responded. She felt the heat from his shoulder against her own, and shifted away from physical contact. He didn't speak or move, but she heard him exhale. They remained so for a long time, then wandered back, Nora to the bedroll under her tarp, Jim to his by the fire.

Jim felt some nervousness about walking into Demersville with its reputation of having bloomed into a raucous settlement. Steamboats didn't provide the only activity there. Bands of Kootenai camped on the trade center's fringes. Demersville boasted a store, livery, blacksmith shop, two saloons, a doctor's office, and barber shop. Reputedly, there was a drunkard justice of the peace, but no jail. Prisoners awaited trial under guard at the local hotel. The broad-minded town boasted both a Catholic and a Protestant church. But how would a Chinese man fare?

Jim Li walked the five miles, leaving Nora with the rifle and shotgun, happy to tend horses, wash clothes, and rest in the sunshine.

Townspeople glanced at Jim with contempt, indifference, or hostility. He'd learned to avoid eye contact with denizens of frontier towns. Hunching a bit, he walked in the muddy street to avoid confrontation until he reached the Protestant church. He stopped to brush dust from his coat and straightened to his full six feet.

A portly man emerged from the frame parsonage behind the equally white church. Jim removed his hat. The man nodded as Jim approached and asked, "Can you tell me where I might find the Reverend McIntosh?" For the first time, he noticed the other's clerical collar.

"His soul is with God. His mortal remains rest in the cemetery. What is your business here?"

"He knew my family in China. I wished to greet him." Jim hid sharp disappointment as the new reverend explained how his predecessor's heart had failed. He added that Reverend McIntosh's wife and daughters moved away to live near family in Ohio. Jim, wanting to weep in disappointment, thanked him.

Once at the well-tended cemetery, he searched through rows of family plots, a Japanese section, and finally stopped at the headstone for the Reverend Douglas McIntosh, servant of God, beloved husband and father. Someone had placed fresh flowers at its base. Jim felt nothing but irony that he came upon both parents so shortly after death claimed them. His questions, the chance to understand, never could be asked or answered. Jim stood as though waiting for his father to materialize. He did not. Reverend McIntosh would keep his reasons and his secrets forever.

Jim headed back to camp with languor combined of thwarted hopes and exhaustion. He'd expected so much. Now the obscured core of his origins remained in mist. A leaf adrift on a wild river, he must move on. His father had contributed Jim's height and large hands. Not his ability. So be it. He would be his own man.

He took comfort in seeing the campfire's dark thread of smoke. He, like Nora, must let the past go and make their future together, something shaped anew, battered by life as both might be.

Nora had gathered firewood and made sourdough biscuits, then washed their travel-soiled clothes. She sat mending rips and tears from rigors of the trail. Jim nodded without smiling as she waved.

He finally approached her. "I found my father buried in the Demersville Cemetery."

She put down her mending. "I'm so sorry, Jim. You deserved to know him."

Jim nodded, then left to fish with a willow pole and feather bobber. The sun warmed his tense shoulders, bouncing its white glare off shining water. Geese flew overhead in a lopsided V. Even nature had irregularities. The day left a taste of bitterness like unripe fruit. He'd arrived too late to know his father. He would accept it in time, and he must also put any anger against paternal abandonment behind him, must seek compassion and detachment.

A trout bit, and Jim pulled it in, dropping the glittering fish into his creel. He fitted a writhing night crawler on his hook and plopped the line into darkening water.

His thoughts drifted to a blossoming dream. Chinese neither feared nor rejected passion. Love existed as a blessing amidst challenges of existence. Perhaps his parents had not differed much, both concerned with spiritual matters. His mother achieved a state of detached holiness that his father, striving for converts, striving to support his wife and two girls, striving for accomplishment of some sort, probably never had.

"Good will, compassion, joy, detachment," Jim whispered as another fish bit. He could achieve the first three, but what about the last? He felt an attachment to Nora that would only grow deeper as they depended on each other in the wilderness. They two alone must find a path out of the dust of illusion.

The next morning as they moved out from camp, Nora stole a look at Jim. His face, even composed, seemed a little wild, as though already affected by the untamed country ahead. His queue hung long and thick, and she found herself wondering what that straight black hair would be like hanging free. She shook her head. A ridiculous thought.

After leaving Demersville, they passed through the broad Flathead Valley. Excited, anticipating entry into the surrounding mountains, they talked of how the trail to come held threat and promise in equal measure.

■ ■ ■ ■

Miles away that night Bat Moriarty's eyes opened, horrified, staring as he lifted a tremulous hand to the collarless neckline of his drenched nightshirt. He'd dreamed of fire again, an apocalyptic conflagration in which he lay paralyzed. As flames licked toward his waist, he'd seen a figure, a man's shape, the face obscured by smoke. Almost weeping in desperation, Bat reached out to the shadowy form whose hand rose and extended toward him. Instead of carrying him to safety, however, the figure's fingers took firm grasp of the ring on Bat's finger, wrenched it off, then disappeared.

Bat turned his head, hair matted, on the sweat-soaked pillow, and stared at the tangled, brassy curls of the woman snoring beside him. He winced as he shook her. The blister-shiny pink scars covered burns on his legs and torso that still caused pain. When she didn't stop her soft rhythmic wheeze, he pushed her hefty shoulder again. "Lou," he muttered, "I need help here."

The woman groaned. "I'm tired. Can't it wait?"

"No, damn you. It can't."

His blowzy bed partner denting the mattress sat up and rubbed her eyes. She looked at his condition and sighed. The springs complained when she swung her dimpled legs over the edge and shuffled to the window, opening it to let air into the stuffy darkness. She lit the lantern and appraised him. "Lord, honey. You had that dream again, didn't you? Let's get you into something dry."

Bat's eyes bored into hers with a mixture of gratitude and resentment. Hair plastered his spooned-in temples. His thin mustache had been shaved away, leaving a vulnerable, pale upper lip. Lou shifted him, pulling the soaked nightshirt over his head as though she were a nurse or his mother. The dark, circular scar of the bullet hole looked black and depthless on his chest. In a high, tired voice, Bat cursed at the pain of moving.

"Doc will be here tomorrow. Today, I guess. Sun's coming up. He'll have all the news from Helena," Lou said, hurling the soaked nightshirt in a corner of the rough plank floor already piled with soiled, sickroom linens.

Lou poured tepid water from a pitcher into a chipped mug and took a swallow from it before helping Bat drink, turning the pillow over to its dry side and lowering his head

251

back down. She watched him close his eyes and drift off, lines crazing lids covering the sockets as he winced in sleep. She shook her head. He'd been such a handsome charmer. All the girls had wanted his attentions. But it was Lou who'd gone into the saloon for Bat when she saw him lying alone, flames lapping at his legs. No puny slip of a girl could have done it, but Lou, daughter of near giants, raised on a hog farm in Iowa, had carried him out the back. Then she hoisted him in front of her like a sack of corn and rode his horse on out of town, not sure what kind of trouble he was in, or if he were dead or alive, just knowing there'd been a fight. She comforted herself in awareness that even when the pain was at its worst Bat didn't call out any woman's name. He seemed obsessed instead with the idea that something had been stolen from him.

Lou ran a brush through her hair and splashed water on her eyes. She let her robe hang open over a stained chemise while she straightened up the ramshackle house, including the second bedroom where she conducted business. There was plenty of that in Clancy. Big-boned and well-muscled, she scoffed at the notion that riding the miners would cause her any problems. What wore her out was taking care of Bat. Anyway, she never thought she'd have him to herself. She made breakfast, planning to tempt the invalid to eat oatmeal sweetened with brown sugar.

Before noon Doc Bentley pulled up in his two-seater. The wiry little man jumped down and tied the reins to the fence. "Hello, Lou. You look done in. How's our boy?" He spoke with practiced, impersonal cheer.

"Bat still has those evil nightmares, Doc. All the time."

"Well, he's in pain. After all, he nearly got burned to a crisp after being shot. Give him time."

Doc entered his patient's room. Bat's red-rimmed eyes burned as intense as the fire that almost claimed him. He grunted and swore as the doc changed his leaking bandages. Lou leaned against the wall, smoked a cheroot, and watched.

"Having as much pain?" the doctor asked, addressing the question to whichever of them might feel like answering.

"Yes. Hell. That laudanum helps some, but it doesn't last long enough," Bat said. "If a man could only get a night's sleep."

"We'll increase the dosage." Doc looked directly at Bat. "I'm doing this as much for her as you. Won't do you any good to run your nurse to death."

"Lou? Nothing could stop her. Some kind of mistake of nature. She should have been a man."

"Life would have been goddamn easier. That's a fact. But don't be foolish." Lou raised her husky voice from the doorway. "No man would have carried you out of that burning whore house."

"You'd be right about that, I guess." He muttered, "My darlin'," as if it were an afterthought.

Doc promised to come back in two days. He told Lou, "I don't like to see a patient on so much laudanum, but you look wearier every time I call here. Your profession demands enough without you caring for a patient possessed by unholy demons."

Lou went back to Bat's room after the doc departed. She leaned over with a heavy woman's grunt and gathered the stained, foul-smelling laundry, taking it to the back porch. A Chinese came by twice a week to pick it up. When she returned to their room, Bat held out a hand. "Sorry, Lou. You're the only one who could have saved me."

She took his hand and sat on the bed beside him. She lit a second cheroot, pulled, and exhaled. "That Chinaman came and got the laundry. He sure doesn't look anything like ole Jim Li from Lillie's place."

"Jim Li? He was at Lillie's? He was the biggest Chinese I ever saw. Half white. Educated better than the miners in Butte. That's where I knew him. How'd he come to be at Lillie's?"

"Somebody said he was looking for a relative. His father, I think."

Bat turned his face away. "You smell like smoke. I can't abide that anymore."

Lou let go of his hand and got up. "Well, there's an old cowboy coming up the walk right now who'll pay good money to abide it," she said.

"Best see to him then. I'm all right now."

After Lou closed the door, Bat dozed in the noon warmth. The dream came again almost at once. He squirmed in the heat, struggling for breath. He heard crackling wood and crashing, shattering glass. Then the figure knelt over him. This time the flames lit the face instead of obscuring it. Bat's eyes flew open as he screamed the name, "Li."

From the second bedroom he heard a man growl, "What the hell is going on in there?"

CHAPTER FIFTEEN

High above the South Fork of the Flathead River, the place called Bad Rock Canyon taxed humans and horses. Unseasonable rains added to Nora's wretchedness. She awakened in predawn to the relentless spatter on the canvas shielding her. Temperatures had dropped. She pulled blankets up to her stiffened shoulders. After awhile, she gave up trying to be warm and climbed out to dress, shivering under her dripping tarp. She sat on a soaked log to pull her shoes on. Everything appeared swathed in fog and misery.

"Pea soup," she muttered, pulling her duster tight.

Jim materialized out of silvery mist.

"We'll wait until it lifts to start, won't we?" Nora asked.

He nodded.

Nora went a short way from camp to squat in the brush, then wash in a shallow stream that tumbled down to the river below. Her cupped hand ached with cold when she splashed her face, her rag towel icy and damp. No wonder her skin had turned dry, her lips rough. Her skirt darkened around the hem with moisture. She curled her toes to keep feeling in them inside cracked shoes. Melancholy visited her with the cold, bringing doubts about what they'd begun. She fought worrying. She had no future in Helena. To escape poverty and actually own land was worth even this discomfort.

She made an effort to be brisk as she gathered firewood. For a panicky moment she lost the sound of Jim shuffling with his load of wood nearby. She called out, and he reappeared.

"We have enough," he said, glancing at the kindling in Nora's arms. They used old newspaper and damp sticks to start a cold fire. Sluggish, pewter-tinted smoke rose, then leveled into the mist's sheen. Forenoon sun arrived at last to burn off the fog. Deer grazed below along the far side of the blue-green South Fork of the Flathead. Their fine, balanced shapes grew distinct on the bank's pebbly, nearly level incline. Heart for the journey reentered Nora.

She scoured their pans with gravel and

creek water, then shook out and rolled up her damp blankets. After Jim harnessed the horses, they began the ascent through and out of the canyon. They got down to walk, both pulling with ropes while the horses heaved against their harnesses to pull the wagon up the incline. All four grunted, panting.

Clouds lowered again, masking mountain-tops and chilling the thin, high air. Nora huddled, turning her collar up and her hat brim down against the beginning drizzle. Vertical strands of torrential gray rain soon pounded them. The wagon lurched and bounced. Jim finally gave Nora the reins and climbed down. He took Wink's bridle and guided the horses over the rocky trail. The steep ascent exhausted them all. Finally at the summit, they roughnecked, locking the back brakes and skidding down the detritus of a washed-out slope at the start of their descent. Nora stifled cries, not wanting her fear to make things worse for Jim. Going uphill had been nearly impossible, and going downhill threatened a fatal runaway. They used ropes as pulleys, fastened on trees to snub their way down when the wagon threatened to pitch out of control. She marveled at Jim's willingness to keep going. She kept learning there must be far more to this man than she'd once thought.

They made a cold, glum camp, putting tarps up, trying to stay dry. Nora shivered until exhaustion brought anxiety-riddled sleep.

Next day, relentless rain soaked through even the tarp covering their gear and supplies. Icy rivulets ran off their hatbrims to course down between their shoulders.

Exhausted by their eighth week of bushwhacking or moving on rough trails, they crossed the river, then stopped beside a small lake. After they'd set up camp, several Blackfeet pitched tipis nearby. A long-haired white giant, a mountain man, greeted them, saying the Indians had permission to be off the reservation as he had just married one of the family, and they wished to see her new home. Dressed in buckskins and moccasins, he looked Nora and Jim over. Nora leveled a flat gaze back at him. She could read in his eyes that he thought this no country for her. She didn't care what he thought. She chose not to think. Thinking took effort.

In early evening, one of the Blackfeet women went into labor. Nora listened dispiritedly to the celebration that followed the baby's arrival. Memories of other newborn life pierced her. Shivering, she cleaned her belongings as best she could in the drizzle, finally stopping to huddle on a boulder under lacy gray-green cedar branches. Images of Helen and Nora's little son hovered on the lake's dark surface. Could she ever stop yearning for her lost children? For Tade?

"Here I am in the wilderness and you still follow me." She cried a little. The hot trickle of tears stung her cheeks, salt burning her raw skin. She raised her head and rubbed her tender face with chapped hands, the nails broken and black. She rubbed one hand's fingertips over the other's knuckles, then scowled at her own weakness. She rose to find Jim.

She always felt better near Jim.

Next day, the sky turned a blue that made Nora think of satin ribbons she'd once seen on a fine Dublin lady's hat. She gasped when they rode over a rise and viewed the jagged grandeur of the Rockies layered to the horizon, but winced when she swallowed. What a time for a sore throat.

She squinted, partly a result of the sky's dazzling bright blue, but partly because her eyes hurt. She rubbed her neck, trying to rid her brain of a heavy fog, then shivered, pulling a shawl around her shoulders. She couldn't be sick. August already and they weren't even at a decent place to settle. Not even to the North Fork.

By afternoon Nora's chest tightened and ached. She muffled coughs with the shawl, willing herself not to feel ill as her ribs jabbed at her lungs with each wagon pitch. Another restless night brought no relief.

Toward late afternoon next day, they reached a clearing by the Middle Fork of the Flathead River. A railroad survey crew camped nearby. Twelve unwashed, goggle-eyed men, as Nora saw them, looked like they'd been living in tents for months. She made an effort to pull herself together, but her face felt hot, her throat full of knives that stabbed when she tried to swallow.

A bearish man wearing a buckskin shirt, leggings, moccasins, and a scarlet voyageur's sash around his waist moved out from the group. While the others gaped at the two seated in the wagon, his voice boomed a greeting. Nora detected upper-class English inflections. Brown hair fanned over his shoulders. A nod to vanity showed in his drooping mustache and carefully trimmed goatee. He was what Rose Murphy would have called "a fine enough figure of a man." Nora's grandfather would have said he had sea eyes — accustomed to scanning great distances.

The colorful character tipped his hat. She nodded to acknowledge his mannerly gesture when a fit of coughing racked her. She couldn't hide this one, and embarrassment reddened her already flushed cheeks. The man's smile faded. Nora knew her eyes must be pink-rimmed, her face chapped from the weather, her hair lank.

He stepped away and returned, offering a dipper of water. She accepted, trying not to groan as she swallowed. She handed it back and stood. The tents and men wobbled. She sat back down, but spoke as though nothing at all unusual had just happened.

"I'm Mrs. Larkin. Nora. I've come to settle on the North Fork of the Flathead River with this good worker I hired." Another fit of wet coughs.

"I'm Beartracks Benton. Mrs. Larkin, let me help you down. You're not well."

"No. We're on our way to the North Fork. We need to ford the river. Every day before winter . . ."

Jim Li climbed out of the wagon and turned to the tall man, their gazes eye-to-eye. The stranger grinned. "Well, I smuggled one tall Chinaman in over Flattop Mountain awhile back. There can't be two of you. Nope, you're he or his twin brother."

For once, Jim lost the customary blank mask he so often wore for white devils. Nora forgot her misery and turned toward him, surprised by his intake of breath. She jumped in. "Well, why wouldn't there be tall fellows in China just as easily as anywhere? There must be more than one of them. Anyway, Jim has been in America for ages. Haven't I known him since I was a girl, myself? He's not all a Chinaman either. Wasn't his own father a white man? His height likely came up from that root in the tree, didn't it?"

Beartracks studied them for a long moment. "That's a fine way you have of speaking, Mrs. Larkin. Don't worry, China Jim, I'll never mention my unlawful pursuits or the company I keep again. Are the two of you — ?"

"We're actually partners. Friends, too," Nora risked the truth earlier than she'd intended. "I don't know that you've seen our like here before, but we're going to settle a place together, share and share alike."

Beartracks only laughed and asked Jim, "What do you know about being a mountain man? Not much from the look of you."

"I know almost nothing. I need to learn quickly."

"That you do, China Jim. I can teach you a few ways of the country, but I won't take you with me often. Not you nor any other except Pete Dumont can keep up with old Beartracks Benton, but I'll show you how to stay alive and keep this Irish girl alive along with you."

Jim bowed. "Thank you. I am ignorant and we have much to do before winter."

Hoarseness made Nora's words sound sharper than she intended. "First, let's get ourselves across that river. Can you help us, Mr. Benton?"

"Yes, but why don't you camp here? These aren't dangerous men, and you're not well."

The head surveyor, a burly, bearded man, joined them. Ignoring Jim, he spoke to Nora, extending his own invitation.

"Thank you, but every day counts dear for us now," Nora responded. She turned to Beartracks. "We were told there's a sort of ferry with cables."

"That's it. There's still light, so if you're determined let's do it now."

Watching Beartracks talk with the survey crew, Nora wondered whether they could trust him. It seemed they had no choice with her sick and the river to cross. It would be a relief to turn the wagon away from the curious men. In her feverish state menace lurked in their unwavering, hungry stares. Clear enough they hadn't seen a woman in a long time. She reached a hand to her aching forehead.

"You are ill. Perhaps we should stay in the camp," Jim said.

"I'm good enough. We have to cross the river. Didn't you notice? Some of them look none too friendly. Maybe it's you. Let's keep moving. I'm afraid here."

"All right."

Beartracks Benton walked beside them. The two men guided the horses as they pulled the wagon on board a raft Beartracks borrowed from a friend. Both men pushed with long poles while Nora huddled on the wagon seat, clutching the reins.

On the far side of the Middle Fork, towering, thick-trunked cedar darkened the trail, creating premature night under hundreds of webby branches. Nora dropped her head to her hands in sick, hot weariness.

Beartracks moved fast. "I have a trapline cabin on Lake McDonald," he announced over his shoulder. "Good headquarters for you tonight, though don't plan on fancy." Scalloped clouds shone pink by the time the three reached the foot of the lake. At Beartracks's direction, Jim stopped beside a rude cabin just above the pebbled beach.

Dimly aware, Nora had a sense of entering a massive, peaceful sanctuary, the more otherworldly because of her fever.

Transparent water lapped over darkening mauve and blue-green rocks near her feet. A smug family of ducks floated communally on its surface, quacking at the newcomers. Forest spread on either side with mountains rising, pine spires pointing skyward — everything pulling Nora's gaze upward. The scene at Lake McDonald's far end won her attention, a wall of mountains dipped and folded in ridges and crevasses, mysterious and unreachable, lovely in alpenglow. Those compelling masses, remote and indifferent, went beyond the rough wildness of any she'd seen before.

"It's paradise," she murmured. "Tade and Helen could be there. Just over there."

Then she collapsed.

Carrying Nora, Jim kicked open the door, which swung wide on rawhide hinges to reveal a packed dirt floor, air stale in the dimness. A few cans of beans sat on a board shelf above a small wood-burning stove. Someone had stripped the rustic bunk, wide enough for two, of bedding. A small table at its foot served as a place to eat or as a desk. A scraped moose stomach covered the cabin's small, square window. Dried herbs and other plants hung from the low ceiling. Their ends startled Jim as they brushed against his head.

He lowered Nora to the plank bed as Beartracks followed with blankets from the wagon. Jim unbuttoned Nora's coat. "She has a bad fever." He pulled her limp arms from her duster's sleeves.

Nora murmured something. Something about flames, but Jim didn't take it in. He lifted her again as Beartracks made the bed.

"Build a fire and get water from the lake to boil," Beartracks ordered. "My woman cooks up medicines. She's off visiting Blackfeet cousins now, but she always makes sure I have her healing herbs with me."

Jim closed the door, worried by Nora's labored breath. He started the kindling ablaze, then fed logs into the stove before dealing with the water.

Beartracks pulled a leather bag from his parfleche. "As you can see, my fine young Chinaman, I have pipsissawa for fever." He pulled out a dried pale purple flower. "I also need bark from willows down by the creek to boil for Mrs. Larkin's fever." He pulled another dried plant hanging in a bunch. "The moccasin flower. Lady's Slipper, some call it. Not so easily found. And wild on-ions."

Sent out to search, Jim stumbled in the dark as he traversed the tall grass along the creek, pushing through the forest's ground cover and fallen trees, quickly gathering what willow bark he could. Once back at the cabin, he watched Beartracks boil Black-Eyed Susan roots and then the Lady's Slipper. Jim brought the herbal tea to Nora's lips, urging her to sip as he lifted her head with one hand, the steaming cup in the other. He left her only to retrieve a jar of honey from the wagon.

Nora labored to take ropey, strangled breaths. Beartracks roasted wild onions in the fire's embers. When they'd cooked soft, he pressed oil from them, mixing it with honey. Jim fed it to Nora by teaspoonfuls. After the mountain man discretely stepped out, Jim followed his directions and spread the extract on a cloth, unbuttoned Nora's shirtwaist, and opened her bodice. He caught his breath before he placed the cloth, in now shaking hands, upon her bare chest. Such beauty made detachment difficult.

Later, after Beartracks had returned, Nora murmured in delerium. "What if he knows? . . . come after us, Jim . . . come up from hell itself . . . can't go far enough. Not far enough." The two men looked away from each other. After an awkward moment, Beartracks slipped out again.

Anxious, Jim sat by the fire stroking Nora's brow with a cool rag. What if he lost her? He wanted to think it impossible, but knew too well how illnesses carried off loved ones. He would be hard pressed if Nora went the way of his parents. It wasn't just that he'd be struggling by himself in the North Fork. He would be alone in his very spirit without this tragic, determined, red-haired Irish woman. He'd been so lonely before her.

He listened to Nora's delerious muttering. Was it the priest's orders, the guilt, that would conjure up such things? Jim hadn't been haunted by thoughts of the dead gambler. Was Nora seeing his ghost in this room? Jim had thought the ring fortuitous. Why feel any guilt at all over using the dead to help the living?

Beartracks returned to boil and measure onions and flowers, pressing and mixing. He left again to reappear long after dark, a small doe slung over his shoulder. He spoke from the doorway. "Let's make a fire outside, China Jim. How's Mrs. Larkin?" He peered into his cabin's fragrant humidity. Nora lay on the bunk in candlelight, grappling for each breath. "More onion," he muttered before they went out. "I've seen it used by my wife and others. Sometimes I've seen it work. Other times the sick ones die. Who knows the reasons? The willow bark is often damned effective for fevers."

Outside, Jim watched Beartracks dress out the doe by the wavering campfire's flames. Beartracks noted his scrutiny. "You need to learn how to do this, China Jim. Mrs. Larkin'll need plenty of good food."

"Yes. If she lives," Jim muttered. He shivered even though the fire heated their hands and faces.

"Ah, fear not, young Celestial, she'll live. She looks to be one of the tough ones. Skinny, but strong. You build up the fire while I spit the meat."

After they'd eaten, Beartracks stood. "I'll spell you."

"No. I must tend Nora. She talks in dreams. She won't know you, or she will perhaps mistake you for her dead husband." Jim bowed.

"That's the first Chinese mannerism I've seen you make. Mrs. Larkin says you have some white in you, is that right?" When Jim remained silent, Beartracks continued, "You're in for a long night. Stay out here and get some air." He flicked a glance over the small turmoil of diminished fire and turned, taking long strides to his cabin.

The mountain man slipped in, a determined Jim following, shutting the door to keep in pungent steam. Beartracks rolled a log over by Nora's bed, upended it, and sat, elbows on his knees, studying her as he dabbed her forehead with cool water. Nora uttered fierce snatches of words. Something about a bat and a fire. Something about a baby boy. Then her face softened. She seemed to be talking to a child. "Helen, acushla, my treasure." Then, "Tade, what do you think of this color? Will it do? Will it suit me?" Her eyes flew open and she peered at Beartracks. "Will it do? Do I suit you in it?"

Jim moved in front of the mountain man and pulled the blanket to Nora's chin. "You're the most beautiful woman I have ever seen, Nora Larkin," he whispered in Chinese. "You must fight this. You must. We are partners."

Her eyes closed and she frowned, rambling on about bats again, and rings. ". . . bring us down, Jim," she sighed, ". . . come up from hell itself . . . after us. I . . . can't go far enough. Not enough. Stay with me . . . don't . . . abandon me . . . I need you . . . need you, Jim." Jim lifted Nora's head to give her a teaspoon of onion and honey. Beartracks left just after Nora pleaded, "Take the baby away, Jim. Take him."

Jim reapplied the mixture on a cloth, which he laid over her perfect breasts. Later he gave her tea from the willow bark and wildflowers. He didn't sleep, but lay on a blanket on the floor, listening to her meanderings.

Jim remained by Nora's bedside for four days and nights, leaving only to gather water or wood. He undressed her, giving up on trying to protect her modesty, as she switched from chills to fevers. She needed him for everything. He bathed her, spooned tea and the honey mixture, and tried to comfort her during incoherent ravings. He scrubbed clothes and bedding in a wash tub retrieved from behind the little structure.

Only once, alone in the firelight, did Jim pause toiling to study the beautiful woman who lay momentarily nude on the rough bed. Trembling like a man enthralled before an object of worship, he moved his hand, not quite touching Nora from the crown of her head, over her throat, over her breasts, over her ribs and belly and the mound below, over her thighs and calves and feet. He sighed, but hearing footsteps outside, laid a blanket over all he'd gazed on, his treasured, yearned-for Nora Larkin, just before Beartracks entered with more herbs and venison.

Toward dawn of the fourth day, Nora's breathing quieted and evened. Jim touched her face, cool, but so pale. Her nightgown and the blanket beneath her were sweat-soaked and cold, but she slept so peacefully he only piled on another blanket. Bathing could wait.

Standing at the open door, Jim saw Beartracks Benton asleep on a bedroll on the beach, his campfire crumbled to red and gray embers. So the mountain man had stayed close during these long nights. Jim walked to him. "She will live."

Inside, they bent over Nora and grinned like doting uncles at a favorite niece's bedside. When alone, Jim again saw to bathing her and airing and changing her clammy bedding. Sunshine warmed the day and Nora still slept, her face to the open door.

CHAPTER SIXTEEN

By late afternoon on the fifth day after their arrival at Beartracks's cabin, Nora came fully awake. Her focus settled first on the sooty, mud-chinked wall next to her. "Jesus, Mary, and Joseph," she gasped, trying to sit up. She fell back, dismayed at her weaknes.

A figure blocked out the brightness of the open doorway. "Nora? It's Jim. Have you chosen to return to me?"

She tried to answer, pressed her fingers against her throat, and cleared it. "Past — past deciding," she croaked. Her hand moved from her tangled hair down what she wore, Jim's shirt. "I can scarce remember. There was a lake?"

"We think you had pneumonia. A fever at least. Beartracks used bark and roots and flowers as medicine."

"And onion." Nora wrinkled her nose.

Jim's laugh caught in a sob of relief. "Onion mixed with honey. We have venison.

Are you hungry?"

"Not for so much. Could you make me a little broth, do you suppose?" Nora closed her eyes, intending it to be for a moment only.When she awoke next morning, the door stood open. Turning her head, she saw blue water and those great mountains she'd noted, but couldn't take in, when she first saw them. Now she gazed at their uneven V's and massive risings, everything as beautiful as Jim Li had described. She said so as he stepped in with an armload of wood.

He brought her a dipperful of water. "Would you care for tea? I've been gathering more herbs."

"You and Mr. Benton saved my life, Jim. I'm sorry now I ever hesitated about trusting him, although I don't suppose I'd agree on his English politics." Unexpected tears of weakness ran down her temples into the tangled hair. "What a witch's bridle," she sighed, raking her fingers through it.

"The important thing is, you agreed to come to this north country," Jim said, taking her hand.

"I've caused us to lose precious time, haven't I?" She let her hand rest in his, the touch comforting and welcome.

"We've used these days to dry out bedding, gather plants for medicine, and Bear-tracks has agreed to travel with us to where we will settle. You opened another door even in your illness."

"Get along. I've never looked so bad. I'm afraid to see the hag I've become, and I smell of sweat and onions. What a charmer. He's never seen a woman so ugly. He's fascinated, don't you see? Do you think you could heat water for me?"

Jim helped Nora wash, then unsnarl her hair. She relaxed under the sensual rhythm of long, steady brushstrokes. His touch felt natural as he braided her now-shiny mane into one long rope. He told her about the days she'd been away from them, his warm hands so gentle she all but purred under his touch. She closed her eyes and tilted her head back.

Having been within Death's reach and escaping made any social restraints trivial. Jim must have bathed her nude body. She should be embarrassed, but felt only grati-tude. Anyway, she'd been, and still re-mained, too weak to care for herself. Jim, gentle and matter of fact, neither looked away, nor made her uncomfortable.

Nora drank venison broth and gazed out at Lake McDonald and the mountains. If she'd died, those massive promentories would still be there. Eternity rested in them.

Beartracks had crossed to the head of the lake to retrieve his mysterious woman, then go on to visit friends at a small hotel owned by a fur trader. Nora felt thankful for privacy.

At the end of her first week of convalescence, she dressed and walked on trembling legs, progressing only a few yards down the beach to rest on a windfallen tree and take in the double scene once above, and once reflected in the quiet water. Nora wanted to take part in the work going on around her. She and Jim, two ignorant pilgrims, shared increasing awareness of how much knowledge they lacked to survive in this wilderness. Now they could learn from a real mountain man, a blessing, too, but she sensed he knew them better than he should from such a brief acquaintance.

A nightmarish dread had haunted her like a malevolent ghost ever since Helena. Even before falling ill, she had nightmares where Bat Moriarty reached for her not in love, but with malignant hate. Noticing Jim greasing the wagon's wheels, Nora labored the short distance uphill. By the time she reached him, she panted, leaning on the wagon. Jim smiled at her. He rubbed his hands in the grass to clean them, stood, and wiped them again on a rag.

"Jim, in my fever did I talk about things best kept to ourselves?"

"Yes, but your words came out all mixed. Beartracks thinks you talked of bats. You only mentioned the fire and ring in broken cries."

Nora nodded, still angry at herself as much as relieved. Why could she never just release the past? Fear and guilt diluted a person like added water took the taste from a stew. She turned back to the cabin. Once there, she stretched out on the plank bed and slept.

Later, she walked to the beach to wash her face and pull back her hair. As she straightened, Beartracks Benton appeared, paddling his canoe toward her. A young Indian woman sat behind him, their matching strokes powerful and certain. Neither waved, but Nora waited, hugging her arms to her waist. She would take care of one worry at least.

Beartracks pulled the long canoe onto the beach in one smooth movement, its hull scraping softly on the rocks. Jagged animal traps lay in the bottom. The girl shot Nora a shy, dimpled smile, then climbed out, spread a deer hide on the ground, and piled the traps into it.

Beartracks and the Indian woman — pretty, with high cheekbones — spoke briefly in a language Nora didn't know. He gestured for the girl to stand before Nora. "My Blackfeet wife, Sweet Grass." Affection glowed in his voice. "Her teaching me about healing herbs is how China Jim and I pulled you through."

Nora extended her hand. "In that case, you saved my life."

Sweet Grass hesitated, then reached out. Her brown hand in Nora's was small and well shaped, but rough, a child's hand. Nora guessed Beartracks to be nearly forty. The girl could be twenty-five years younger. Sweet Grass moved away.

"I hear I talked nonsense when I was taken ill," Nora began. "You're not to think it had any truth in fact unless I talked about my husband Tade, or my little girl, Helen. They died within two years of each other. It was a loss that takes me still at times." Nora bit her lip, realizing too late that her rush of words had just compounded the problem. Why had she spoken of the past at all?

"You talked about bats and diamond rings, even threw in a fire. Quite an imagination when you're sick. Do you have an imagination when you're well? Ever imagine good things?"

"Such as what, Mr. Benton?" Nora flinched. She'd brought a new danger to them. She made an effort to hide her dread and be casual.

"Me, for one. I'm a trapper, hunter, guide, poet, artist, tracker, and I do love to rest these sharp old eyes on a pretty girl. At least when Sweet Grass there has her back turned." He closed the four corners of the hide. He packed his traps into a wicker backpack and flung it and the hides over his shoulder. He turned to her again, the lake and mountains shining at his back. "But it's not so often I see one like you standing right in front of me on a late summer afternoon."

Nora tilted her chin. If she'd learned one thing at Lillie's, it was that some men always wanted to satisfy their carnal needs. "Sure, and I didn't just get off the boat, Mr. Benton. I'm a widow. I'm used to men's flattery, although I don't give such nonsense any weight at all. Not a bit of it. And it shouldn't matter whether Sweet Grass is watching you or not."

Beartracks Benton grinned, accepting her response in good nature.

"I should go back," Nora said. "Jim could use what little help I'll be."

"Where is China Jim?"

"Fishing down the shore."

Beartracks leaned against the wagon. "It's none of my business, but you and China Jim . . . I've heard of Irish women taking up with Chinamen. I'll tell you, what neighbors you have won't like it. Be clear that he's only your labor. We'll stop at Hogans' on our journey. Sweet Grass will stay on here for awhile. Nan Hogan disapproves of our union. Mixing races."

Nora bristled. Jim was so much better than any man, any person, she'd met since Tade. "You know, I came from landless poverty. People never liked to see tinkers coming down the road, always wanted my family gone as soon as Da finished mending and shining the dented kettles and pans missing handles they handed him. I learned early on to ignore small minds and their mean opinions."

She glared in defiance. They'd tried so hard to make it clear there was nothing of romance between them. Still, there had been those moments at St. Ignatius. Her face heated. Did she harbor secret feelings? Did Jim?

"We're not sweethearts. Jim told me about this Flathead River country. I couldn't come alone, could I? We're business partners. But if it were more, how could it be any others' business? Why would I care what they think?"

"Reconsider that. You're alone up here. Folks depend on each other."

"Well then, they'd better not go jumping to conclusions, had they? Folks have been doing that about me all my life. Jim, too, come to that. What we do or don't do is our business." Nora threw down a leaf she'd been examining.

"As to your coming with us, that's a grand thing because we have a lot to learn. This country is so lovely. I haven't seen so much green since Ireland, but it's forbidding, too. I'm grateful, especially now, for a man who knows its ways to join us." She'd learned from Lillie and her girls how to use such flattery to advantage, to deflect his assumptions about her and Jim. She knew enough not to close the door too rudely on hopes of seduction when dealing with men able to help her reach her goals.

He hesitated. "I have an idea where you should settle. You don't have to tell me if I'm right about this, but white men don't often come up here unless they're running from something. A woman is rare. Plenty here have left their previous home between sundown and sunrise. Nobody questions anybody else, so I won't ask why you were afraid someone would find you."

"There's not a soul after us that I know of," Nora interrupted. Bat was dead, wasn't he, she asked herself.

"Well, the law comes through sometimes. Your traveling companion might attract attention. He's not here legally. I know because I'm the one who smuggled him in. Sweet Grass remembers him, too. But we won't tell because it's a lucrative trade, slipping Celestials across the border."

Nora met his eyes. "I left a difficult life behind me. None of it is your business. My past is not your toy."

He nodded soberly, taking no offense. "True words, young daughter of Erin. Now there aren't many come to stay here. Most settle on the east side of the North Fork. But there's land on the west side, too. We could ford the North Fork. I'll show you a spot I've sometimes thought would make a fine place to build a home. You'd be hard to sneak up on."

"I'll speak to Jim about it. I don't expect he'd mind being away from people. It's what we expected."

"I come through often." He took off his hat with another wicked grin.

Nora turned, revealing only her profile,

running her hand over huge, flat leaves of a plant hung with red berries. "I've never been a prostitute if that's what you're thinking," she said. "I've had some troubles. I lost my husband. Lost my wee babes. Lost my work. But I'm here to be a landowner. That will take all our attention, mine and Jim's." She gave him a quick glance before returning her eyes to the plant, mastering herself again. "We'll be grateful to you for riding with us and for all you've already done, wherever we settle."

Beartracks replaced his hat. "As you wish, Irish lovely, but my hearing is sharper than most. You said you lost a daughter to diphtheria, but then spoke of babes. And you begged someone in your delerium to take the baby away."

Nora inhaled and turned. "I don't know about any of that. I was sick out of my head. Well, I feel worn out entirely with all this talk. Mr. Benton, do not bring up my past ever again." After a pause, she patted the broad leaf of the plant. "A person could use these as plates," she said with a forced smile. "What do you call it?"

"Devil's Club," Beartracks answered. "Watch out for the thorns."

Nora nodded and gave him a steady look. "Always good advice, I've found. Watch out for the thorns."

By mid-September Nora felt stronger, the trio had rested, repaired, and mended belongings. They bid farewell to a smiling Sweet Grass. Nora departed with a mixture of eagerness to make progress and regret at leaving the sun-dappled lake and the comfort of even a rustic shelter.

Beartracks's cabin reminded Nora of little homes in Ireland's wild places. She remembered traveling in her da's wagon and wondering about the barefoot children who played in muddy grounds outside their open doorways. No children here, she thought with a pang, never again for her.

She squared her shoulders and reminded herself of what she was about. Land and a home where she could live without interference. That seemed all the more important after her talk with Beartracks about likely objections to Jim. How she yearned for peace and dignity. They'd have neither if they couldn't prosper here, at least enough to make a living.

She still felt shaky at times, sweating and a bit sick. Jim had concocted more tea. Nora drank the tepid liquid from a jar, agreeing to "anything but the onions."

Beartracks and Jim alternately walked and

took the reins beside Nora. The trail became rougher and narrower. "It's little better than a cow path," she muttered through rattled teeth.

They moved around the lake's west side, catching glimpses of blue water and deep green mountains through gigantic spears of ancient pine, fir, and aspen. Nora loved to watch the leaves shimmer in the breeze, but hard chucking against rocks, stumps, and holes in the trail claimed most of her attention. They skidded down terrifying inclines, roughnecking, locking the back brakes. Nora weakened with every jostle. When one slope nearly threw her off the wagon, she lowered her head, hating her tears.

Beside her, Jim pulled in Wink and Cotton before she realized he'd noticed her distress. "I'm sorry," she said, brushing away tears with hands hot and swollen from gripping the wagon seat. "I hurt all over from being jarred so, and I know I can't walk. I'm holding us back."

Jim slid to her. He lifted her onto his lap, his arms around her, legs braced on the wagon floor. "Beartracks," he called. "Come up here to take the reins. Nora's too weak, so I will hold her." It was the first time Jim directed the other man. Beartracks set his jaw as if to object, but stopped on noticing

stairs to a small room with a dormer ceiling and a window that framed snowy mountains. She dropped her bag and sank on the bed, rubbing her eyes. "Sure, and I don't have all my strength back yet. I worry night and day about slowing us down."

Nan turned maternal. "You do need to rest. No man alive can take proper care of a sick woman. Have a liedown. We eat at seven sharp."

Alone, Nora opened her collar and pulled off her dusty shoes and grimy stockings. She undid her hair, lay back on the lumpy mattress, and touched the rough log wall beside her before closing her eyes. Hours later she opened them. The light had faded. Highspirited men's voices drifted from below. She swung her feet to the rag rug and peered out the open window. Beartracks stood, weight shifted to one foot, talking to another bearded man in the corral. The second man, Nora assumed, must be Fred Hogan. He gestured broadly, telling some joke. Their boistrous laughter filled the yard, lazy and carefree. Jim was nowhere to be seen.

Nora sighed in envy. These men guffawed over some trivial happening, while she'd landed here beset with problems on all sides . . . herself weak as a newborn rabbit,

Jim with a damaged shoulder, precious time lost. She splashed her face with water from the bowl on the dresser and redid her hair. Having done her best, she descended the narrow stairs to join Beartracks, the Hogans, and two Canadian fur trappers for a dinner of elk steaks, mashed potatoes, greens, and rhubarb pie. The jolly Canadians and Beartracks swapped stories of trapping and hunting on the North Fork where Nora and Jim would be settling. The men drank whiskey after dinner, but Nora declined, instead sipping homemade dandelion wine with Nan.

"The girls should be careful of Beartracks Benton," Nan began as she settled into her sturdy rocker by the fireplace. "He breaks us ladies' hearts. He knows how to charm with gentlemanly ways, but he's near wild as the mountain lions. My husband has known Beartracks to eat the breast of a wild bird raw when he doesn't want to take time to cook it. Think of that when he tips his hat to you. He's a bad drinker, but he can sure spout poetry. They say he came from one of the great families, a younger son. He left for Canada because of some scandal. Now he's a remittance man. His family pays him to stay away from them."

Nora shuddered. What sort of guide led

them? She wished Jim were beside her to discuss it, but he wasn't welcome in the narrow-minded Hogan household. She fought down a wave of anger. Beartracks had one thing right. They'd do better to charm the Hogans instead of bucking these new neighbors. Perhaps in time Nora and Jim could erase the Hogans' prejudice. And they needed Beartracks, no matter he ate raw meat and, worse yet, hailed from England.

Chapter Seventeen

They started out from the Hogans' at dawn, roseate streaks tinting broad snowcaps. Progress came hard in clod-strewn ruts. Nora's energy waned by afternoon. They'd spent most daylight hours moving through cedar, fir, and lodgepole. Huge, moss-blanketed boulders hid mysteries within their massive interiors. At times Nora found herself eye level with tops of huge larch, their trunks continuing down plunging, tangled slopes to merge into roots. Deer bounded over half-decayed windfalls or lightning-blasted stumps.

They camped at a grassy patch near a stream gilded by late-afternoon sun. Nan had packed huckleberry preserves for their biscuits. Nora had never tasted such sweet, purple richness.

"Just wait," Beartracks told her. "You'll be gathering huckleberries in buckets for pies, syrups, preserves, or to eat right off the bush. Griz fatten on them."

That night, Nora heard boots crunch followed by the hiss of shifting logs as Jim rebuilt the fire the sleepers encircled. Through half-opened eyes she watched him crouch over the flares, throwing his cheekbones into relief. His hair hung free. A warrior. She thought of Nan's words about Beartracks Benton eating the raw heart of a bird and closed her eyes, blotting out thoughts of men refined or crude, and how they could be newly formed in this wilderness. The sleep of exhaustion reclaimed her.

By afternoon next day, they came to a place to ford the North Fork of the Flathead from its east bank to the west.

"It seems I'm always crossing water to start a new life." Nora spoke aloud without realizing.

Beartracks grinned. "West is a good direction for new beginnings. It signifies mystery and adventure." Then he grew serious. "No bridge or ferry here, though. A river with no bridge."

They checked supplies, knotted and secured the tarpaulin ropes. Nora sat far back in the wagon, Jim in front with Beartracks, who guided Wink and Cotton into the current's ripples. Nora's fingernails bore into a rope when icy water splashed over their wheeltops. "Saints preserve us miserable wretches," she muttered as the current's power swung the wagon sideways.

Beartracks cursed the horses, whipping the reins. At last, Wink and Cotton lunged and clambered onto the western bank.

"We're safer here, are we?" Nora asked, after crossing herself in gratitude that they'd survived the ford.

"Safer from surprise visits," Beartracks responded. "It's all wilderness from here into Canada. I run my trapline through the Belly River region into Alberta. It's pretty country. I'll show you the place I'd build a cabin where wolves could sing weary settlers to sleep at night." The wagon lumbered over rough ground, stopping in a sun-dappled clearing. A creek ran across one side to the river that separated them from the rugged panorama of the Rockies to the East. "This is it." Beartracks made a sweeping gesture.

"It is a fine place," Jim said. "High enough to let us see soaring mountains there and other ranges into Canada and west. We have abundant water and will see anyone crossing toward us."

"I'm no rancher, but I'll help you build your cabin before winter. Can't leave a pretty girl to freeze." Beartracks tipped his hat. "Pretty Nora from Ireland." He looked steadily at her as Jim assumed that mask-like expression of displeasure.

Nora turned a full circle, taking in all of it — stream, peaks, grassy clearing, and towering moss-draped pines. Good country for fishing, hunting, and planting, everything they needed. In time they might even run cattle. She looked up at Jim and nodded. He smiled and returned her nod.

She spoke with a catch in her voice. "It has water and the clearing to put the cabin on for a start. It will be home."

Overhead, a red-tailed hawk rang out a piercing cry.

An hour later Jim paused from unloading the wagon. Nora watched him study the massive mountains aglow in the setting sun. "What are you imagining, Jim?"

"Ah, mystery in crags and glaciers, spirits in waterfalls and lakes. An image of my mother becoming an immortal at the top of the world just now evoked her presence. This place must be a good home for us, Nora. It must and it will."

They set up camp. Their belongings appeared paltry stacked in haphazard piles on the ground, but Nora liked the sight of her tarp lean-to against the vault of forest. A surge of hope filled her. Guilt followed. How could she be happy with Tade and Helen gone and her boy in Butte? How could she feel almost like a child on a picnic? She had no right. With that realization she saw the forest darken, and she shivered in the lengthening shadows.

Jim approached. "As I said, I thought of my mother earlier. She gave me to her sister. But I believe she still accepted joy in her life. Joy after grief is not forbidden. In time she became one of the immortals, a good, protecting spirit."

Nora smiled, soothed by his understanding. "Thank you, Jim. You were right to bring us here. This wild place has such peace and challenge both. We'll not have time to dwell on the past with so much to do."

She knew as she spoke that the past could not be banished altogether. Still, the dead shouldn't hinder the living. She'd begun to feel a healing, something about wilderness only the word sacred could encompass. Could it be that after all the ugliness and sordid turns, she'd been given a spiritual rebirth among the monumental peaks of this world? She revolved slowly, again absorbing her new home.

She set to work building a cook fire. This place might be sacred, but it would, she already knew, call on every reserve of every strength the two partners possessed. And she must do more than survive. She had to prosper to repay that debt owed Bat Moriarty's widow. Only then, according to the priest, could she redeem her soul.

Beartracks said his farewells. They watched him ride off, leaving them to a mix of fear and relief at being by themselves again.

The last thing before entering her bedroll, Nora removed both shoes and stockings to curl her bare toes in the coarse, cold grass until they reached the hard dirt above its roots. "My land," she whispered, overwhelmed again. "Land I'll one day own. No one will take this home from me." She knelt and dug her fingers into it, her eyes closed against tears. When she opened them, they met Jim's, watching from beside the fire. "We made it, Jim," she said. "We pulled it off, for certain, and look at the odds."

"We will make a fine life here." Jim hesitated, then bowed and walked into the darkness.

Nora peered, but couldn't see him. Why did he bow? Out of respect? Didn't he know by now she recognized him as her equal and more? She brushed dirt and pine needles from her travel-soiled dress.

Later, warm in her bedroll, she considered three men. Tade had been so simple and good, a man of ability and decency. Then feckless Bat replaced him with that devilish, dangerous charm. She'd desired them both, the passion for Bat born of deprivation. Now she traveled with a third man. While she admired him and acknowledged that she journeyed with an attractive partner, she didn't want and wasn't ready for love. She still mourned Tade and Helen and grieved for the little boy in distant Butte.

She dreamed of clearing trees, meadows of shamrocks replacing them. In the morning the shamrocks had vanished, but the jagged Rocky Mountains rose to a sky so radiant Nora squinted to look at it. Above her a pair of bald eagles flapped broad wings and coasted, their raptors' eyes raking across every detail of the newcomers' activity. Nora hastened to light kindling for cooking breakfast, proud to have a start on Jim.

She toted a bucket and towel down to the stream. As she lowered herself into the scratchy brush, she wondered how long it would take to build a proper privy. After washing in the frigid water, she rubbed hard at her face to restore circulation. When she lowered the towel, she stared into porcine eyes. Nora screamed. The black bear woofed. Brush cracked and crashed as each raced up an opposite bank.

Jim tore through bushes, pointing his rifle as Nora staggered to him. "A bear! A great black thing!"

"Where?" Jim, hopping on bare feet, stepped around Nora. Finally, he chuckled and lowered his firearm. "It didn't follow you. You're all right."

"All right? The beast fair to frightened the liver out of me. Is my hair all-the-way or just partly turned to white?"

Jim nudged a log over for her to sit on. "Learn to use this rifle. And keep it with you."

"Right. I'll not live here defenseless."

Jim's smile faded. "We must both learn to live in this hazardous beauty, to understand and respect it. Careless, we could lose everything. It is not enough to have arrived."

"Why are you sounding like a judge?" Nora laughed at Jim's solemn pronouncement. "As you see, I've quite recovered after meeting old Black Bloomers. I'm more than ready for that cabin we've planned. Let's eat and start building."

■ ■ ■ ■

When they took stock after breakfast, Nora's bravado faded. She shuddered at how much work lay ahead. Winter could arrive as early as mid-October. Beartracks had promised to return in a few weeks, but hadn't specified the day. He'd already done more than they had a right to expect. For now, there was only Jim and Nora. But, after all, wasn't that what they intended?

"Let's build our privy first, then the cabin," Jim suggested.

Nora nodded. "In winter we'll tell tales by the fire. I'm that fond of stories. I know plenty about the little people that you won't have heard."

Jim gave her a quick look. "Chinese tell legends of spirits."

"Do they now? Good, so. Well, where shall we build our fine house?"

They agreed the cabin should face the river and great wall of mountains beyond, enabling them to observe anyone crossing. Nora had never shaken the sense of being followed, although none living had reason to trail them. "We'll see those peaks shining the very minute we step out our door in the mornings if we place our home just here," she said.

They would build one big room, fourteen by sixteen feet, with alcoves containing bunks curtained off for privacy. Easier to keep warm that way. They would make their own table and chairs, and position the wood-burning stove facing the door.

Jim remembered how to fell trees from his woodcutting days. He used the axe to make a V-shaped wedge in a hemlock, positioning the cut so when sawed through it would fall into the clearing away from other trees. When the tree crashed and bounced to the meadow floor, Nora went to work with hatchet and saw, cutting away branches, saving the softest boughs for mattress ticking. She savored the scent of pine needles and hewn wood, that freshness of new beginnings.

In the days that followed, Jim dug a hole and cut timber for the privy. Nora snickered when he carved a half-moon in the door. They maneuvered the little building into place and drew straws to decide who would use it first. Nora pulled the shortest blade and walked with straight-backed dignity into the structure, her eyes sparkling, her face pink.

The two managed eight or nine trees a day.

Dull from exhaustion, they burned slash in nightly bonfires that cast orange sparks toward remote constellations. Jim said Orion stood guard over them with his sword.

Nora abandoned any effort at clean clothes. She removed her sawdust-smeared dress at night, slipping on a nightgown, grateful that no rust-brown wood chips or scratchy bark fragments clung to it.

They lived on fish, beans, biscuits, and sourdough pancakes. As their bodies grew stronger, so did their companionship. They worked as two halves of one purpose, toward one goal. Jim's shoulders broadened. Sometimes, too, Nora felt his eyes rest on her during evenings when they lolled by the fire, tired and satisfied with another day's progress.

After three weeks, Beartracks strode into camp. He threw a fresh-killed doe on the ground and pushed his hat back with one finger, grinning at the stacked timber. "Not bad work for two banged-up pilgrims."

"We have blisters on our poor hands for reward." Nora held hers out to display proof.

"I'll show your China Jim how to make you beaver gloves for winter, Irish. Keep you warm."

Nora stuffed her hands in her pockets. Some kinds of warmth frightened her. She remembered the heat of Jim's shoulder against hers as they rode on the wagon, how sweat glistened on his throat during long, hot days of building.

Later they all ate venison and laughed over Beartracks's adventures. He raised his cup in salute. "You pilgrims have done well, but I'll stay to help finish your cabin. You people are too jeezely interesting to leave alone."

With mattock and spade, Jim overturned rocky earth, then tamped it down for a floor. Nora spread wood chips over the evened dirt. Jim and Beartracks stretched rawhide over the chips on pegs driven into the ground. She forgot to worry about her looks, her hair often half-loose around her face.

"We'll fix a better floor if the weather holds," Jim promised. "I need to learn hunting and trapping skills from Beartracks, although I hate to leave you alone."

"I'll grow used to it. I might even enjoy a few nights all alone here."

September turned to October. Aspen leaves shimmered like coins, then fell to decorate pine branches, transforming them to Christmas trees, or spiraled down to hide among tawny bracken, bright yellow lost to approaching winter.

Nora's blisters hardened. She scarcely recognized her own hands with their splitting fingernails and ugly yellowed, callused palms. She grew used to waking half asleep, stumbling to the creek, and splashing icy water on her wind-burned face. By midday, sweat-soaked clothes dried on her back.

Nora wore her ragged coat with sleeves now smeared by mud and sawdust, when after several weeks even midday remained cool. It wasn't symbolic anymore, just a necessary garment.

Strength she'd taken for granted and then lost returned to her. She healed in body and lifted in spirit, even discovered easy laughter again.

As the log walls grew, Nora touched their rough surfaces in wonder. She carried mud to chink the walls. She'd never been certain of owning another real home after Dublin Gulch. It seemed less like a second chance than Nora being transformed into a different woman altogether in this place. For certain, she felt nothing like that naive girl who'd arrived in Butte, America. Sometimes she could remember Tade and Helen without pain. Sometimes it felt actually good to think of them. Providence showed mercy at last, she thought.

Jim's one extravagance had been boxed glass windowpanes wrapped with painstaking care. Thanks to real windows, they'd see the mountains even on wintry days. No windows in the alcoves, though. "No need to let in cold," Beartracks insisted. "You'll thank me in January."

He showed Jim how to use the mattock to make roof shingles from cedar logs. They hewed timber, framing in a door with elk hide hinges. Jim built bunks while Nora stuffed pine boughs into ticking. Beartracks suggested they gather the reedy stems of bear grass, knot and dry them over winter. "Untie them in spring to replace the stuffing. You'll find it softer."

Aspen leaves fluttered down in sweeping showers until the trees appeared bare and fragile. After glowing lime-green, larch formed pumpkin-colored bands on mountain slopes.

"I can't trust my eyes." Nora laughed. "Pines turning fall colors."

"They shed their needles. You'll walk through drifts of them soon," Beartracks told her.

"What a grand place," Nora sighed, putting a hand on the small of her back as she straightened. "There's as much magic here as in the old country."

Jim agreed. "How easy to believe spirits live all around us, even here."

Nora smiled and brought up familiar themes. "I don't know as some of the wee folk might not feel at home here. I believe I will."

Hardened ground turned too cold for any but fitful sleep and stiffened joints. Nora moved into the half-finished cabin, awakened by each predawn after a few restless hours to look out at moonlit spears of frost-whitened grass. Dressing in the dark, she could see puffs of her ghostly exhalations even inside the cabin.

Beartracks left for a week to return with fresh meat, bear paw snowshoes strapped on his back. He whooped at the sight of the cabin and lean-to and at added cords of firewood he'd warned them to cut and stack before snow arrived. All that remained was to trim and caulk two cabin windows and set in Jim's glass panes.

In three days their home sat ready to inhabit. That evening would be their first indoors together. Nora used the space under her bunk for the tapestry satchel that had come with her on that long-ago journey from Boston. She patted its threadbare sides, an old friend.

Their first meal would become familiar fare, venison with wild onions dug up by Nora and potatoes purchased from Nan Hogan. Before dinner Beartracks asked, "I almost forgot. Hogans are making a trip down to the valley. Do either of you have letters to mail? Back home perhaps?"

Awkward silence descended. The friends Nora knew before lived by strict rules. Rose would be shocked beyond words that Nora slept under the same roof with a "heathen rat-eater," not to mention her stint in the brothel. Patrick would mutter, "I told her so." No. No letters to post. What if Rose got a letter and thought to tell Bridget?

Nora drained the potatoes as bitterness rankled. She had no comforting memories of her infant boy. She imagined Bridget with her little son, thinking how much better off he must be than if Nora had dragged him up to the wilderness, Bridget with Nora's own child's head dreaming on her shoulder. She frowned. "Why would the likes of us have letters to post? We'll let the past join the past and welcome to it."

Beartracks cocked his head, owl-like, and shrugged. Jim said nothing. Sullen silence threatened to chill their housewarming. With effort, they regained their spirits when Nora served the meal. Nora expected their guest to stay, but he gathered his gear after supper. "I have a place I can still make tonight," he explained. "I think it might be harder in the morning."

Nora washed the dinner things as Jim brought in wood to add to the fire, then went out again to feed the horses. Nora heard a whispered patter on the roof. "Larch needles?" she asked pointing up with a spoon as he came in.

"Snow. We finished the cabin and horses' lean-to just in time." Jim brushed wet white patches off his jacket.

After a pause, Nora voiced what they were both thinking, "And the privy." Laughter swirled away any lingering tension. Nora stoked the fire and put on water to heat, then sat down at their table still fragrant with new wood, Jim across from her. The Catholic and the Taoist became lost in, if not prayers of thanks, prayerful attitudes.

Jim spoke first, "Beartracks left something. He brought you a special present from Nan Hogan. Rhubarb wine. Famous all over the North Fork, he says."

They poured the wine, clear as water, into tumblers. As they toasted to their accomplishment, the wind moaned around their new home's corners. That night temperatures dropped to levels that could kill. Snow piled in blue drifts as dusk shaded to night, fall to winter. Inside the warm cabin, Jim lit coal oil lanterns and brought out a deck of cards. The two played poker.

Nora dealt like a professional, beating him first, then teaching him with skills learned from the girls at Lillie's. The fire burned while smells of logs still sticky with sap hovered strong as incense. When the card games ended, Nora stretched and walked to the window, peering into flying snow. Jim rose to stand close behind her.

"This place suits you."

Nora replied without turning. "It does. We've built ourselves a fine shelter for winter, even if the floor is a bit on the freezing order."

She saw a reflected Jim hold up his hand as if to stop her. He pulled on his coat and left for a few moments to return powdered with snow, dropping a bundle to the floor. He knelt to unroll a black bearskin. "I believe you and Black Bloomers met before. He frightened you by the creek, and now he must pay the price by keeping our feet warm forever. We'll put him beside your bunk."

"Why, Jim," Nora began, "when did you do all this? I thought you were just practicing your shooting in the early mornings."

"I did practice. But one day I saw the fellow. As you know, Beartracks also taught me how to dress an animal and tan its hide, how to hang meat from a tall limb. It's called a cache. Animals can't reach it and it stays frozen in winter."

Jim spread the lush hide out to its full size. Stepping to the window, he pulled the inside shutter down, then raised it again. "You can prop it partway open at night. Just be sure you don't mind if curious animals like this fellow peek in."

"Critters. I don't mind them. It's people."

"The man who made you feel that way no longer lives."

"He paid for it, right enough." Outside, spires of old-growth pines swayed, roaring in the rising wind. A cold blast made Nora shiver. She closed the window.

Jim appraised her. "You are coming back to life. We have our home."

"Aye, Jim. It's ours and it being on our land means everything. If we file a homestead claim, if that's ever possible, it will be what they can't take away."

Jim stepped back, smiled, and bowed.

CHAPTER EIGHTEEN

Later that night, Nora made coffee. Seeing Jim in the lamplight reminded her of their evening in the Bonds' home. It seemed long ago, but Jim looked as handsome as on that night, even taller, straighter, free of white culture's constraints.

"Easterners hire Beartracks as a hunting guide," Jim said. "He suggested they might want to take meals here. We could pack lunches, make fruit pies to sell, some from our own garden. We'll have a job keeping deer out, of course. We can raise chickens, too, but the same job keeping cats away from them."

"Cats?"

"Mountain lions. We'll see grizzlies, too, looking for food in the spring. If one wants to break in, Beartracks says it will." Jim talked on of forest fires, flooding, and more. "Avalanches can bury a man so they never find him until spring melt — bury animals

— whatever's in their way. When the mountain starts to growl, we must watch out."

He insisted on escorting Nora to the outhouse holding a lantern high as Diogenes, scanning the woods until she reemerged. He steadied her when she stumbled on a slippery root. Nora, somewhat embarrassed and knowing there would be times Jim would be away hunting, resolved to go on solitary trips in the dark after this. When they stepped back inside, a skiff of powder swept in with them.

"I'll say my good night." Jim smiled and went to his alcove. Nora could see the movement of his undressing, a blurred silhouette behind calico.

Pine boughs tossed outside. Sounds like crashing waves, she thought. Like winds that blow in from the sea. Being inside a sturdy shelter on a stormy night was to be blessed.

Unable to sleep, Nora finally picked up a lantern and the rifle and stepped out, just wanting to watch winter's first snow sweep across to the river. When she returned to the warm room, she found Jim sitting by the stove. He patted the bench. "Sit with me awhile. We'll be snowed in tomorrow. No need to rise early." Nora joined him. His hair fanned over his shoulders, blue black in flickering firelight. He looked to be a warrior of some ancient conquering people. He'd never looked as strong and at ease. He sat so still she thought he'd forgotten her until he turned to search her face.

"Do you ever think you might be more than my business partner some day?" His eyes held hers. His question had really been a statement of desire, and now he waited.

Nora inhaled. Even though she'd pondered the same question, she found herself unready for him to be so direct. "That's not how we started out, Jim. No. Maybe it would be more honest to say I'm not ready to be like that yet. I've grown closer to you. I trust you. I see that you're a handsome — a well-knit — man. Only, I'm trying to move on in a different way. I couldn't stand more loss. It's only peace I've been needing since so much happened."

She didn't say that she still wondered at times if she were truly anything more than an opportunity, a means of conferring the status of a white wife. But she knew for certain that he smelled of pine and wood smoke. Doubt and desire. The ancient rhythm of wanting and love within reach. Was that to be the rule of their life? Is that all he felt?

Jim smiled. "It takes many tributaries,

many waterfalls, to feed a great river, one worthy of respect. But sometimes, in a dry season, even a fine wide river must wait for the heavens to open and the rains to come down to let it flow as it is meant to do."

"Well some droughts never end. Then there's just an empty desert. I can't have more children."

"No deserts exist in the North Fork," Jim said. "Here the rains come and the forest will swell green until it leaves us so content we won't want anything else. I have no need of heirs. I am quite aware of the difficulties of mixing the blood, the cultures."

She nodded. "Well, I'm sorry, but I'm not ready for such thoughts. I'd better go to my own bed so we can both be getting ourselves some sleep. It's been a day."

Jim nodded. "Good night. Expect a different world when morning comes."

Aware of Jim's presence just the other side of her alcove curtain, Nora undressed kneeling on her bunk. She slipped a flannel nightgown over her head, then pulled a wool shirt over that and dove under the blankets. Despite their dense weight, she shivered. Warm light glimmered from the lanterns and stove grate. Nora curled, watching it brighten and dim like auroras playing over the calico. Jim, protecting and wanting her, sat just on the other side, keeper of the fire.

She awakened before dawn, aware the wind's howl had died away. Dim light still shifted through the curtain. Jim had banked the fire. She'd shoved her shoes under her blankets to keep them warm and free of mice. Now Nora pushed her feet into them and pulled a blanket around her shoulders as she went to the window. Using her wooden hairbrush, she scratched away the thick white rime. Snow-filled clouds had lifted. The full moon poured its bluish, skimmed milk light over the meadow. Stars patterned the sky at angles and ellipses, squandering their myths and archetypes on the vast, unpeopled landscape.

But it wasn't empty. A purposeful shadow progressed across the blank expanse toward the river and snow-covered peaks levitating in the dark. Nora thought she might be seeing a distorted shade of mountain lion or wolf, but then realized it was Jim carrying the Winchester. He disappeared. A veil of snow falling from a branch obscured his shadow.

"Come back, although I may never be ready for you," she whispered. "Do I really mean that? I'm young to put such desires away." A strengthening life force worked against memories of the lost, beloved, innocent dead still able to rise and command her future so easily. She'd tasted both lust and love. No longer young in heart, could she still give herself to a man, even a fine one?

"What a ways I've come from Connemara," she muttered. "From Boston for that matter. But I'm standing in my own place, a landowner." She straightened her shoulders and rebuilt the fire.

Jim had heated leftover coffee before leaving. Nora ran her thumb along the rim of his cup. "Well, he'll be back. He fits the life here well enough, it seems," she murmured, setting the cup down and turning to her alcove, more empty now than snug.

When Nora rose hours later, Jim's boots sat outside his alcove. She dressed in haste and started fresh coffee. She stifled any impulse to enquire where he'd been when he joined her. Both took care to be courteous while discussing tasks to finish before winter. Later, they steamed and bent fir to curl the front end of a toboggan, sawing and nailing round bucket covers to hold containers they'd put on the toboggan for hauling water and other necessities. Pulled over snow to the creek and back, it would carve furrows that turned dark blue at twilight like ink lines recording each day's efforts. Jim later declared they looked like Chinese calligraphy.

Among other chores, he cut fresh cottonwood bark to feed Wink and Cotton and shoveled rationed oats and prairie hay into their manger. The horses would be thin by spring, but would fare better next year in a real barn. The cottonwoods died from losing the stripped bark, but Jim and Nora would burn the dead wood. Hope fueled their labor, hope that they could prosper in this rough country.

Each winter day, fragrance of fresh shavings from new floor planks mixed with the rich smokiness of larch burning in the stove. Nora had poked rags into every spare inch when they'd loaded the wagon in Helena. Now she fashioned them into a multicolored rug.

She reveled in creating an environment so clean and new. Still memories tumbled in, twisting her with every thought of the priest's conditions. Remembering Bat and how Jim had taken the ring added to her unease.

Faith had returned in the monumental solitude of the North Fork. Spirituality reborn. But to Nora, spirit and Catholicism melded into one divine, demanding whole. It would take so long to earn absolution by paying the money to Dierdre. Nora couldn't speak of it again to Jim who understood so much, but would never share her ingrained guilt and fear of damnation. She just had to wrest her own means of salvation from this wilderness. Guilt linked to Bat Moriarty would be a long time fading.

One early winter morning Nora unlatched the door to see a herd of elk big as horses under a floating sea of antlers. Their whispering murmurs carried from the meadow like waves. She beckoned wildly to Jim who picked up his rifle, aimed, and fired once. A great bull fell. The herd crashed away to the river, leaving their dead sovereign, his immense, inert head reddening the snow. The once regal animal's tongue flopped out of his gaping mouth. Nora felt a stab of pity mixed with giddy joy in storing enough meat to last until spring.

Just as they prepared to sit down to elk steaks that night, pounding shook the door.

"Open up, pilgrims. Beartracks Benton and Sweet Grass have come calling."

Nora blushed at their praise for the wood floor, the rug, the store of food.

Next morning Beartracks invited Jim to go along to check his lines. "Learn to be a trapper and then teach Irish here. In fall I trap beaver, otter, and mink — bobcat and lynx — winter it's marten, ermine, and fisher. Sometimes I catch raiding wolverine."

A visibly pregnant Sweet Grass stayed behind. During those five days the women formed a friendship in spite of occasional stumbles over language. Nora shared memories of pregnancy, mentioning Helen, but never the son whose name she didn't know.

Sweet Grass taught Nora how to make snowshoes beginning with steaming the fir and bending it, similar to what Jim and Nora did to make the tobaggon. Nora wrapped rawhide left to right on bent frames, fastening the front and back strips together, fashioning the webbing, and tying on boot-fastening strips, fourteen by thirty inches of hard-won wood and webbing. Her fingers ached, but she reveled in growing self-sufficiency and eagerness to show Jim. She even made and wore leggings and moccasins, shortening some of her heavy skirts for easier movement outside.

Nora took a rare look at the calendar on December 25, shocked that she'd forgotten

Christmas. Strange how she could love this place with such satisfaction, then be yanked back to her past, both bright and dark. She pictured Christmases in Butte, the Larkin family so contented. She pushed away more disturbing memories that could only bring tears, and said a quick rosary. She prayed for patience in the matter of the ring payment, adding a petition that nothing destroy the peace of her and Jim's home, that her sense of approaching disaster be unfounded, that it might just be shadows from the disastrous past. And she prayed for her son, enjoying his first Christmas so far away.

After breakfast, she tossed out suet and bits of biscuit and pancakes as gifts to jays, chickadees, and magpies, relatives of the ones in Ireland that bring good luck when you greet them. Ravens sailed overhead like dark ships, making hoarse, complaining cries of foreboding. She reminded herself again that Bat Moriarty had met his end at Lillie McGraw's. No one else would want to hurt Jim or her.

Snow on timbered slopes formed a herringbone pattern of green and white up to the snowpack on gleaming peaks. Legions of fat snowflakes drifted earthward, landing with whispers like those of sated lovers. Nora's heart lifted. Intimacy grew here in ice curls within small hidden worlds of wood and moss. Grandeur rested in ever-changing light on mountains. Nature presented sensory gifts for which she'd been starving. Forgotten well-being restored itself in her.

As confidence grew, Nora enjoyed Jim's leaving her alone while he checked traps. Yet she liked his reappearances more. She puzzled over those quickenings. Could her heart know better than her mistrustful head? She so looked forward to the sight of him striding to the cabin, bearing furs to sell in spring.

By January, winter clamped down so hard even the wooden floor chilled the cabin dwellers' feet through their buckskin moccasins. Nora stuffed scraps of hide into cracks in contracting walls. Jim chopped through thick creek ice for water.

They fashioned snowshoes to sell in spring. Worry over money threaded through their thoughts like animal trails through the forest. They calculated money and what could be done with it, those long silences of the journey north now giving way to lively speculation. They talked of land boundaries, the possibilities of running cattle.

Jim never reintroduced his wish that

something more might grow between them. Nora appreciated his discretion, but some nights her alcove became a lonely place. She would unexpectedly want to touch his shining black hair, rest her hand on his shoulder — then reminded herself how she erred before. She must never create such pain for herself again. It would kill her.

At Jim's urging the two went together to check traplines in February. They pulled their tobaggon north as the rising sun washed pale rose over all, deepening the red-brown branches of mountain mahogany. Rust-brown V's of dropped pine needles flecked the snow. After weeks of bone-freezing, skin-cracking cold, a warmer eastern breeze puffed at them, a giant's exhaled breath. By the time they reached Beartracks's trapper's cabin at Kintla Lake, wind-blasted pines complained and flung themselves, roaring back and forth like lunatics.

That night the uproar ceased. Coyotes yipped out on the lake's thick ice, hushing at once when wolves howled their feral, drawn-out harmonies. Feeding chunks of wood into the fireplace, Jim caught another sound, a reverberating growl from above, grumbling like a displeased god. It brought back a winter years ago when he'd heard that rumbling from the Chungnan Range. Then he remembered Beartracks's warning about when the mountain thunders. Jim left Nora sleeping in her bedroll while he walked out in the dark to study the mountainside looming behind the cabin. Slabs of snow might slide, triggered by new layers bearing so heavily the old ones broke off. The mountain resonated another anguished moan. Jim went inside to drift, still dressed, into restless sleep.

Louder rumbles brought him full awake. He sat up shaking Nora. He grabbed her just as she finished shoving her feet into boots. Their shouts whipped away, lost as snow on the mountain tumbled and pulsated in an overwhelming bellow. The enraged god descended, cleaving a chute down the ancient forest. They stumbled out of the cabin into a black and white jumble. Floundering, falling, they scrambled to the lake. To Jim, their dash seemed a slow hallucination rather than its actual frantic speed. The wind bent them as it did people he'd seen in prairie blizzards.

Trees and branches flew past. The force knocked both Nora and Jim face down. She crawled to him. Man and woman gripped each other, clutching the blankets they'd dragged from the cabin until the wind snatched the cloth, whirling it away. Tree-tops and branches sailed overhead, the tremendous sickening crack of old trees sounded like the snapping of giant bones. White powder rolled and purled high on Boundary Mountain as a half-mile snowslide gained momentum. After what seemed hours rather than mere minutes, the slide finally came to rest nearly against the cabin's back wall.

That colossal roar diminished. When its last echo faded, Jim and Nora struggled to their hands and knees, gaping at the mountain. Jim pushed himself to stand on wobbling legs, then retrieved the blankets caught on debris. Ravaged trees stretched in that one long, snowy chute up the mountain. Jim covered Nora with a tattered remnant and helped her stand.

Northern Lights appeared . . . vertical green, rose, and blue veils in darting, sinuous, vaulting undulations. Jim and Nora turned to each other, mingling tears and laughter.

Wordless, they embraced. Instinctively, hungrily, still alive, they drew together, mouth finding mouth. They broke apart only to lean against each other, then walk back with sensual purpose blessed by shimmering aurora overhead. A wall of snow, trees, and rock rose fifteen feet behind the cabin. Oblivious to anything but desire, the two went inside.

Jim rebuilt the fire. Nora lay watching, grateful to have him, grateful they'd survived together. They slipped each other's torn clothes away. No reason existed for haste. They paused for slow, arousing kisses. Their hands explored each other's bodies until Nora drew him down. Jim's mouth again sought hers. She lay, palms open, as though awaiting a gift. He stretched low over her. His mouth sought her breast and he suckled there, grasping it, moving it as she moaned in pleasure. Then he kissed lower and lower down her body. He slowly opened her thighs as though she were a flower. He held her hips, giving her a pleasure shocking in its forbidden, unknown warmth. Never had she felt such sensations. She gripped his head as he carried her away on high waves of desire. She arched against him, shattered with joy, then floated down the crest until she drifted to a still pool of sated fulfillment. Slowly he entered her and she moved with him. She controlled the pace of his passion and felt the bliss of giving him such pleasure. It felt as though they'd done this many times — out of need, out of love, out of everything treasured in the other. His cry of release carried her name, as though its sound alone meant more to him than life.

They held each other in the afterglow. "I swear," Nora whispered, "I'll never take a day of our life together for granted."

He kissed her forehead. When they slept, her fiery red and his black hair swept in a circle of ying and yang around their heads, eternal as love had been even before they met and greeted it, inviting it to stay with them always.

When they awoke, Nora stretched like a satisfied cat. "Well, I believe we've done it now, no going back to servants and partners."

Jim rose on his elbow to smile at her. "No, I want to marry you. I wanted to be your partner, but that was never the only thing. I journeyed such a long way thinking it was for my past and to find my father, but it was not. The past is nothing. You are my present, my future. I love you."

"I will be your wife, for certain," Nora said, opening her arms in joyful invitation. She, too, set the past aside as she felt his smooth skin, his hard body, his very goodness under her hands.

After generous passion, hand in hand they

opened the door to dazzling sunshine and the sparkle of suspended frost crystals. Complacent whitetail deer stepped on the snow-blanketed lake, nibbling from strewn branches.

After resting a day, Nora and Jim loaded their gear and started from Kintla toward home, eager to be where they'd created their new world, their sanctuary.

Chapter Nineteen

In Clancy, Bat's chest wound and burns proved slow to heal, leaving shiny lurid scars on his legs, hands, and torso. Lou conducted her professional life while caring for him. Although they slept in the same bed, he left her alone thanks to physical weakness and a fastidious aversion to being with a woman so used. The walls between his room and her "office" were thin.

Anytime Lou let his supply of laudanum run low, Bat cursed in frustration, hurled his crutches against walls, and lurched through the house flinging out the contents of drawers in a frantic, scrabbling search. As a result, Doc continued to furnish heavy doses to the gambler.

Lou became the laudanum keeper. She could handle Bat as long as she fed his need.

Bat had dreams. In one he lay on his old bed at Nora's house, she in her dressing gown, red-gold hair falling over her breasts and down her back. As she lay supine, he turned to gather her underneath him.

For the first time since the fire, Bat's body responded to desire and he slipped into Lou, whose hands, after a few astonished seconds, reached to stroke his back, cupping over his thin, wing-like shoulder blades as if she could hold him buried in her, keep him from flying away.

Before they finished Bat awakened, but didn't stop until release came. Then he flopped away, shuddering a little in pleasure's aftermath. "My God, Lou. You're still damn good at your work. Must be all the practice," he sighed.

"You're my work. My hardest work," Lou muttered, pushing herself up so her veined white breasts, brown nipples the size of quarters, drooped over the blanket's tattered edge. "Here." She opened the drawer of the nightstand and took out a nine-inch cigar. She scraped a match on the lantern base, lit the smoke, and pulled on it. She blew out a puff and handed the cigar over to Bat. "I saved it for this occasion," she said, "but I near gave up on ever smoking it."

Taking it with him, he rose naked and tipped back a bottle to finish the last drops of laudanum, throwing the empty out the open window. It hit a rock, shattering the night's peace. He studied Lou for a long moment. His look held no emotion, but softened as the drug took effect.

"We need to move on, honey, if you're planning to get all the bottles of that you want," Lou told him. "The miners won't be here much longer with gold playing out." Bat had been practicing at cards, sitting by the table in his robe, coaxing his dexterity back, shuffling, cutting, dealing. Poker was his game, but he could deal faro or run keno. She continued, "I want to go with you. I'm sick of these dirty miners. This hellhole is nothing to me but bad smells and bone weariness."

Bat leaned out the windowsill, looking in the direction of a scrawny bush where bottle shards reflected white moonlight. His thoughts formed quick and decisive. He still felt weak, but could walk again. He eyed his reflection in the mirror. The fire hadn't scarred his face except that pain had carved lines into his forehead and from his elegant nostrils to his mouth. Pallor and purple circles under his eyes were prominent new features. His hair had thinned a little, aging him before his time. Easy confidence had been replaced by a watchfulness, permanent apprehension of a man who'd been stripped of valuables while he lay bleeding and help-less.

Bat felt certain, after hours of going over the scene, that it had been Jim Li who pulled the ring off his finger and left him to the inferno. Lou said she didn't know anything about where Jim Li had gone. Lillie McGraw had closed her operation, and they heard she'd moved to Denver with a new husband. The girls scattered, mostly to opportunities in the prosperous West Coast.

Bat nursed a bad feeling about going back to Helena. He'd been involved in the fight that caused the fire. The law might have questions. Also, Dierdre might have placed one of her infernal personal ads there by now. Anyway, Jim Li wouldn't stay in Helena. A Chinaman who wanted to disappear with a valuable ring would likely head for a city with a Chinatown, someplace to trade stolen goods and blend in with his own, maybe even go back to China, marry, have sons, live like a lord. The very thought drove Bat to a teeth-grinding fury.

Bat intended to find Jim Li, but needed money to do it. He could pimp Lou. She'd do whatever he told her, but they needed to be someplace where he could get into a good game.

"We're leaving all right," he said at last.

"What would you say to California?"

"San Francisco?"

"Why not, but Denver first. We don't have enough to go straight there. We'll have to make odd hops. Know anybody you can work with in Billings? I'm thinking Billings, Bismarck, drop down to Deadwood, then Denver, then San Francisco. Then we'll do it all again. A big loop."

"You're never going to stop looking for the big Chinaman, are you?"

Bat growled. "When I find the son of a bitch, I'll collect my ring or its value, then put him in the ground."

"Well, I hope we make it to San Francisco. I've always wanted to see that city before I die. I hope we have money. I also hope you never see the Chinaman again because if you find him, you might forget how much you need me." She sat up and studied the man staring out at the night, then slid back down in the limp sheets. "And I am useful to you, honey. I'll always be useful to you. I wish you'd develop a need for me as strong as for that laudanum. Up until tonight I'd almost given up the idea that I'd ever be more than a nurse and supplier."

She rolled over, face to the wall. After a long revery at the window, the man who talked of killing climbed into bed and curled against her back like a child. In minutes he succumbed to the laudanum, his coarse breathing the only sound in the darkened room. Lou lay awake.

He woke just enough to hear her next words. "My dream of life is like yours, honey, but with one big exception. If we get out of Clancy, if we make a new start, I want to make you forget this revenge on the Chinaman. That'll only lead to worse trouble for both of us."

Nora took time from preparing pelts to plan spring work: a garden, seed for hay, fencing, a deeper root cellar, perhaps a summer kitchen by the creek, but most important, a real barn.

The Hogans appeared one day. Jim had trekked away to scout for fall traplines, and Nora found herself glad for company after days of solitude. They brought a pair of skis with poles for her to try. She'd mastered the business of snowshoes, lifting her leg high then stepping down flat footed, moving through snowfields she'd have sunk in up to her hips otherwise.

Nan's ski instructions presented new challenges. "Bend your knees a little. Lean forward, then steady yourself and push off with the poles."

Nora started, flopped into soft snow twice after false starts, then discovered a long, gliding rhythm and blood-warming speed. She and Nan, exhaling icy fog as they visited and laughed, skied that night below a full moon's radiance. Nora followed a gleam of trail, flanked by towering old growth like enchanted trees in a fairy tale. She wondered where Jim might be, hunkered over some little fire. An image rose of his black hair rising like wings to glide over the blue-white ground toward her. Without him the scene turned empty, the charm broken.

Foreboding ambushed her. Could anything happen to Jim? Could she lose him, too?

At first Nora heard only their conversation and the suserration of skis on snow. Then the wavered chords of wolves in full voice purled from the north. She thrust toward the sound. "Listen to them, Nan." Her voice rang eager and strained. "They sound wild as banshees. Is it a spell they're casting?"

Nan shook her head at the Irish notion. "You're imagining things. You'll go crazy as a hoot owl if you let your imagination run wild out here. Let's go back. Wolves make me nervous."

Nora felt reckless and a bit rebellious. The

wilderness, that feral harmony, called to her in the night so full of untamed secrets and opportunities. She and Jim belonged to this place beyond expectations. It claimed them as much as they it.

But sensible Nan wanted to turn back to the cabin. Nora followed without argument.

The only other visitors through that winter were moose, elk, and coyotes. Beartracks arrived every few weeks, bringing reports of a healthy baby daughter named Dawn Mist, and concern that Sweet Grass had been ailing since giving birth. He also spoke of fellow mountain men, events in Canada's Belly River country, and talk that in spring there would be a box car railroad camp at Belton, the name now given to the place where Nora and Jim first met their jovial mentor. There were expectations of a completed railroad from the east side of the Rockies to Kalispell.

In May, rivulets of melted snowpack gushed into creeks and rivers accompanied by incessant rain. Mud, icy pools and puddles, opaque sky above ghostly mists made up the universe. At last the June sun drove off such clammy wraithes and silvery monotones. Rocky ground sucked the frigid, pooling water into itself.

They hooked the horses to plow and broke ground sprinkled with dashing yellow glacier lilies. Nora intended to plant a half-acre vegetable garden. Jim deepened the root cellar.

One late afternoon when earth burgeoned green, Nora stood in the rectangle of her future garden. Stumps scattered over the half-acre rendering made straight furrows impossible.

Beartracks appeared, riding his bay horse hard over the bank. He slowed near her. "Nora, Sweet Grass is worse. She wants you. If you're willing, we'd better start tomorrow. Early."

Nora pulled off a dirt-stiff work glove and raked back her disheveled hair with her fingers. "I'll come. Who has Dawn Mist?"

Beartracks, looking tired and drawn, lowered his pack of furs. "The fur buyer Snyder at the lodge across the lake sent a Blackfeet woman who's come to help, although he won't spare her for long. None of the medicines are helping." He paused and viewed Nora's efforts as if glad to change the subject. "Other folks get rid of stumps with dynamite."

"Dynamite, is it? Nobody told us to bring that." Nora gestured for him to walk to the cabin with her.

He hoisted the furs again. "Well, it's what people do. Then your rows could be —"

"Straight as string. The stumps are a nuisance and they take up space better used. Where would we get this dynamite?"

"The camp at Belton could spare what you need. Anyway, you and Jim should see it. Folks are settling near my place. They call it Apgar after my old friends the Apgar brothers, one of them anyway. No wives yet, but several men put up cabins. When the railroad's finished, their families will follow."

"Families. Is she really so bad, Beartracks?"

He frowned. "Not well, Irish. Not well at all. Her spirits are low, like she's given up. We try everything, but she weakens. You must see our Dawn Mist. A good-natured infant, although some would fault her being mixed like China Jim."

Nora nodded. "Of course."

"We'll stop at Nan and Fred's."

Nora looked down at her mud-splotched skirt, shaking the caked hem. "Well, it will take me a bit to be ready."

Beartracks nodded at the moccasins and leggings. "You're not such a pilgrim any longer, and it's only your first spring."

"I've always gotten along in the place where I land."

That night she bathed and laid out decent clothes, a gray dress with a jacket and the old straw boater with the green ribbon. Although moccasins were comfortable around the place, she pulled out her worn, heavy black shoes, so cracked and curled she took time to rub tallow on them. The old desire to be respectable returned. She didn't want it to seem to townfolk that she'd forgotten all the ways of civilization while making her home on the North Fork.

Jim insisted one of them should stay to keep working and tend to Beartracks's horse. As she rode away on the wagon next morning, Nora felt a pang looking back at him bending to work in the garden. They'd become a family of two during the long enforced winter. Passion overcame the little irritations of close life in the cabin. They'd emerged with a love, respect, and dependence more absolute than Nora had ever known.

Instead of the clear alpine water Nora had crossed last autumn, the North Fork swelled up swirling, the color of milky tea. While Wink and Cotton balked, then stepped into the water, Nora clung to her wagon seat, feet braced hard in her worn shoes.

Beartracks grinned for the first time since arriving. "Relax, Irish. Think of blasting all those stumps to tarnation. I know pilgrims. As tired as you get of wintering in your cabins, you're shy as fawns come spring."

"No," Nora lied. "I'm not afraid to venture out. It's the wild water, the bumpy road. Everything's come through winter so different."

"You're a strong, healthy girl now. Not sickly as when you stayed with us. Not like Sweet Grass is."

He had the right of it there, Nora agreed. North Fork life had been good for her, had given her the fulfullment of a man's love, what she'd thought never to have again.

The wagon rolled through webbed shadows speared by white flowers. Nora marveled at all the tints of green as they passed moss-covered boulders high as castle walls and fallen trees, their circular root systems upended like shields.

"I wouldn't be surprised to see fairies here. You know, the little people."

"Little people, big people, too many people of all sizes when the railroad's done," Beartracks muttered.

CHAPTER TWENTY

Winter hadn't altered Nan Hogan. Nora could swear the woman wore the dress she'd met her in the summer before. Spring sun had already tanned Nan's handsome face. Her cheeks glowed from the heat of baking bread.

The Hogans had other guests. An arrogant British aristocrat had come hunting trophy mountain goat, his guide none other than the famous Pete Dumont. Nora had first heard Pete Dumont's name from Lillie McGraw. She would not pass on Lillie's greeting, however. The memory of Lillie's place made her cringe.

A woman dressed in black traveled with them, her dark hair and hazel eyes set off by gold nugget earrings. The men, Pete and Beartracks catching up on their respective winters, noticed Nora who summoned all her dignity before stepping into the room, extending her hand, wishing it were softer or she'd worn a glove. Pete Dumont made a sweeping bow. "Mrs. Larkin. Beartracks told me he'd brought a pretty girl to the North Fork. I am Pierre Dumont, but all in these mountains call me Pete."

The nobleman interrupted. "Beartracks brought a beautiful titian-haired goddess, a Hibernian Helen to inspire poets, a face that could launch a thousand ships." The woman at his side narrowed her eyes.

Nora, not noticing, remembered with a stab how she'd chosen Helen's name, but took advantage of a rare literary reference she knew. "I'm not one the Greeks and Trojans would fight over, sir," she said with a wary smile. "Just a settler trying to hold her land."

"Admirable, Mrs. Larkin." He bowed stiffly. "Lord Smith-Gordon. This exotic creature is my friend, Miss Clementine Dasher. You Irish have done well in America. I applaud your ambition."

Nora nodded to hard-eyed Clementine, knowing instantly she was an independent version of the girls at Lillie's. "Us people, is it? Your countrymen haven't given us much choice now, have they, my Lord?"

Beartracks leapt in. "Well, well, Nora has a partner." He described Jim.

Nan laughed, describing their disheveled

arrival until tensions melted. Both Nora and the English lord remained formal, unable to avoid or ignore their heritage as ancient enemies.

After dinner the men retired to the barn for serious drinking, and Clementine excused herself. Nora settled by the fire with Nan who had winter stories of her own about a man who arrived at their door nearly frozen, or the moose that took up residence near the barn and liked to listen to the hired man play his harmonica. She couldn't top Nora's avalanche experience, though. Nora left out the resulting passion.

Next morning Nora dawdled in her room, not wanting to breakfast with the aristocratic trophy hunter and his haughty mistress. After finally hearing them ride off, she went to Nan's kitchen. Beartracks appeared. Pale, he winced when Nan rattled the cookware.

"Sure and I don't know why you men drink," Nora said.

"We know why when we're doing it," he said, pulling up a chair and sagging into it. "We just can't remember in the morning."

They arrived at Apgar by late afternoon. A pockmarked Blackfeet girl sat on a log in front of Beartracks's cabin looking miserable. A chubby baby kicking moccasined feet lay across her knees. When Beartracks called, she gathered the infant against her shoulder and walked toward them. She spoke to Beartracks in Blackfeet. He whirled and ran to the cabin. Nora stared at the somber girl for a moment, then followed.

Sweet Grass lay in a doeskin, bead-decorated dress. Folded little hands clasped a rosary. Her skin had the gray pallor of death, her features the stiffness of frozen wax. Beartracks knelt, his head on her hands.

"I'm so sorry," Nora murmured, touching his shoulder. She'd miss the soft-voiced, helpful girl with her dimpled smile.

After silent minutes, Beartracks rose, jaw set, and went about enveloping his wife's body in an elk robe. He carried her, followed by Nora and the Indian girl, now hefting the baby and a spade, far into the forest beside the big creek that ran from the lake. Nora gestured that she would take the four-month-old. Beartracks dug the grave.

Nora studied Dawn Mist. Intense brown eyes, slightly uptilted in a heart-shaped face, studied her right back. Nora cooed, stroking the baby's shock of black hair, then a small brown hand. The infant grasped Nora's finger. Nora fought tears, remembering her own babies. This little girl now lived as motherless as she lived childless. She shifted the baby, bounced and patted her as Beartracks lowered Sweet Grass into the forest earth to lie forever within the cedar-laden bank.

Trudging back, the Indian woman spoke earnestly to Beartracks who gave one gruff response. Nora held Dawn as the woman strode ahead into the cabin to emerge carrying her parfleche, climbed into a canoe, and raised her hand once before paddling off across the lake.

Nora glanced at Beartracks. He shrugged. "She had to get back."

Carrying the baby toward the cabin, Nora looked back at him. "Come in and tell me what you intend to do with your enchanting daughter."

Inside, she prepared canned milk and mashed cooked apple for Dawn Mist. Beartracks watched, then spoke. "I want you and Jim to take my daughter. Take her and raise her."

Nora didn't answer, but focused on the infant. After feeding Dawn Mist, she heated water, bathed, and changed her. It seemed she'd done it before only yesterday. There'd been an empty ache in Nora's arms for so long. But would this be right?

"You're her father, Beartracks," she said after Dawn Mist fell asleep. "What exactly are you proposing? Do you want us to keep her for only awhile, or until she's grown?"

"My life is in the mountains. I can't raise a girl, and if I ever wanted to go back to Merry Old England, God forbid, my people would never accept a half-breed bastard. Sweet Grass and I never married actually." He nodded. "No, you and Jim take her as yours. You're a mixed bunch anyway. You ought to have a child underfoot. Make you more of a family."

"What if Jim says no?" Nora realized she'd as much as admitted she wanted this orphan.

"Find somebody who will — or take her back to the reservation — although most of her relatives died off during the starving time in '83 and the smallpox epidemic. Those people still live hard. It's how I took up with Sweet Grass. She strung along with me until I just gave up and accepted her as permanent. I'll never do that to another woman. Dumont's smart to stay unfettered. Anyhow, Dawn is half white."

Nora rested her eyes on the sleeping baby. Providence offered her this third chance at motherhood. She found the words to tell Beartracks about Helen, finding it easier to talk about her even though her blonde chatterbox had been quite different from this exotic child. "I'll tell you what we'll do," she said. "We'll take Dawn with us, and I'll put it to Jim. His big heart will carry the day. You'll visit from time to time so she knows you. I'll be her legal guardian. Put something in writing. What do you say?"

Beartracks sighed in relief. "So it's up to China Jim? He can't refuse you. That's a great relief. I'm going into Belton. I'll bring back dynamite in the morning, and we'll start back."

Alone with Dawn, Nora pondered what she'd just done. She began a low Celtic lullaby, and eventually slept beside the child, her treasured gift.

Chapter Twenty-One

The Hogans greeted Nora and Beartracks as they stopped on the return trip, happy to have the long-awaited supplies. Nan said Pete Dumont had planned to spend a night at Nora and Jim's cabin, then leave Clementine there while they went up to Kintla with the Englishman. A doubtful Nan added it was kind of Nora to take in Beartracks's "little half-breed."

"She is a blessing for me," Nora retorted. "And her name is Dawn Mist. We'll call her Dawn."

That same night, Pete Dumont brought Smith-Gordon and Clementine to Nora and Jim's cabin. Clementine bathed in their galvanized tub. Jim made up Nora's old bed where the exhausted woman dropped into hard sleep while the three men played long games of poker. Smith-Gordon fancied himself a sharp player. "I met Clementine at a house in Storyville in New Orleans," he told them. "She was a faro dealer come down from Chicago. One of the best. I'm keeping her with me for the time being . . . an entertaining woman in every circumstance. With her hair pulled back, the golden nuggets match golden flecks in her eyes. What fellow doesn't enjoy being in close proximity to gold? Or a woman of such varied talents?"

Jim, having played poker many times with Nora on long winter nights, realized that Smith-Gordon wasn't the player he believed himself to be. The Englishman made it clear he didn't think much of Jim at all. He ignored him, keeping his endless stories and observations directed to Pete. Slowly, Jim began to play improved hands. By dawn he'd won a sizeable sum from the astonished aristocrat.

"I never knew a Chinese to outplay an Englishman." Smith-Gordon glared.

"China Jim here is full of surprises," Pete said, pushing the pot toward their host. "I'm beginning to think he can do just about anything. But cheat? No. Nora's man is honest."

Next day just after reaching the river, Nora and Beartracks ran into the hunters. Lord

Smith-Gordon had a large, tawny mountain lion slung over his pack animal. The nobleman smiled, definitely in a fine mood.

Approaching home, Nora noticed Clementine Dasher saunter out of the cabin. "Sure this place is becoming as crowded as Boston," she muttered to Dawn, who cooed from the sling that held her across Nora's chest.

Jim stepped forward, his hands gripping Nora's shoulders after she climbed down. She held up the baby. "Our friend Sweet Grass passed away, poor girl. And we've much to talk about. Look at this beautiful child left motherless."

"Yes," Jim said as he studied Dawn Mist, whose expression puckered at this stranger's face. "I see we do."

Beartracks greeted Clementine. Smith-Gordon and Pete went to the barn to hang the lion.

On their return, Clementine's eyelashes fluttered. The nugget earrings bobbed. "I missed you, my lord."

The Englishman extended his hand. "Miss Dasher, Clementine — would you favor me with a walk out of doors? All this riding has quite given me a need to stretch my legs."

Clementine took the proffered hand, stood, smoothed her skirt against her thighs, then swept out the door. Nora watched her take the slim aristocrat's arm, tilt her chin, and gaze into his pale blue eyes. "She knows how to keep him intrigued," she murmured.

Pete and Beartracks grinned and drifted outside.

Nora changed Dawn and placed her on Jim's old alcove bed for a nap. In low tones, Nora related Beartracks's request that they raise his daughter. The smell of cut wood surrounded them as they gazed out open rectangles intended to become windows that faced the soft undulations of the Whitefish Range. "This baby needs us, Jim. I think we need her, too. Beartracks won't interfere. He'll be like an uncle. You'd be the father she needs, and I — would be her mother."

Jim hesitated. "You propose we take this child and love it as our own? Could you do that?"

"I could. You must remember I know what it is to care for a little girl."

Jim's expression softened. "My parents did not raise me, but my aunt White Plum did. I believe I brought her some joy. If you wish, we will make this little English-Blackfeet baby our daughter."

"Thank you, Jim. I trusted you'd say just that." Nora kissed him, happy tears filling her eyes. He walked to the alcove and picked up the sleeping Dawn Mist.

"Here is our child," he said. "Now, our future holds much more than we could have dreamed. And something else to add to your joy. All our poker practice paid off. I won a sum from the Englishman last night. It meant only hurt pride to him, but I believe to you it means salvation. For Dierdre Moriarty perhaps it means help for her family."

"Jim, is it enough?" Nora rushed to him.

"Just enough."

"Well, what some would call your ill-gotten gains is the lifeline I feared would never come. You've been my redemption once again. I love you so." Nora embraced him and their daughter. The heavy burden of guilt she'd carried ever since Helena rolled away. They leaned into each other as a puff of pine-scented air breezed in. Harvest time approaching at last.

They would ask Beartracks to see the money sent to Michigan from a Kalispell bank. Nora composed a note to Dierdre to enclose with the bank draft. She thought for a long time, then told one last lie, simply writing that she and her husband had known Moriarty and before his death he entrusted them to send his savings to his wife and children.

While Clementine and her lord walked out together, Pete surprised those indoors by pencil-sketching a radiant Nora holding Dawn, a protective Jim bending over them.

When the others finally returned, Clementine wore a triumphant, gloating smile.

Smith-Gordon patted his companion's hand. "Friends, I'll proceed to San Francisco from here. Miss Dasher tells me it's a rollicking city for one with my interests. I suggest we depart at dawn."

Before the Englishman and his mistress rode out next morning, Clementine nodded to Jim, her eyes flashing less than gratitude. "Thank you for making me comfortable. I'll remember meeting a Chinaman in the mountains. Especially one who cost Smith-Gordon so dear at cards."

She mounted and sat tall on her black gelding beside the Englishman on his horse. Not exactly beautiful, she had high color, a narrow face below her arched brows, prominent cheekbones, and an aquiline nose. Striking, Nora thought. Clementine Dasher must be what they meant by a striking woman. Clementine gave them a wink as she lifted her hand in a dismissive farewell gesture. Lord Smith-Gordon touched his heels to his bay stallion that pranced a little before trotting through the meadow to the river where Pete Dumont waited to raft them across.

Jim spoke first. "I am glad to wave farewell. I sense ill fortune follows that woman. She visits it on those who enter her sphere."

"Do you think so? Then the English lord is in for it. I don't mind about his ilk getting their due." Nora nuzzled Dawn.

Beartracks laughed. "The English lord is helping himself. Nobody else gives a damn or likes her. Well, I'll be on my way to Kalispell with your winnings. I could use a spell in town. My father has probably sent me a little extra by now."

Nora and Jim thanked him, then turned in wonder to their new charge, forgetting Beartracks, the English lord, and his dark mistress.

Jim blasted the first stumps three weeks later. At ease with dynamite, he turned a quizzical look on Nora before she retreated away from the noise with Dawn. "Remember whose country brought the world fireworks?"

"Whose?" Nora teased.

Jim shook his head at such real or feigned ignorance of China's brilliance and placed each load. Explosions shook the cabin and upset Wink and Cotton, but the precious window panes, taped as a precaution, held.

Just before supper a week later, Beartracks whooped from the road. He reported the money had indeed been sent to Dierdre. The bank president even telegraphed Michigan to be certain that Bat Moriarty's widow still lived at her old address.

Nora stepped away from the men to offer a quick prayer of thanks for this news.

The friends ate together. After awhile Beartracks stood. "A delightful meal and better company. Well, I'm off to old Zeb's." He smoothed his hair front to back, the crown of a wide-brimmed hat tilted on his head. "Zeb's a surly scoundrel who partnered with me twenty years ago. Pete said he's settled three miles from here."

In the morning, Beartracks broke out of the trees, driving two jersey cows ahead.

"You'll need a better fence for these bossies. Zeb's dead. A bear. Wasn't much left of him to bury."

"Poor man." Nora ran her hand down one cow's ample flanks. "Such fine animals," she murmured. "We've dreamed of starting our own herd."

"Why don't you just take them? Use their

milk for Dawn. Zeb was a loner. No family."

"We'll make good use of them, for certain," Nora answered.

After dinner they talked at the table. She touched on the subject of Zeb. "I know he was a sort of friend to you."

"He was a hard man in bad times. Not many of us left." Beartracks frowned.

In the morning, he was gone.

"He left the best of himself with us," Jim said, picking up Dawn who smiled now at the man who'd become her father.

Nora again loved the look of the land in spring, dotted with white three-petaled trillium, yellow glacier lilies, blue harebells, and white beargrass. But summer held its own rewards. Scaring ground birds and field mice, Jim cut wild grass with a scythe, bundled it for Wink and Cotton, then plowed the meadow before planting timothy for hay.

Nora planted her half-acre garden in potatoes, rhubarb, squash, beans, and onions. Her hands were long past worrying over. She seldom paused to glance in a mirror. She thought only of Jim, Dawn, and the land. She blasted out two stumps by herself after Jim showed her how. They cut down jack pine. Hard work left them sun-scorched and exhausted at the end of each day, but with a second clearing by summer's end. They figured meeting the cost of more cattle, even a small herd of twenty or so, would be hard, but possible. They finally built the real barn that gave the place an air of permanence.

One evening after the long day's labors, Nora and Jim rested on a rough-hewn bench on the porch, sipping buttermilk cold from the crock always submerged in icy mountain waters. The baby's babbling accompanied the sunset change from yellows to pinks to blues on the mountains.

Jim spoke of what they'd both noticed. "We have not seen much of Beartracks Benton."

Nora only shrugged. "I suppose he's got his own business to attend to."

Jim leaned back, admiring the view. "He may want to give us time to settle in with Dawn . . . it may hurt him to see her."

"It was a strange time with Pete, Clementine, and her Englishman. Beartracks giving up his daughter almost got swept aside. Do you still believe Miss Dasher brought bad luck?"

"She probably will never return to hurt us. Just a foreboding I attach to her. All I want is a peaceful life with you and Dawn Mist. No one else matters." He reached over to tuck a blanket up to their drowsy daughter's chin.

The mountains altered to dark hulks as early stars presented themselves, faint at first, but nothing in the world could stop their coming like schools of still white fish in the darkening river of the night sky.

CHAPTER TWENTY-TWO

The North Fork, 1902

Each year they bought one or two head of cattle. They kept their herd in the hills part of the year, then brought it down for fattening on Evening Star Ranch, as Jim had persuaded Nora to name their place. They enlarged the cabin to include two real bedrooms. Nora canned venison, berries, made rhubarb wine, and packed butter in crocks for trading. Dawn gathered eggs from the hen house.

One winter night, Nora sat by the stove, studying Jim as he read a book borrowed from Nan Hogan, his hair falling loose on his shoulders. Nora often found herself stirred by his muscular grace, his strong, slender hands. That she warranted this elegant man's love still surprised and gratified her at times. Their nights of passion differed from any she'd known. Jim, a creative lover, brought her to sensual heights. The sense of the forbidden, his dark hands on her white skin, knowing no pregnancy would result, the surprises in joining their two cultures, all of it flowed together in a torrent. Her body matched his in desperate eagerness.

Of course, the Hogans and others cast disapproving looks when Nora and Jim openly became more than business partners.

"Did they think we were stony saints?" she'd asked Jim. She mused on how they could never have become what they were anywhere else. On the North Fork, they created new lives, new selves.

She set aside her mending and rose to stand beside him. "Is that poetry you're reading?"

"Yes. Keats. About a young man and woman who run away together on St. Agnes Eve. That's tonight."

"Sort of like what we did." She reached out to touch his cheek.

"Yes, each loves the other beyond all else."

Nora knelt before him, her hand on his knee.

Jim laid the book aside and covered her hand with his. "Are you happy?"

"I am. You brought me back to life. You redeemed me. We have Dawn Mist."

"Will you still marry me?" They'd spoken

of marrying every year, but wondered whether an official would perform the ceremony.

"Yes. I've wanted it since the avalanche, but I didn't know how we'd do it. I've heard from Nan there's a priest in Midvale near the Blackfeet reservation. He must be used to marrying whites to Indians. Do you think he'd marry an Irish-born to a Chinese?"

"When the snow melts. We will become beyond reproach, even in the eyes of your church."

"And Nan Hogan. Well, perhaps not Nan."

In June Nora and Jim asked Beartracks to caretake their place for a week. Nan agreed to take Dawn Mist, who'd come to think of the Hogans as an aunt and uncle.

Beartracks commented that he didn't see why anyone had to go to all the bother. What did a few words from a priest make?

"The difference between heaven and hell," Nora answered.

"Ah, the afterlife," Beartracks said with a condescending smile.

In fact, Nora was thinking of her earthly past.

The night before they left, Nora couldn't sleep. She burrowed into their quilts in the crisp night and reflected. When she left Ireland, there could be no turning back. When she left Boston, it was also for good. But none of the previous moves had the finality of the day they forded the North Fork of the Flathead, the river with no bridge. Once on the west side, she and Jim created a new way of life combining East and West. Had anyone told her she'd marry Jim Li, raise a mountain man's daughter as their own, and live in the wilderness, she'd have called the speaker witless. There would always be those who'd turn their backs to the pair of them. Still, together and properly wed they needn't care about anything else. Hadn't they built a shelter sturdy enough for all weathers?

They stayed at Beartracks's cabin in Apgar, boarding the train next day, traveling east over the granite faces of the Rockies at Marias Pass to the village of Midvale. Nora spotted a small clapboard Catholic church beyond the tracks.

As they crossed to it, carrying their satchels, a white-haired priest emerged, raising a hand in friendly greeting.

Jim took the lead in broaching the subject.

After he understood their circumstances, the old Father smiled. "You know, I've married many whites and Indians here. I'm a bit of a rogue and a rebel on that point," he said. "Most of the unions hold firm and no harm done. Certainly not the harm of living in sin. I wasn't expecting to perform a ceremony today. I'm due to leave for a funeral in Browning this evening, then on to Great Falls, but we'll take time. I'll send the proof of marriage to the courthouse there. Wait here while I find a witness."

Benches substituted for pews inside the clean, one-room church, and windows looked out on sweeping flower-carpeted prairie. Nora tucked her arm through Jim's as they stood in sudden stillness after being outside in wind that filled their ears. The seriousness of finally marrying, the permanence of it, impressed them.

The priest, Father John as he informed them, entered with a young woman who smiled shyly and handed Nora a bouquet of Black-Eyed Susans. After the brief ceremony, Nora Flanagan Larkin Li and her husband signed the Bible in the little Midvale church.

Nora explained to the priest that she'd become a United States citizen while living in Butte after Tade's death. He expressed no concern over Jim's lack of citizenship. He said that no Montana judge he knew would bother to question Nora's right to remain a citizen even if married to a foreigner or simply living with one.

Content, Nora accompanied her tall husband, whom she'd known as her spiritual spouse for years, into the bright wind-cleansed day.

"Like the first day of the world," she murmured into the wind that carried her words to all the unknown places beyond.

By the time she reached age forty, Nora expected nothing more than life with Jim, together raising merry Dawn Mist who often revealed her mother's dimples and Beartracks's sense of fun. Nora and Jim husbanded their land, no longer improving it for themselves alone.

But on a late summer day two years after they married, a stranger walked over the rise of the river bank and strode toward her, clicking a willow branch along their cross-fence. She'd started skinning a coyote Jim had shot to stop its threatening the cattle. Not a job Nora enjoyed and she felt annoyance at this interruption that would make odious work last even longer. Since she didn't recognize the skinny youth who approached, she picked up her Winchester 30-30, cradling it in one arm as she stepped out from the barn's shadow to let him see her. He must have used their raft to cross, she thought.

Nora waited, a hard, planed-down version of the soft rounded girl who'd boarded the train in Boston. Fine lines branched from the corners of her eyes, and a light copper bronzed her skin. Frontier woman now, she handled the rifle with confidence wrought by experience.

The boy, hair tawny with a hint of red, strode toward her, but slowed when he saw the gun. The two scrutinized each other like wary animals. She figured him as just an adolescent, some runaway boy about fifteen or sixteen, dusty clothes frayed and a little outgrown. A burlap sack hung over one shoulder. He stared at her from brown eyes, then flashed a smile that showed perfect white teeth.

"Stop there, boyo," Nora ordered. "What business have you here?"

"I'm searching for Nora Larkin and I've had the devil's own time finding her," the boy answered.

Nora nearly dropped the gun, grown so heavy on her arm. "Who are you?" She gulped the last word down as her throat constricted.

"Nora Larkin's son Michael. Would you

be the woman I'm looking for?"

"I am." The mountains danced behind the boy. The meadow blazed up in shimmering amber flames.

"Before she died, my mother . . . or I believed her to be until she lay dying . . . Bridget that took me in and raised me . . . told me about how you are the mother I was born to and how my father died, and you couldn't look after me so you gave me over to be raised by her and Michael, my dad." He shifted his weight from one foot to the other, letting the willow branch slip from his fingers. "They both died of the fever. All the money from the house went for debts, too."

He raked a hand through his hair. "Before she passed away, she told me to find you in Helena. I found out more about you there from that fat banker, Sean Kehoe. I just met and spoke to him by chance in a saloon where I was sweeping up and all. Imagine. He told me where you'd gone. Said you'd done some business." He stopped fidgeting and gave her a direct, almost challenging stare. "So I've found you."

Nora listened in disbelief. Her friend Bridget dead? And this boy? Could this be her son really come to her as she'd dreamed so often? Nora gasped and took a step forward. "You're him?" She lay the gun on the ground just before her knees buckled. She knelt beside it, looking helplessly up at the boy with the sun at his back and the contagious smile replaced by panicked concern.

"Don't faint," he pleaded. "Oh Jesus, I swear you're white as a ghost. Lower your head. Please, Mrs. — Mrs. Larkin — Mrs. Nora."

"Water. From the bucket."

The boy searched frantically from one side of the long porch to the other before he spotted a water bucket. By the time he raced back, water sloshing over his dust-caked boots, Nora had struggled to her feet and staggered to the bench.

"Thank you," she said, taking the dipper with a trembling hand. She gave it back to him to replace, still not trusting her knees. She stayed put, taking him in with mixed wonder and fathomless need.

Michael walked to the far side of the porch to replace the dipper, paused a moment, then swung back toward her. His wool jacket and his pants might be travel smudged, and his boot leather crazed with dust-filled cracks, but she recognized Bat Moriarty's self-assured walk. With her recovery his smile returned, and she saw

Bat's fateful good looks in it.

"Well," she said in a husky voice, "from all I can see Bridget and Michael did a fine job of raising you. I believe I did the right thing when I sent you to them in Butte, America."

"Butte, Montana. Nobody says that other any more. It's 1904, after all."

"Pardon me."

"Sure. You've been way up here for awhile, I guess. Once I found out, I had to find you. How many fellows have their dying mothers tell them a story like that?"

"Not too many, I suppose. What, exactly, did Bridget tell you about me and yourself?" Nora took her eyes off him for the first time and lowered them to her hands.

"She told me everything. How my dad died in one of the big cave-ins at the Never-sweat. There was one every year for awhile. Just about everybody he worked with back then is moved on or dead. Mother told me his name. Tade Larkin. She told me how you moved to Helena to keep a boarding house after he died. Why didn't you just have me and stay in Butte with your friends? Or else, why didn't you go ahead and get the boarding house in Helena and keep me?"

"Well." Nora reached back to untie her

bloodied apron. The slow movement belied the speed of her thoughts. She folded the cloth and tucked it under the bench. "Well, now, it's a long story. Give me a minute to let me think how best to tell it."

Nora gazed desperately at the mountains, trying to clear her stunned mind. Bridget had only told the boy half the truth. She'd been friend enough to protect Nora, or perhaps she'd just been mother enough to protect Michael from knowing the sorry fact that his father was a skirt-chasing, shiftless, gambling man.

Nora inhaled. "I made a bad investment of my savings and lost all my money from selling my house — that very house in Butte you grew up in. Mrs. Leary, who was to be my partner, lost her money to the same crooked bankers. She went off to live with her son in Great Falls. I was in terrible sad shape, grieving after your father and then your sister."

"I had a sister?" Michael's eyebrows shot up.

"You had an angel of a sister. Like you, only she had angel's blue eyes. We named her Helen for that queen all the armies fought to keep. Only I couldn't keep Helen. She went to be with Tade when she was a wee girl."

"How did she die?'

"Diphtheria. A fierce disease. Just when I thought I'd brought her through it, she went like that." Nora lifted a hand and dropped it. "We were living with Mrs. Leary. She had a half-Chinese servant there named Jim Li, and Jim was — like you — looking for his folks — his father anyway. She paused. She was getting off the subject that would be pressing to Michael.

He frowned. "Why are you telling me about some chink?"

Nora's head jerked and she glared at her son. His words shook her out of the mix of dream and desperate imagining she'd been in since he appeared, the sun behind lighting him like he was an archangel come to stay. She stopped spinning a new fabric for her life's story and narrowed her eyes at this boy from Butte. The mountains and amber meadow stopped dancing. She took a full breath.

"Jim Li is the person who risked his life to deliver you to Bridget and Michael when I was so very ill with no money. I didn't expect to live, so I sent you to them. Jim saved my life and became much more than just a good, honest friend to me. He's like all of us, boy. He's more than just the look of him. I found that out."

"A Chinaman? What do you mean he risked his life?"

"He's half Chinese and traveled with a white baby. What do you think I mean?"

"But what's this Chinaman got to do with anything now?"

Nora sat again. "He had a stake of his own and wanted us to be business partners since it would be easier for me to do the buying and settling of the land, me being a woman, but white at least, and him with a Chinese look. They were treated badly enough in those days." She paused and frowned. "I guess it isn't so much better now. Well, I was penniless and weak from sickness and about given up to despair no matter it's a sin, and he asked me to come up here to help get some land we could survive on, and I said yes."

"But why didn't you take me?" The inevitable question. The hardest to answer.

"I expected to die," Nora answered, looking at the mountains. At least that part was true. "I'd grown sick in body and soul. I wanted you to have a good life with a father and mother both. Even if I lived for awhile, I expected to disappear up here. I just felt you had a better chance with Bridget and her husband. You'd go to school. Weren't they good to you?"

Michael shrugged. "Mother was fun and pretty and kind to everyone. My father, well, strict and quick with the back of his hand if I sassed him." He frowned. "You never even tried to find out about me. After you got well, I mean."

"Your mother and father, for that's what they were after taking you in, had the right to raise you without interference. I promised that in writing."

"Well, you and this Chinaman? What about you?"

Nora gave him a level look. "You might as well start calling him Jim Li for that's the man's name." Then her expression softened. "Oh, we worked together until we fell in love. You'll understand why I did when you meet him. We went to Midvale and stood before a priest. We've been married and happy to be so."

Michael walked out in front of her. He studied the clouds gathering over the mountains, then turned toward the cabin, now a rambling story-and-a-half structure. He walked to the end of the porch to study the outbuildings and the summer kitchen down by the creek. For the moment he seemed finished with questions.

"Would you like to see our place? We've poured ourselves into it. It's a hard life, but we've kept body and soul together here better than most. Our few head are running up on the high pastures just now. We call this Evening Star Ranch. Jim fancied the name." Nora's voice showed her pride.

"I do, too," Michael said. "Do you have a brand?"

"We do."

"You should have an arch with the brand sign on it." When Nora laughed, he scowled.

She wished she'd been more tactful. "Well, now, perhaps you're right. But you see, so far we don't own the land outright. I'll file for homestead papers as soon as the government makes that possible. We've already made all the improvements they could want and more. When the time comes, would you help us put up that grand arch for the entrance?" It was as close as she dared come to asking him to stay.

Michael looked young and uncertain thinking over her question. Nora saw none of Bat in him then, more her own expression when she readied herself to make some vital decision. "Maybe I won't be able to stay that long. I'm just passing through. I'm on my own now, going to see the country for myself."

Nora hadn't touched Michael, but now she stood and lifted a tentative hand toward him, withdrawing it after a light brush against his rough wool sleeve. "I've thought of my son that I gave up every day for nearly sixteen years, Michael. I've wondered what you looked like, about your schooling, your friends, even what you like to eat. I wondered, but I never expected to have you standing here before me. Never expected such a miracle at all, but now that you've come, I ask you to stay awhile at least. Stay on. Let us get to know each other. You may not like all you come to know." Nora paused. "It's not an easy life, but give yourself time to make up your own mind whether to go or live here. Give yourself a chance to know Jim. He's a fine man."

Michael's shoulders moved back as he straightened. He held out a hand. "Well, let's shake on it then. I'll stay awhile. Thanks for asking. It wasn't such an easy job getting here, you know."

Nora held out her calloused hand and felt it enveloped in the long, slim fingers of Bat Moriarty's son. But the smile that met her own had a warmth about it that Bat's never had.

"Let me show you about," Nora said to her boy. "Jim is off hunting. He'll be back soon. Won't he be surprised to meet you?

There's someone else will be with him. You must meet Dawn as well."

Chapter Twenty-Three

The leather strap hanging around Dawn's neck and shoulders secured a round basket heavy with purple huckleberries, leaving her hands free to find the best berries to nibble. It had been a good day. Jim hunted while she picked through a patch thick with ripe fruit. After he rejoined her, a small buck draped over his shoulder, they rowed across the river in their second boat, noting the first on the far side. Dawn ran up the bank. Mama would be so admiring of such a harvest.

Dawn wore leggings and moccasins below a loose, blue and white gingham dress. Her hair hung in braids looped behind her waist. Small and delicate, she appeared younger than she was, but people remembered her face. A brow with a widow's peak, eyebrows like little birds' wings, lustrous brown eyes tilted above high cheekbones, a small straight nose, a sensuous mouth, and dimples when she smiled. Jim and Nora had been given only Dawn Mist, but they knew and cherished the value of such a gift when they'd expected to be childless.

She flew up the worn path. At the sight of the twist of nearly transparent smoke from the chimney, her smile widened. Mama must be baking a day early.

Dawn undid the strap as she reached the porch, pushing the door open with her back, calling, "Mama! Guess what we found today." She swung round, and nearly dropped the basket. A boy stood by the table, a boy who looked perfect as a high waterfall or flying eagle or running mountain lion could look perfect. Dawn stood like a stupified doe, the boy equally transfixed.

Nora stepped from the dimness behind him. "It's you who'll never guess what I found today. Or who found me. This is Michael, my boy that friends took to raise as their own when I fell on hard times in Helena. Michael, this is our adopted daughter, Dawn Mist. Dawn's mother was a lovely Blackfeet girl. Her da who asked us to raise her for him is Beartracks Benton, a trapper originally from England, but we like him anyway."

Michael was the first to act. He moved

toward Dawn. "Can I help you with your basket?" She shoved it at him and he stepped back, holding it awkwardly.

"Is Jim on his way?" Nora asked. Speechless, Dawn shot her an imploring look. Nora added, "I'll just meet him. You two fetch us some buttermilk. You might as well get used to each other. Michael's going to stay on."

Dawn cast her a glance of pure dread as Nora left, hurrying toward the distant figure of her husband.

Not only was the exquisite child-woman poised before him half-Blackfeet, she lived here. Her skin was brown, her hair black, and he saw moccasins peeping out from the outlandish gingham shift. Most of the girls he knew in Butte, like the boisterous Murphy brood, were solid, fair-skinned colleens who giggled before Mass behind square, blunt-fingered hands. They rolled their blue eyes before stepping into confession to confess what? Impure thoughts about the cocky young miners who winked at them and asked for dances at festivities in Hibernia Hall?

This girl presented something new. Wild without earthiness, feminine without flirtation, and strong without bulk. When she finally raised her leaf-shaped eyes, she tilted her head and studied him. Michael, who'd broken all the adolescent female hearts in Butte, found himself acutely aware of his frayed sleeves and cracked boots.

"Well," he said giving the basket a little push onto the table, "did she say something about buttermilk?"

Dawn beckoned him and turned to the open door. Michael stood beside her in an instant, noting that her head with its straight part running from the widow's peak to the nape of a slender neck, only came up to his chest. Still, she moved so quickly toward the creek that he had to take long strides to keep up.

They reached its bank, covered with wild roses and other flowers whose herbal fragrance billowed up in the wake of Dawn Mist's fluttered rush. Michael weaved on his feet.

"Wait, Dawn," his voice tremulous. "Do you mind if we just sit a minute? I've been walking for days. I haven't eaten since yesterday noon." He sank down to a moss-cushioned log and raked parted fingers through his hair. Dawn pulled the buttermilk crock from the water and turned to him. A blinding dazzle of sunlight danced on the water's surface behind her. She always seemed to be stepping out of light.

"Here." She climbed the bank, causing a sweet commotion among the roses. A pine squirrel scolded from somewhere in shadows across the water. Dawn unwrapped the crock and removed its cover.

Michael drank the cloying buttermilk in gulps. When he'd finished, he drew his sleeve across wet eyes. "It's bright out here."

The perfect oval face turned toward him and broke into a gentle smile. "You'll be all right with us. Mama says we live in paradise itself." She spoke on in a calm, unhurried voice, describing their lives.

"What about school?"

"Ho, there's been some talk of one. Up to now, Papa and Mama have taught me to read and figure. I know a lot about China and Ireland."

Nora called both their names as though she'd been doing it all their lives, and Dawn slowed to Michael's pace as they sauntered back. He paused to appreciate the sunset spilling its colors over the mountains. He remembered, though, he had another stranger to meet.

"We've increased our household," Nora called when Jim came close enough to make out her words. "It's Michael, my son. He's here. Just came walking up the road like you, as fine as you please."

"How did he come all the way from Butte?"

"By feet and raft, I guess. Poor Bridget and Michael died. But Bridget told him about me while she could, only she gilded the lily. He thinks Tade was his father, believes he died in a cave-in a year or so after the real explosion that took him. I don't want to set him straight just now, maybe never. Anyway, please watch your words around him."

Jim's smile turned uncertain at her last words. "I believe the truth to be best." But seeing her jaw set, he bowed to Nora, something he saved for special occasions. "Michael, Taipai, is here. What good fortune."

"Well, yes, of course. He's a fine lad. He's going to be with us for awhile. Forever, if I can keep him. We might as well learn to act like family. After all, we are, aren't we? Come on. It's long overdue, this meeting, wouldn't you agree?" She pulled him into the cabin.

Michael sat at the table, corralling emotions that ranged from relief at finding Nora, niggling anger against her that he tried to ignore, and his aching awareness of Dawn

Mist. He saw the long black hair swept across Jim Li's buckskin-clad shoulders as Nora and the man approached. Michael squared his own. His father scorned the Chinese. Michael, Sr. insisted Celestials would take Irish jobs if given half a chance. Michael grew up believing all Chinamen smoked opium, gambled, and fought in gangs for territorial rights in Chinatown.

Bridget used to talk of how hardworking Chinese were, but Michael's father only snorted in disdain and bragged about manhandling them. Michael and others snowballed or stoned unfortunate Chinese found walking alone yoked with balanced bundles of laundry. One finally drew a pistol from his black sleeve and fired in the air, scattering howling Irish urchins into the Finnish neighborhood where the rock throwing became their usual deadly battle between those two ethnic groups, yet another hatred nurtured over family dinner tables.

Disoriented, Michael had landed himself in this unimaginable situation. Was the strain of finding Nora over? Just beginning? Both? His own mother happy with a Chinese . . . *married* to a Chinese!

Nora and Jim entered. Jim, bigger than he'd looked from a distance, lowered wood beside the stove and extended a hand, confident pressure in its grip.

"We met fifteen years ago." Jim's eyes crinkled in a warm smile that made it difficult to be wary or remember his father's contemptuous labels. Michael half-returned the smile. The man's serene voice sounded somehow familiar. "You are Taipai, Evening Star. I gave you that name on our journey from Helena to Butte, America."

"Nobody calls it that anymore," Michael stiffened, fighting the urge to rub circulation back into his hand.

Not offended, Jim laughed. "I told you the story of my life that night. You were the first person in America to hear it all."

"I don't remember." Michael looked hard into the man's eyes.

"It's a much longer story now. With a much happier ending thanks to this woman you have found. I welcome you to our home."

There was hardly a trace of accent in the big man's speech and he moved with a pride and freedom Michael hadn't seen in Butte's Chinese. Still, his mother married this man. Was it right?

They finished the meal of venison stew and huckleberry pie just as footsteps sounded, followed by exaggerated pounding on the door.

"It's Beartracks." Nora grinned at Jim. "I'll let the man in."

Before Nora reached the door it burst open, and a giant in buckskin leggings, a blue shirt, and a broad-brimmed hat ducked as he entered, tossing a pack of furs into the corner.

"Aren't you a sight for sore eyes?" he roared, hugging Nora.

Michael stood and the stranger inspected him up and down.

"Beartracks, my own son Michael is here. My son and Tade's."

"How — ?"

"It's a long story, but before you hear it, Dawn will get you something to eat."

Dawn smiled at Beartracks. They gave each other a brief embrace.

"I came here from Butte," Michael said.

Beartracks nodded, but, and this both surprised and disappointed Michael, didn't ask questions. Instead, the man's eyes followed Dawn as she brought him a dish of stew and bread.

After last cups of coffee, they moved to the porch, sharing each other's news as stars bloomed into the blue-black field of the night sky.

Beartracks caught them up on the Hogans. Later, they played whist. Michael

385

watched Beartracks in amazement. One of the weathered old mountain men on the outside, he seemed civilized. Michael heard a trace of English accent, too. Nora's red hair and Michael's own almost put them in the small numbers here. The two sundarkened older men seemed different from any Chinese or English he'd seen, but his contacts had been limited in Butte. There Irish, Welsh, Finns, and a few others had their own neighborhoods. The Chinese, except for a few colorful restaurateurs, kept to themselves. As for the Indians — a half-starving few lived in a pathetic camp by the dump — otherwise he hardly ever saw one. Dawn Mist, Beartracks Benton, and Jim Li sat before him in relaxed dignity. He couldn't picture these three degrading themselves before anyone.

So exhausted his closing eyes saw the room double-imaged, he heard with gratitude Nora's suggestion that they think of sleep. He'd thrown his thin bedroll in the barn. When he asked Beartracks if he slept there, too, the man laughed.

"Not under a roof on a night like this. A corner of the meadow suits me. Why don't you sleep by my campfire? Stop being a pilgrim. That's what China Jim and Nora did."

Michael had a growing sense of being in the presence of a legend and, last surprise of the day, for the first time in his sixteen years he'd contracted a case of hero worship. Then too, this man was Dawn's natural father. Michael still struggled to sort out his feelings about Nora and Jim. A little distance might help.

When he emerged with his bedroll, he stopped. His mother and Jim huddled together, speaking in low voices. He heard Jim's words, ". . . walking into shadows. The truth can rise like fireweed after a conflagration. It won't stay under the earth no matter how you might wish it to. It must send up shoots."

Nora's gave an unintelligible answer, but Michael saw her shake her head, then stop as she noticed him.

"Did I interrupt something?" Michael asked.

"No." Nora walked toward him. "Jim and I just share a slight difference of opinion." She hesitated and then gave him a quick embrace. "I'm so glad you've come, son. Welcome. Welcome."

Michael leaned into her, his arms still loaded. "Me, too." No better words came to him.

He saw Beartracks disappearing into the night, striding as though he could see without straining, and half ran to catch up. They camped on soft grass next to the timothy meadow. The creek sounded its drawn-out whispers. The fire crackled, hissed, and sighed, then settled, shifting into a steady, low flame.

Beartracks recounted how he'd arrived from England, a young rake who'd caused nothing but trouble until his wearied family sent him to America.

"How'd you learn the mountain life?"

"Pete Dumont, the Indians including Dawn's mother. Some I learned just stumbling around by myself. That and from the critters."

Michael tossed a stick in the fire. "Can I go with you sometime?"

"Start with Jim Li. China Jim picked up the life here faster than most." He grinned. "You should have seen those two when they first showed up. Nora so sick she could hardly sit in the wagon, but giving orders just the same. She looked pretty even like that."

"She is pretty, isn't she? They said my dad

who died was good-looking, too. Is that wolves?" The long, feral keening harmonized and wound among tree spires, then spiraled into the thronging stars.

"Sound good, don't they? Time for sleep, boy. Big day tomorrow." Beartracks rolled his blanket around himself, turned away, and slept.

Michael awoke once in the night and saw Beartracks adding sticks to the fire, illuminated in the flare of the flames, his eyes half-closed, but seeming to miss nothing of the night that padded and blinked around them.

That fall, Nora took Michael over the entire ranch. He learned how to survive and even thrive on the North Fork, in its natural rhythms, rounding up and branding cattle, cutting and hauling hay, trapping and hunting game. He came to think of Nora as his mother as surely as he had Bridget. As they hiked or rode, she told him about her life in Ireland. Pieces of the puzzle of Michael's life cascaded into place.

Jim hunted alone, his coming and going unpredictable. Sometimes he took off with Nora for a few hours. On one occasion Michael asked Jim if they had trouble from neighbors. Jim stroked the board he'd just hewn. "This is a place where people live as they can. They know us and treat us well by now."

Chapter Twenty-Four

Ignorant of either Michael's existence, or Nora and Jim's whereabouts, Bat Moriarty and Lou left Clancy in 1890, traveling for the next fourteen years by stage and rail, retracing journeys with stays that lasted months or sometimes as long as a year in Billings, Bismarck, Deadwood, and Denver. Best of all, several times they hit San Francisco. That harbor city never lost its gleam as a gambler's utopia. From the wide-open Barbary Coast, to the opium dens and cribs of Chinatown, to the French restaurants with private rooms, the city never failed as a jewel-bedecked haven for vice. They spent more time there than the other western cities and towns, but Bat would never settle down. Restless and hunting, he always returned to his search for Jim Li.

A cool detachment belied Bat's intense determination to win. He joined or organized all-night rounds in saloons and hotels.

In spite of never seeming to sleep, he won often. Lou, frowzy and voluptuous in red satin or velvet, stood at his shoulder when he played. She always carried a large red handbag that matched her dress. Lou stored laudanum in that red purse, enough to keep Bat calm.

"She's my luck," he told those who wondered out loud.

Bat Moriarty intrigued others, a detached, steady man with scarred hands and preternatural skill with cards. When the games finished early, he wandered alone through Chinatowns of cities that included them. His eyes glittered in the glow of streetlights, focusing on any tall Asians, ignoring the birdlike calls of caged prostitutes.

Although Bat's face had escaped the fire unscarred, suffering left his skin drawn and lined. His black hair turned white. His one overt concession to the inferno's ravages was that he wore fingerless gloves of gray kid leather. He became known for them and for the vulgar, deep-voiced woman in red who hovered over his games, leaving only when he signaled her to go.

Lou settled for her nurse-lover role. She purchased and measured out doses. If Bat sometimes disappeared for a night, she neither questioned nor complained. When his black moods exploded into blows, she endured them. His success at cards made it unnecessary to go back to her old profession, and she gained a certain status in western saloons and bawdy houses as Bat Moriarty's good luck charm.

Only one thing troubled Lou. More than the nights when he didn't lie next to her, it bothered her that Bat asked everywhere about the Chinaman Jim Li. Lou remembered Jim, and she knew something else. She knew he'd befriended Nora Larkin. If anyone would know about Li, it would be Nora. She remembered how the pregnant housekeeper went into labor the night of the fire and called for Jim Li, but Lou never told Bat. Who knew where the woman had gone? She'd heard that all but Lillie's favorites had scattered to less accident-prone establishments.

On the evening of April 17, 1906, at the St. Francis Hotel in San Francisco, as Bat and Lou passed the front desk, a dark-haired woman with gold nugget earrings registered. Her unblinking hazel eyes scanned the room like a raptor's hunting for prey.

Once in her rooms, Clementine Dasher luxuriated in a long bath. She'd just returned from London, the affair with Smith-Gordon over for good. Ever the aristocrat, he'd been generous at their parting. Now Clementine prowled for a new life, a new patron.

She dressed in a low-cut black velvet gown with a three-inch black choker and long black gloves. She glanced at her reflection in the mirror and saw a face still arresting. Satisfied, Clementine left her suite and made her way toward charming sounds of violins and tinkling crystal floating from under the grand dining room's chandelier.

She noticed the dashing gambler and the big blonde he escorted. He looked languid and bored. His heavy-lidded eyes met Clementine's, and he inclined his head almost imperceptibly. She smiled. He abandoned the ample-bosomed lady at his table, approached Clementine, and bowed. "Excuse my intrusion, but I should know you. Did we meet in Chicago some years ago?"

"Please sit down — Mr. Moriarty." The name leapt out of hiding. Bat Moriarty. Older. Carefree no more. That much she intimated from the lines around his eyes and in the tightness of his mouth. He reminded her of resentful men she'd known, those capable of rationalizing cruelty. Something had happened to the gambler who used to make her sisters at the bawdyhouse surrender to fits of hilarity . . . or swoon.

"I can't abandon my companion, but would you join us, Miss — ?"

"Clementine Dasher. We met ages ago in Chicago at dear Ma Touchwood's establishment."

"Ah. The lady is frank." Bat pulled out her chair. She noted the fingerless gloves and fingers branched in scars. She hoped he noted the long line of her slender back and fragrant slope of her bare shoulders. However, he remained unmoved to investigate further.

Lou received Clementine with guarded courtesy, but chatted at ease enough when Clementine let her know she shared a past similar to her own, albeit a rung or more up the whores' ladder by the look of her. In a few moments, Lou grew uneasy all over again when Clementine touched the fourth finger of Bat's right hand.

"Bat, you sometimes used to wear a ring, a memorable diamond. Don't tell me you lost that gorgeous thing in a wager."

Bat flexed his hand. "No wager — in a fire. A damned Chinaman named Jim Li stole it off my hand while I lay helpless. I'd give a year of my life to find him."

"But isn't this lucky? I met this man while on a hunting trip through the North Fork of the Flathead River in Montana. He was with an Irish woman . . . a Nora Larkin."

Lou jumped, emitting a startled hiccup.

"Nora Larkin?" Bat swung his head to Lou then back to Clementine like an angry bull. "Nora Larkin?"

"That's right," Clementine said. "Your thief lived with her. He cost my companion, Lord Smith-Gordon, a tidy sum when they played poker."

"By god, little Nora Larkin," Bat muttered. "Lou, what do you know about this?"

Lou chewed the inside of her cheek while fiddling with her napkin. "She worked at Lillie's as the housekeeper. It was Jim Li brought her to Lillie. She went into labor the night of the fire. After that they must have partnered up. I swear I didn't know anything about it."

Bat blinked. "Did Nora and Li take a baby to the North Fork? What was it, anyway?" he tried to sound casual, but Lou wasn't fooled.

In a belated attempt to save her place at least as a tarnished good luck charm, she forced a shaky laugh. "No. I heard from one of the girls who came through Clancy that Nora Larkin sent her baby boy off to live with folks she knew somewhere."

"There was no little boy on the place when we stayed there," Clementine added. "No, wait. Before I left, the Larkin woman rode in with a baby girl, an Indian orphan she'd taken to raise."

Bat closed his eyes for a moment, then opened them and pushed his plate away. "Lou," he ordered, "time to go upstairs."

Lou cast a triumphant glance at Clementine. Bat still meant to keep her with him. One suspected act of disloyalty wouldn't change anything. She rose unsteadily, pulling the tablecloth sideways with her. Clementine slapped her hands on it in a startled attempt to save her wine. Lou sniggered, staggering into a surprised waiter.

Bat gripped Lou's upper arm. She winced, and they proceeded up the stairs, one of Lou's shoulders higher than the other where Bat kept her soft white flesh billowing out between his scarred fingers. At their door he pushed her through, slammed, then locked it. He struck her a blow to the side of the head with his fist, another to her stomach. She fell to her hands and knees, retching.

"Bitch. You held out on me. You knew where they were."

Lou gained enough breath to struggle to

her feet. "No, just that they knew each other. What difference did it make? I didn't know you knew Nora Larkin. Don't I always try to help you, honey? Remember who saved you from the fire?"

Bat stood breathing in harsh intakes like sobs. Reason returned to his eyes. "Yes. You saved me from the fire. You did. Get me a dose, Lou."

Lou limped warily to her handbag and measured out the medicine as though for a child or invalid. She recapped and dropped the bottle back in her purse, poured water onto a cloth, and wiped off the spoon. She sighed at her reflection in the wall mirror. "Your good luck charm can't go downstairs tonight. You gave it a shiner."

Bat's head tipped against the back of his chair and he sighed. "Stay here then. I don't give a damn. I can win without you. I'll audition the tall blackbird — what's her name? Clementine, Clementine, won't you please be mine, Clementine . . ." His voice trailed into drugged sleep and he dozed, sighing at intervals.

Lou studied him. He meant it. This time he'd leave her. She slipped the laudanum supply out of her bag and lifted the window to cool night air, setting the bottles on the fire escape landing.

Two stories below, a man cursed, trying to calm his distraught horse. The animal reared, frantic. The struggling rider looked up and saw her. "Sorry for the language," he called up. "He's usually so calm. Something's got him spooked."

Lou shrugged and closed the window. She held a wet cloth to her swelling eye. After two hours, she shook Bat's shoulder. "Wake up, honey. Time to win."

Bat awoke feeling sluggish, splashed water on his face, and put on a clean shirt and vest. He walked out the door without speaking.

Clementine had moved to a table in the saloon until he beckoned her. During the game she stood like a raven at his shoulder, but he lost. He threw down the cards in disgust at 4:45 a.m.

As they walked to their rooms, Bat asked about the North Fork. Where exactly was the Li family? Clementine described the route of her journey with Smith-Gordon and Pete Dumont. "I'd like to see that Celestial humbled. He humiliated Smith-Gordon at the game, and it was a lot of work for me to make that fool aristocrat feel proud again." She fingered Bat's lapel and raised her eyes. "Why are you with that awful woman? You could think about moving up." Then she sighed.

"Good night, Clementine. Good to see you. You've been useful." Bat Moriarty wasn't thinking about moving up. Something else consumed him.

Bat walked toward his room, relieved to be rid of Clementine. His instinct for luck still untouched by laudanum addiction, he'd felt a prickle on the back of his neck when Clementine stood behind him like a perfectly formed, malevolent shadow. He'd known such women before, and they weren't always prostitutes. Deirdre had a bit of it in her, women who appeared all soft and desirable and then drained you until they left a void only bad luck could fill. And usually, a woman like Clementine passed bad luck coming in as she slipped out, her skirts brushing against the grotesque shape of it as she made her escape.

As he progressed down the dim, quiet hallway, thin anger invaded Bat and fattened with each footfall on the red carpet. His tired saunter became a furious stride. By God, Lou hadn't seen the end of this. It was her fault he'd lost.

A great tearing jolted the bottom of the Pacific Ocean. The San Andreas Fault had awakened. One of its walls slipped one way, another thrust the opposite, and that parting opened the ocean floor with a tremor that shot toward land like a bullet. The tremor, about to devastate a great city, raced toward it, tearing open the earth's surface as if it were thin cloth.

Bat turned his key in the door to the room where Lou had fallen into fitful sleep. He yanked her out of bed, wrenching her arm as the tremor wrenched, twisted, and snapped everything in its advance. Lou cried out as Bat backhanded her. She fell against the heavy armoire, cracking her head hard against its corner before slumping to the floor, her eyes, one bruised, gazing expressionless into Bat's.

He nudged her with his boot. Her glassy stare might have belonged to a china-headed, cloth-bodied doll. He dropped to his knees and shook her. "Lou? Lou, wake up. I need a dose. Lou!" He slapped her, and the doll's head swung to the side, still painted into a vacant gaze.

Bat growled, more afraid this time than angry. Then he heard a rumble from something vast and deeper than his own chest. A demonic force flung him away from Lou's body. He rolled against the bed just as the heavy armoire crashed over her. Its opened doors spilled red satin and velvet around her body. The water pitcher tottered, then shattered on the floor. The bed danced across the room while the mirror and pictures jigged off their fastenings to drop beside overturned lamps and chairs.

Bat alternately pressed against the floor, rolled against walls, or tossed up to land with a grunting thud. The roar stopped — the cacophony of walls, roofs, cornices, and glass breaking and jangling, crumpling and juddering stuffed his ears. All movement ceased. Bat sprawled amid the wreckage, testing his limbs for obedience. He turned to Lou.

"I need it, Lou." He sat up and reached for her handbag. The laudanum wasn't there. He screamed in fear and rage just as the second shock hit. Sounds of wrenching, smashing, spattering, and thumping drowned out his voice. The delicate tinkling as laudanum bottles danced to the edge, then off the wrought iron landing was too slight for him to hear.

Silence. Bat stared at Lou and swore. How had he been so stupid? It was Li's fault. Li had started the whole chain that brought them to this. He'd gone over it a million times. If the Chinaman had only pulled him away from the fire — the pain of the burns.

Now Lou lay dead.

Bat forced the trauma-warped window open. Dust rose outside to nearly two stories. At first there was nothing. He might be alone, a sole survivor. Then he heard sounds of human misery, groans and cries of pain and fear.

He stepped around the fallen armoire. The door to the hallway opened partway on sprung hinges. Among white-faced guests, a maid, cap askew, hurried toward him. "It's an earthquake, sir. Manager says all the guests must come downstairs. There's danger of another shock, and it's safer under arches. The place might collapse around our ears."

"I'll just grab a few things."

Bat stepped back into the room. Only the distracted maid had seen him. Trembling, he righted a fallen chair, and sat, forcing his thoughts to order. In minutes, he slipped out. Let them find Lou alone, killed by a fallen armoire.

Pale, bloodied, disheveled survivors, many still in nightclothes, crowded the lobby. Bat heard one ask a waiter where a doctor could be found. "There's a temporary infirmary in the saloon," the man answered in a foreign accent. "One of the hotel guests, a doctor, has set up there."

Clementine lay in the infirmary, her arm in a sling. The overwhelmed physician, a bloodstained bandage covering his own ear, didn't notice Bat's starved look as Clementine took a small dose of laudanum.

"She'll need more of that, won't she?" Bat asked.

"It would ease the pain later, but I can't give her any more. There's but one bottle left in my bag and others need it."

"Of course, I'll sit with Miss Dasher."

When the doctor turned to answer another patient's question, Bat slipped his hand in the bag. His fingers closed around a bottle. Clementine whimpered in uneasy sleep as Bat strode out, pocketing the laudanum.

He walked through the full lobby into the street, tipped back the bottle, and drank. Dazed hordes milled around him, caked by dust, some with torn and stained clothes, some carrying bundles, pets, living and dead children.

"I finally made it to hell," Bat muttered. Another shock threw him off balance. A store crumpled nearby. Falling beams and mortar mixed with breaking glass. Bat swallowed more laudanum.

"Fire!" He heard the cry and grimaced. It was true. He was in hell. He'd been there before and remembered. Heat and flames licking, crackling, popping, orange arms thrust skyward. And the pain. There would be cataclysmic fires after this. Still, the Fire Department would handle it.

He staggered a little. The aftershocks terrified those shuffling past. Bat decided to blend in with them, like parading with ghosts. Bat overheard that the firefighters' hoses were rendered nearly useless. Damaged pipes — empty cisterns — little for the firemen to do but make firebreaks. He also heard talk of looters, rings, and other jewelry stripped from corpses, stores and saloons plundered.

He looked for a hospital. A hospital would have drugs, and he would need laudanum again soon. Amid downed wires and the bodies of humans and horses, living people, dogs, and cats rushed past him, postures contorted in horror.

He found a hospital where the injured were being bandaged, but medicine seemed in short supply. Bat walked outside. Smoke burned his lungs and eyes. Fire raced toward him only this time he didn't lie helpless. This time he could move. That is, nothing physical prevented him, but he seemed stuck as Lot's wife, only turned to dread in human form instead of a figure of salt.

His anguished eyes found the street sign:

Larkin. "Ah. Nora. Nora Larkin. Had my son, have my diamond. I'm going to follow Nora. Nora Larkin, I'll follow you. Find my prey . . . make him sorry . . . make you weep." He slouched up Larkin Street toward Nob Hill, following the signs reading Larkin until guided away from the fire.

Near Nob Hill, Bat turned to look back at the city. Smoke rose nearly two miles into the air and he heard a new sound added to the din from below, a kind of thumping. "It's dynamite," a voice behind him announced. "The crazy sons-of-bitches are blowing up intact homes to make firebreaks."

Bat hesitated, then turned toward the group who'd gathered to watch the destruction of their city. "I need laudanum," he said. "Is Chinatown still standing?"

"Yes," a jaded-looking man answered. "A man can get anything in Chinatown. That won't change."

Bat headed east at a staggering trot. Some buildings lay in rubble, but others stood. Almost involuntarily he noted the men, measuring their height. Silly when he'd just learned his man dwelt in Montana's wilderness. Bat reached an herb shop as the proprietor was locking the door. He convinced the merchant to transact quick business. The owner analyzed Bat's ravaged face and sold him two bottles at an inflated price.

Bat stepped outside. Dynamite had brought about more conflagrations. Terrified people raced ahead of flames whose searing heat blasted his skin. Cursing, Bat ran. Just another one of the panicked crowd, he stopped, panting for air, leaning his hands against his knees, head down.

"You there. Yes, you. Follow me." A tall, heavy-featured young trooper in an Army uniform held a bayonet-mounted rifle on Bat.

"Where are we going?"

"Move." A rough prod in the back accompanied the order.

At the touch of the bayonet, Bat's calf muscle twitched against the Bowie knife sheathed in his boot.

"Stop here."

They'd come to a pile of bodies. Bodies of every size: burned, crushed, bloodied, reeking of death, waited to be loaded onto wagons pulled by exhausted draft horses. Bat retched and glowered at the trooper.

By the time the last corpses lay stacked on wagons pulled off by half-dead horses, the smoke-filled square sat all but deserted. Only troopers shouted and prodded at remaining conscripted civilians. The soldier who'd forced Bat to load the dead separated from the others for a moment.

"My God," he said. "Look at that."

He pointed his gun at a small dog dragging a singed rat bigger than its nemesis, the dog's teeth sunk into its throat. His young captor's attention diverted, in one swift, practiced movement Bat pulled the Bowie up and threw it. The blade lodged in the trooper's back. Bat retrieved the knife and wiped it off on the dead soldier's uniform.

Bat picked up the gun next. He moved to an alley from which he saw that by some miracle the St. Francis Hotel still stood. Bat stared at it. Lou. Had they found her? Was Lou's body in some charred pile? Sinking to the ground, he rolled to his side, slipped out his bottle of laudanum, and swallowed. He drifted into black, dreamless oblivion.

Disgusted shouts of dismay woke him. Bat hung back long enough to watch the St. Francis Hotel burn at last. Then he ran. At the Ferry Building, he found boats making profitable trips across the Bay to Oakland where refugee camps sheltered the dispossessed. Bat Moriarty, stinking of sweat and ashes, decided to be among them.

found Nora, Michael gained respect for Jim in many ways. The man from China could outwork any Michael ever saw. Jim could also be patient. He taught Michael ranch work, how to construct outbuildings, break horses, hunt, check sets on the trapline, hay, break ground, deliver calves, and brand cattle. He taught with precise care as though preparing his student for a great responsibility.

Michael took off to check traplines or hunt when he reached the point where the curve of Dawn's breast or a glimpse of bare leg drove him to wakeful nights and irritable days. This last season of waiting promised to be hardest. To do things right, to marry Dawn, he had to ask Dawn and then Nora, Jim, and probably Beartracks Benton. They would give their blessing. However, they would want them to wait at least a year, then have a real wedding with a priest to keep Nora happy. Dawn's Catholicism mixed with Blackfeet spirituality. Jim remained a believer in gods, spirits, and immortals. Michael knew it cost Jim Li a piece of his heart whenever he crossed the North Fork. The older man had a true fear of water spirits.

But with Dawn, Michael always found new delights. As well as he knew Dawn, moods came on her that mystified him. He would never finish exploring the country here or his Dawn Mist, never know everything about either. And that gave him pleasure.

And she loved him. His friend. His girl. He slipped her silky hair through his fingers. She turned to the mundane work of milking, her cheek against the cow's flank. She shot a stream of milk to the one-eyed cat, barely missing the boy who wanted her so much.

For now Michael tossed and turned at night, damning the slow swing of the winter sun and slow arrival of long rains to melt winter's snow. Those same rains swelled the runoff that turned the river into a raging milk-and-coffee torrent.

A week later, Michael had just finished chores when he heard Nora. "Michael, we're going to Belton."

He waited in the kitchen while Nora spooned sourdough batter for pancakes. Dawn sat near him, poring over her lesson. Jim had gone to check traps. "Why Belton today?" Michael finally asked.

Nora turned from the stove. "Our butter is plentiful, and we can trade. Besides, we've been hearing more about them opening the strong while unheeding colors rippled in the limitless sky.

When June 15 finally arrived, Michael and Nora weren't the only North Fork residents to board the train at Belton for Columbia Falls, there to change to the "Gallopin' Goose" for the short run to Kalispell. The Hogans and others already seated greeted them. Michael sensed tension. Still, it turned into a kind of party descending from the mountains into the broad Flathead Valley.

At the Grand Central Hotel, Nora started to register two rooms for her and Michael. "Not that we'll spend much time in them," she muttered. "We'll have to be first in line. We'll have to be up at 4:30 — make that 4:00 a.m., Michael."

"Look, Mother, why even get me a room? Why don't I just go to the courthouse around midnight? You can join me as early as you want after you catch a few hours' rest."

She paused, then nodded. "That's a grand idea."

Michael's heart bounded. He could finagle one hour of freedom to taste a few of Kalispell's forbidden treats, at least a cold beer in a saloon. He waited for Nora in the dining room and stood politely when she appeared a few moments later, dressed in a short blue jacket with a matching blouse and skirt.

A second man pausing in the doorway of the hotel saloon caught his breath when Nora smiled at her son waiting in the high-ceilinged dining room. "Nora Larkin," the man whispered. "Still lovely. How can that be?" He stepped out of the dim archway, pulling his hat at an angle, but sliding a glance after the woman being seated at a table set with crystal and fine china. Then Bat Moriarty noticed the striking young man flashing a white-toothed grin. Bat recognized the charm that comes from wearing physical beauty like a coat the wearer believes it would mean nothing to discard. He'd learned the falsity of that belief.

Bat took in the breadth of the boy's shoulders, the long, slim fingers picking up a glass. "He might have come back to her from Butte," he murmured. "Could just be." A smile skimmed over the gambler's gaunt face, unguarded for a fleeting moment.

He came to himself again when a group of raucous homesteaders herded through the lobby. He heard one call, "Nora. Michael. We thought you might be here."

"Is your mother keeping you on a short leash, boy?" A bearded man boomed.

Bat swung away into the summer evening, his gloved hand smoothing the brim of his bowler. Horses, buggies, and the occasional horseless carriage passed on Main Street, but the gambler didn't notice.

Nora Larkin had walked within feet of him, and now dined with their son born of one night together. Strange, he never gave much thought to the brats left behind when he deserted Deirdre in Michigan. But since learning Nora had given birth to his child, Bat had often speculated about him, how he looked, how he might turn out, maybe only because he'd never laid eyes on him. Well, now he had. It didn't change his mind about the score he'd come to settle. He reached into his breast pocket and pulled out the flask Patsy had filled with laudanum. She'd proved a loyal girl, but he'd be damned if anyone would control his doses as Lou had done.

Bat turned toward the saloon where Patsy worked. Her face brightened when he pushed open the swinging doors and crooked his finger, motioning her to join him. Of course, she would.

They always did.

He spoke to her, then left again to watch and wait.

Chapter Twenty-Six

Michael rushed downstairs to the lobby and out the hotel door, looking eagerly at the lights of Kalispell. Especially the lights of the saloon.

Patsy faced the swinging doors Michael stepped through. He hesitated, then idly watched the pretty girl excuse herself from conversation with a plainly disappointed logger before she approached him. Poised with his bedroll against his hip, the rangy boy knew women noticed him, but had never been subject to such a brazen advance.

"Hello. Like a little company?" He returned her smile, and noticed her sudden look of being off balance.

"Guess I'll have a beer." He didn't realize his voice, his smile, too, resembled those of another of the bar's customers.

"Buy me one, good lookin', and I'll protect

you from the vultures." She inclined her head.

Michael observed a magenta-haired whore taking his measure, her scowl turning to a leer.

"Why not? Just one, though. I have to be someplace pretty soon."

"Your girl's place?"

"No, the courthouse steps. I'm filing a claim as soon as they open up. Well, my mother is. We've got a place up on the North Fork."

"Up on the North Fork. That's the end of the world. You live up there alone, just you and your mama and the grizzly bears?" Patsy motioned to the bartender who brought beers. They picked them up and moved to a table sticky with spilled beer and peanut shells.

Michael laughed. "No. There are a few others."

"I heard there's a Chinaman up there married to a white woman."

Michael shifted a little in his chair, then gave her a hard look. "That would be Jim Li. A good man." He drank down his beer. "I'd best secure my spot, or my mother will give me a tongue-lashing that would silence even this place."

Patsy hoisted her unfinished glass.

■ ■ ■ ■

Michael headed down Main to the court-house, feeling loose from the alcohol. That night he slept curled against locked double doors at the courthouse entrance. A few others arrived later and sprawled, sleeping or murmuring, wrapped in blankets on the lawn. Michael dreamed of Dawn Mist, unaware that under hand-shaped leaves of a nearby oak, Bat Moriarty watched first him, then the purposeful, womanly figure of Nora Li striding through the graying dark.

Nora felt certain Michael would be first in line for filing their claim, Jim's and her dream about to come true. Nora Flanagan Larkin Li would own land free and clear, a beautiful place, too, even if it would never make her wealthy. It was already their home. She started as a tall man stepped out of the shadows. She couldn't make out his face as he pulled at the brim of his hat. "Sorry," was all she heard. She hurried past and forgot about him, intent on finding her son.

Once she did, Nora sat erect on the step beside Michael, hat and handbag in her lap, until the Clerk of Court and other county employees arrived to open their offices. First inside, Nora and Michael went to the lower floor to the door marked Land Office. Nora paid her $5.00 and filed her claim. They ascended the stairs like sleepwalkers. In outdoor sunshine, they read the document over and over.

"Wait until Jim sees this," Nora whispered. "Our family owns land. It will be yours after Jim and I are gone."

"Mine and Dawn's. And our children's. I'd like to talk to the priest about a wedding."

Nora beamed. The children were young, but their marriage would keep them all together. "I'm pleased if you'll agree to wait one more year for you both to be a bit older. It's good you'll stay on the North Fork. In spite of Dawn's beauty there are those wouldn't see past her being half-Blackfeet so would count your wife less than human. It's still that way for Jim and me."

"To hell with them. I can protect her." Michael's face reddened with anger and some disappointment at the proposed delay.

"Protecting innocence in ourselves is hard enough, my boyo. Protecting it in our loved ones may be impossible." She paused, glancing to the spires of St. Matthew's Church. "Ah, now, we'd better stop nattering about the souls of others and see to the dark spots on our own."

Afterward, they went shopping before boarding the train for Columbia Falls, then switching to the main line for Belton with other jubilant homesteaders.

A figure now wearing a duster and wide-brimmed hat pulled low above the white stubble of an unshaved face boarded the last car of the Gallopin' Goose. Celebrating homesteaders paid little attention to anyone else. Bat pulled the crown of his hat over his eyes and closed them. He hadn't been to bed, but anticipation wouldn't allow him restful sleep.

The Great Northern reached Belton after dark. Bat waited to be last out, then walked to the Belton Hotel. Since Nora and Michael weren't there, he left, following the sound of voices. He spotted mother and son in a team-drawn wagon heading across the bridge that now spanned the Middle Fork. He heard Nora talking, her words silvery and light, like moonbeams on water. "It will be good to be at Apgar again."

Bat cursed in a hoarse whisper. He'd have to get a horse and follow them. He didn't want to call attention to himself by taking a room at the hotel in this mountain hamlet where, even with the railroad, a stranger might be remarked. Some bewhiskered busybody would strike up a conversation, and Bat didn't feel like talking. He wanted to be sharp, savor every moment.

He rousted the livery owner, picked out a big gray, and fastened his portmanteau to the saddle horn. He paid a high price for the gelding, but needed a mount with strong lungs and legs. He rode slow and quiet on the bridge and on to the edge of Apgar to a spot hidden by evergreen and moss-hung larch. He unsaddled and hobbled the gray, lit a cigarette, closed his eyes, and leaned against the reedy bark of a towering cedar, waiting for first light.

Night dragged. To avoid unwanted attention, he hadn't built a fire. He ached from cold by the time the mountains across Lake McDonald hulked black against graying sky. Then Bat grunted and pushed stiffly to his feet, his brain sluggish from the thin air and lack of sleep. Splashing water from McDonald Creek on his face, he shuddered from the shock of it on his stubbled skin.

He led his gray past a collection of buildings, cabins mostly facing the lake. Mist hovered above its glassy surface, clouds flagging the cirques and peaks at the water's far end.

Bat walked to a lean-to beside a cabin

where he spied the ample rumps of Nora and Michael's team in the shadowy interior. Bat remounted, guiding the gelding toward the North Fork. After a short distance, he stopped behind a stand of willow and huckleberry and waited, absently stroking his mount's twitching neck.

An hour later they drew near. Michael's voice could be Bat's own. Then he heard Nora. He couldn't make out their words, but both sounded happy. Excited. Making plans. The muscles in Bat's jaw tensed in a spasm of fury. Nora Larkin had profited from Jim Li's theft. Well, they were in for a nasty letdown. Vengeance had chosen her moment.

He permitted his prey to roll out of sight. No one would intrude between them. The day warmed. He relaxed because he hadn't lost them, hadn't been stopped. As he rode, he listened to birdsong, the plod of the gelding's hooves, and the distant lilt of a woman's voice from an old memory.

Hours later, Bat lifted his head and observed Nora and Michael stop at the Hogans'. He skirted the meadow, watching them unharness their team and enter the house. He moved to the cover of trees. The gray disliked sorting its way off the trail, the forest a tangle of fallen, rotting vegetation and new growth. Bat cursed. It would be another cold, fireless night.

Full daylight. Bat sat up flexing cold-stiffened fingers. A pair of deer fled, white flags vertical, when he hunched over the stream to drink and splash his face. He swallowed laudanum. He couldn't remember when he'd last eaten. It didn't matter. He felt sharp — the blade of a knife — the head of an arrow. He hadn't given detailed thought to how he would do it. Now he didn't think it necessary to plan. Nora and their son would lead him.

He swung astride the gelding and turned at the meadow's edge, moving through a sea of bubble-like white bear grass, blossoms higher than his mount's knees. Nora and Michael looked like dolls readying their team. Nora embraced the large woman who walked them to the wagon and waved them on their way.

Bat trailed at a safe distance. A strange thing happened as he rode. The colors around him, of trees and the panorama of mountains to the east, became unnaturally vivid, almost glowing in their outlines, the grass like green fire. In spite of the laudanum, his heart hammered. He felt a new sensation. The other lives he'd taken were accidents or based on the impulse to survive, self-defense as he remembered them. This was different. The pronounced greens lit with an almost yellow-white tinge. He struggled to keep from becoming too distracted for clear thought. There would never be another chance, or a better day.

Nora and Michael crossed the river. At the landing, the North Fork flowed broad and high. He watched their wagon dip and disappear down the bank, then after moments, rise up on the other side and keep going. He moved upstream and forced the reluctant bay into roiling water.

On the opposite bank, he checked his revolver, the Bowie knife sheathed inside his boot.

Jim and Nora made love that night. He knew she felt pleased for him, the claim filed in her name, but meant for them both. Elation rose in him like sap in a young man Michael's age.

It had been a fixed happiness that his love for Nora grew and intensified. Although she physically resembled the women he'd first seen in Butte, her thinking was as a person who was part of the life here, part of the wilderness, one with him. She flowed with it. His wife was neither frail nor fragile, more like some wildflower flourishing where he'd brought her, nourished and strong.

Jim also gave his joyful blessing to the children's marriage.

He lay in morning's first light, stroking Nora's breast, firm as a girl's. She slumbered after so much love. He moved his hand to her cheek, kissed her forehead, then extricated himself from their bed, pulling on his buckskin shirt, wool pants, and worn boots. Nora sighed, turning away from the door. He paused to appreciate the fall of her still lovely hair over one white shoulder and the mound of her womanly hip under the quilt. Drawn to go back, to arch over her again, instead he closed the door behind him. There would be time after the day's work.

He ate biscuits with Michael and went outside to begin mending the plow blade. Later he would hunt, scouting for next winter's trap line as well. Jim imagined anything might come into the sights of his Winchester that day, a black cougar, an albino elk — anything.

Today Nora would rise and reread her claim document, then gather her baskets to accompany him across the river to search out medicinal plants and roots, heal all, onions, spring beauty, and mint. Dawn had gardening and baking to do at the cabin. The other three would camp across the river that night, return in the morning, and plan a family engagement celebration. Perhaps the four of them could talk about the future after they returned tomorrow evening. It pleased him that the results of his and Nora's work would pass to loved ones.

Bat crossed downstream, watching from the forest's cover. He spotted Jim Li and cursed, fingering his .45. The tall man had become a muscular giant, long hair hanging over buckskin-covered shoulders, a Chinese mountain man. Li carried a rifle. Nora, a pack over her shoulder, had a knife and digging tools hanging from her baskets. Li also carried a pack, going somewhere on foot. The stalker bared his teeth in a grin. This would be easier than he thought. He could pick his time. He watched Nora and Jim walk side by side toward the river, joined by Michael when they reached the bank.

He rode the gray back across the water after seeing them row to the far side in a small boat. He pulled up on a stand of aspen, tethered the gelding, and, panting, followed on foot.

Jim planned to scout good places for traps

on Bowman Creek, then make camp at Bowman Lake where Michael, hunting on his own, would join him. Nora motioned that she planned to dig for herbs on a ledge a distance from her husband. He nodded and moved ahead, thinking they would fish at the lake if Michael didn't find other meat by evening. Jim stepped into the icy creek up to his knees to check a likely pooling spot for a beaver trap. He took comfort in knowing the water ran too shallow for a man to drown in it. The bloated water spirits couldn't reach up from unseen depths and pull him to them.

His side vision caught movement in the brush. A bear? Then over the soft rush of water, he heard the click of a hammer being pulled. Turning, he caught the revolver's gleam. The shot came simultaneous with the image.

Jim twisted, falling forward to his hand and knees in the creek. His shocked reflection stared back, then the gaunt, ravaged face of a man long dead above him. The face wavered in the water, but its mouth moved as a hand clutched Jim's hair, yanking his head back.

"Remember me, Li? It's Bat Moriarty. Moriarty, the man you left for dead in a burning whorehouse. You stole my ring and

I intend to kill you for doing that." Bat forced Jim's head into the water.

Jim saw her then. One draped hand reached above the ghost's pale, watery features. His heart broke for Nora as the spirit pulled him down. But the ghost vanished and a small, porcelain woman took its place, bowing and laughing, holding out her arms.

"Welcome, my son. How I have longed to talk with you."

No longer feeling pain or cold, Jim moved toward his mother, borne on watery light toward the fulfillment of an old longing.

Michael yelled, running through the trees. "No! No! Jim! Let him go, you bastard!"

The white-haired killer released Jim, stepping from the water with a mad, triumphant glare.

Michael raised his gun and pointed. "Pull him out. Now."

A grim, weary smile met the order, and the man bent back toward the stream. "Don't give orders to your father," he said as he turned again. The knife flew so fast Michael missed the flick of its wielder's scarred wrist.

Michael fired just before the blade sliced his arm. He dropped the gun as Jim's pale attacker fell, clutching his chest. Michael staggered to the creek. With his good arm he pulled Jim out and onto his stomach and pushed on his back. Jim coughed and groaned, blood running from his shoulder.

Michael moved to the assailant who whispered, "You just killed your own father, boy."

"You're Tade Larkin?" Michael asked it as a reflex.

"Bat Moriarty. Ask Nora Larkin about me. About the ring."

Michael heard the sputtering exhalation of death. Blood dribbled from Bat Moriarty's mouth.

Then Nora was there, holding Jim, tearing off his shirt to see the wound. Michael sat on the ground in shock.

"The bullet went through," she said. "I'll put cold water to staunch the bleeding. If it won't quit we'll have to cauterize. Build a fire, Michael."

Michael started to shiver hard, cold to his belly, and in pain now from his freely bleeding wound. He slid over to her. "I'm hurt. He got me with his knife before I shot him." The forest shaded now into dim gray-green and he knew it would be dark before long, and colder.

Nora scooped up moss and plastered it

against his arm, tearing a strip from her skirt. Michael awkwardly fastened it in a clumsy knot with his right hand and his teeth. Nora told him to hold a piece of Jim's shirt against the bullet hole while she scrambled to gather sticks and light a fire. She lit a stick and without speaking twisted Michael's hand off Jim and pressed the twig's burning end on the bleeding wound, front and back. Jim's eyes rolled back as he fainted. Then Michael heard the crashing of a large animal through the trees.

Michael scrambled for his gun until he heard Beartracks's voice. "Don't shoot. It's me. I found this big gray tethered by the creek and then heard shots. My god, what's gone on here?"

Michael's arm had bled through the moss and ineffective bandage. When he tried to rise, his knees buckled and instead of speech, his voice caught in a sob of relief. The darkening forest spun around him.

"All right, boy," Beartracks said. "All right. Stay there. My god, Nora, somebody shot old China Jim? Who did this?"

Michael heard no answer and closed his eyes to the sound of cloth tearing.

"Drink this." Michael gagged on Beartracks's whiskey, then grasped the bottle and took a manageable swig. It seared his throat, but his stomach stopped quivering.

"What happened?" Beartracks asked again. "What took place here?"

Michael related the story in a few sentences. Nora held Jim, who didn't regain consciousness, but moaned. She tore more bandages from her skirt and wrapped blankets around both her wounded.

Beartracks got up and nudged Bat's long thin body with his boot, then knelt to search the pockets. He pulled out a bloodstained flask, opened it, and sniffed. "Laudanum. There's no identification." He pulled the fingerless gloves off the corpse's hands and studied the vein-like scars and the bony face with its blood-crusted stubble of white beard. A consumed, terrible visage.

"He was evil," Nora's hoarse voice declared. "There was a fight in Helena. Jim thought Bat was dead and pulled the diamond ring off his hand. We sold it to come here. His evil followed us. I sensed it always but didn't understand how it could be."

"His ring?" Michael asked, fastening on the almost magical image. "His ring?"

"I'll explain tomorrow. It's Jim's and my story, long overdue for the telling."

Michael fell into a sleep filled with death-ridden nightmares and pain. At one point he opened his eyes to see Beartracks waving a torch at some creature whose eyes glowed just beyond the body of the man who claimed to have been Michael's father.

In the morning, Beartracks made a travois to carry Jim, weak, but now awake. Michael rode as Beartracks led the gray pulling its burden. Nora walked beside them. She felt half-dead herself, her hair a snarled tangle. Once the wounded and she were rowed across and settled at the cabin, Beartracks took a shovel back across the river to bury Bat Moriarty in an unmarked grave.

Jim sipped broth, then slept, Dawn watching over him. Nora joined Michael on the porch. Her heart lurched at the sight of his rigid profile. "I'm that glad you're alive. I wouldn't know what to do if . . ."

Michael glared from pain-sunken eyes. "Are you? Yeah, I know you are. But I want to know everything. Is it true? Did I shoot down my own father yesterday? Who was he? Who are you?"

Nora locked her gaze on the craggy, indifferent peaks across the river. She felt Michael and herself, the others as well, to be so small. Belief in their insignificance soothed her, gave her courage to start. She told everything, from meeting Bat on the train to Butte, to Tade's death, to Bat as her lodger and finding out he had a family, to her pregnancy, to Helen's death, to meeting Jim and working at Lillie McGraw's, and finally the fire and the ring and sending Michael to Butte. She even told about selling it to Sean Kehoe.

Michael stared at her when she finished. "Who else knew about this, about this Bat Moriarty?"

"The Murphys. Bridget and Michael. A priest, no two priests. But don't you see? It doesn't matter. If Tade had lived, he would have been your father."

"Well, he didn't. This scarred-up, murdering, drug-fiend gambler was. Hell, I have brothers and sisters. You should have told me. You were a whore, too, weren't you? You're still not telling everything. I killed my own father." His voice broke and he twisted, turning his back on her.

Nora flared in anger. "I never was. I never was an upstairs girl!"

Michael only gave her a bold look, shrugged, and strode back inside.

Nora heard Beartracks's voice speaking to Michael from where he was having a late breakfast after his grim task. "You killed a man. I remember my own killing of a liquored-up trapper one rendezvous. I was barely twenty. That man wasn't even a relative, and I still hate the memory. But you have a life here. Whatever Nora's done, it's been to have and provide a decent life. She and Jim have been fine parents to Dawn."

Michael's response broke Nora's heart. "Well, not to me."

and I will miss the freedom we've
shared this past winter when we leave this
house and live quietly . . . I dread this. She
might have been your parents to Dawn's
Michael's happened . . . the Nora's been so
Will marry me.

CHAPTER TWENTY-SEVEN

For six weeks, Michael let only Dawn change his bandage, using a mix of beeswax and tallow on the wound. He ate on the porch and slept in the barn. As the cut healed, he resumed what chores he could, never speaking to Nora.

One day he went to the barn to throw his gear together.

Dawn Mist appeared in the doorway, her form flat against the outside light.

"How is Jim today?" he asked. He hadn't spoken to Jim either, but remembered the conversation between Jim and Nora the night he'd arrived . . . Jim trying to convince Nora to be truthful. He understood now what it had been about.

Dawn took his hand. "Mama and Papa are resting in their room. They're so troubled. Can't you forgive her?"

He shook his head. "I can't stay around them."

"You can't leave me." Dawn's voice rose in protest.

"We can both leave."

"Leave here?" Fright sparked her eyes.

"Ride with me." He stroked her cheek. "Come with me. I love you. We'll get married."

"But Mama needs us. Beartracks says Jim won't be able to work for two more months."

"Neighbors will help. Beartracks will provide meat. Come with me. I can't stay. I can't be around her."

"What will we do?"

"I'll hire on somewhere. It'll be all right."

"You mean to leave no matter what, and I can't be apart from you even if it breaks their hearts. All right, but you know Mama loves you."

Camped in the meadow that night, leaning on one elbow as he poked at his small campfire, Beartracks heard, then saw, the gray with two riders pass by under the vast sky with its countless stars. He sighed. There'd be the devil to pay with Nora and Jim, but he didn't think anyone could stop the youngsters. The boy had to be on his own for a while and Dawn had to be with the boy.

443

He'd start following in the morning, tracking them until they settled somewhere. Then he'd report back to Nora and China Jim. He lay back and gazed up. A long-tailed comet crossed the constellations in impersonal silence, the ancient stars unshaken, unmoved.

A good thing for them, he decided.

Next morning Nora gave vent to her regrets while giving Jim a gentle sponge bath. "If we'd never taken that cursed ring. I've wished it before, but never more than now. Of course, I know for certain you believed you took it from a dead man." She fixed tormented eyes on Jim's. "I kept my promise to the Father in Helena and gave its worth to Deirdre."

"Do not think you create that much difference in this world. We cannot remake the past. There is nothing to do. Just bad fortune for us all." Jim reached out, wincing at the pain in his shoulder.

She wept against his good shoulder. "I don't even know how Bat found us."

"How does an owl find a rabbit? If it waits long enough, it spots some little sign." He tipped her chin up and they kissed. "Bear-tracks will return as soon as he sees where our fledglings light to build their nest. We haven't lost them forever."

Nora tried to stifle a wish that Jim had been more alert when Bat stalked him in the soft ground, in the hushed green by the creek. She shooed away the thought that there must have been some foreign smell, some shadow, or at least some flight of startled birds.

Beartracks followed Michael and Dawn, camping one night, then on to his cabin at Apgar where they spent a second one while he camped down the beach. In the morning they rode east toward wind-blasted Marias Pass. They rode for days along the bare, sun-drenched eastern slopes, the terrain turning to prairie.

At Midvale, the two visited the clapboard Catholic Church. Beartracks assumed they might be saying confession. When they emerged, however, shaking hands with the priest who followed them to their horse, Beartracks grinned. "Married, by damn," he muttered.

They remounted and rode on to a ranch, a huge spread with the finest house for hundreds of miles. There the journey ended.

Beartracks waited two days before cantering under the brand-inscribed arch. Piano music, perhaps Chopin, wafted through the tasseled parlor curtains to evaporate in the dry, ceaseless prairie wind.

He knocked. The tune broke off. He doffed his hat and bowed slightly when the door opened. A tall, elegant woman lifted her eyebrows. Beartracks introduced himself and asked if Michael and Dawn worked at the ranch. The woman frowned, asking if there were trouble.

"No. No trouble at all. I know their folks, though, and they'd never forgive me if I passed this way and didn't bring back news of the youngsters."

The rancher's wife invited him to follow her through the house and back door. Dawn hung flapping sheets on the line, wind tugging at her braids and skirts. Two little girls played with dolls nearby in the shade of a cottonwood. Once she took in Dawn's joy at seeing Beartracks, the woman waved at her daughters and returned to the house. Dawn and Beartracks visited to renewed strains of Chopin.

Dawn wept as she told Beartracks she felt homesick. Their employers behaved in an impersonal and firm manner. Not mean, but with something unsaid, some attitude that announced Dawn was not and could never be as good as they. She, who had been cherished in Nora and Jim's cabin on the North Fork.

She sniffled as he patted her shoulder, but told Beartracks she now carried the name Dawn Larkin. After all the confusion, that's the name they chose to use. "All these changes. Sometimes people act so rude. You should have seen the stares we got in Midvale. I saw some Blackfeet women. I think I'll visit to see if any of them knew Sweet Grass."

Beartracks nodded. "I know something of this life in two worlds. You won't find it easy. Your mother's cousins live on the Blackfeet Reservation. You'd do well to find them." He fought to stifle a flash of anger. Michael should have kept this lovely, happily sheltered girl away from so-called civilization.

He left, telling Dawn he'd visit from time to time. He told her to greet Michael.

He pulled the brim of his hat in a cool, polite gesture to the rancher's wife as he left.

Jim healed over the next months. One morning in late spring he returned from a long walk to tell Nora of a dance being held at some new neighbors, the Muellers'.

"Oh, I don't believe I'm in a dancing mood. They'll all ask about Michael and

Dawn. You and I do best to keep to ourselves even now we're all legal and legitimate."

Jim persisted until Nora changed her mind. On the afternoon of the dance, she took pains to look better than just tidy for the first time since the children ran off. She wore a soft blue dress, trimmed in white lace and buttons. Her hair, less fiery, more the color of bracken in autumn, still caught the light. Waiting for Jim, she pulled a white shawl around her shoulders and gazed toward the mountains. The Blackfeet were right to call the Rockies the backbone of the world.

"Backbone. Sure and I need backbone, too," Nora spoke aloud. "That and pride. Folks will know our Michael left. All our business. As bad as in Ireland."

Leading the horse, Jim walked to her. He put his long fingers on her waist, lifted her easily, and sprang behind her. His breath stirred the blue ribbon and unruly tendrils at the nape of her neck and she felt for a moment like the hopeful young woman who'd arrived here so long ago. Leaning lightly against him, grateful for his recovery from the bullet wound, she felt her mood lift.

The ride took them overland through heavy

forest to Mueller's meadow. Outside the house, a middle-aged woman seated at a piano on one corner of the wooden platform played "In the Good Old Summer Time" while dancers turned and swayed. Tables laden with bread, pies, salads, and roast game strung in a line away from the house. Neighbors greeted them with welcoming shouts and Nora realized they were recognized now for themselves, not just an Irish-Chinese oddity.

Nan Hogan put her arms around Nora in a welcoming hug. Others did as well. After all the years, Jim had earned the respect, if not the affection, of his neighbors. There were smiles and friendly calls of, "China Jim!"

The piano player commenced "In the Good Old Summer Time" again.

"It's a lovely tune, but doesn't the woman at the piano know any other melodies?" Nora asked.

"No. As a matter of fact, she doesn't," Nan answered. "But it's a good tune to dance to. We'd be in trouble if she only knew hymns."

Nora felt almost happy dancing in Jim's arms. No more stares, at least among these neighbors. Stars wheeled behind Jim's head. Nora relaxed into the fun. She danced with bewhiskered men and shared news with neighbor women. After keeping to herself since Bat's raid, she blossomed in the nearly forgotten ease of simple neighborly chats.

At midnight, the North Fork residents shared a feast, toasting the Muellers with homemade rhubarb wine, transparent as air. The pianist resumed "In the Good Old Summer Time." A nearly forgotten sense of belonging washed over Nora.

"Here," Jim said, taking off his deer hide jacket and swirling it over her shoulders like a cape. She drew the jacket around her, aware of the heat from his skin and the wild, earthy scent of pine and wood smoke that clung to his clothes.

Jim watched her with a little smile. "There can be almost nothing like doeskin," he said, "for keeping us warm."

The night tinted indigo to lighter blue just before the pink flood of dawn. The exhausted pianist played the last chorus and punchy, laughing dancers stopped for a breakfast of fish and sourdough pancakes served with elderberry or huckleberry syrup. Afterward, they prepared for their long rides home. Jim lifted Nora onto the big appaloosa. They crossed Trail Creek, water sparkling over its rocks until Nora turned away, dazzled by the brightness. She saw them then, a stag with magnificent antlers, one notched in a distinctive mark. The doe beside him paused at the water's edge as if to see what this human couple meant, entering their morning.

"Look," Nora whispered. "Hart and hind, as we'd say in the old lands."

"Stag and doe. A pretty sight," Jim said. "We'll see their fawn with the doe soon."

The appaloosa moved through light slanting over pale lichen-draped green branches down to curving ferns. "But, it's an enchanted place. I never think otherwise. I still expect to see the wee folk."

Jim said, "If one showed himself, somebody would shoot him or put him in a cage and haul it over to Apgar like Andre L'Hommidieu does with his mountain lions."

"Perhaps not. They're clever, more so than we mortals."

"That would not require too much."

They rode on in silence. As the sun warmed her, Nora's head drooped, nodded, and the landscape's images doubled. She leaned back against Jim. Then, remembering his shoulder still gave him twinges of pain from time to time, she straightened.

"It's all right," he said. "My shoulder can still stand the weight of a little wife like you."

Nora leaned back again, feeling slight movement as he continued to guide the appaloosa past shining spider webs and scolding squirrels.

She woke at the cabin. Jim lifted her down and gestured toward the woodpile, indicating he'd chop wood after seeing to the horse.

"We're about out of meat," Nora said.

"Not for long. I'll hunt."

They left early next morning to go to the Kintla cabin. Nora dressed in men's pants and braided her hair in one thick rope below her wide-brimmed hat. When they forded the creek near the rustic cabin, Nora using a walking stick for balance from flat rock to flat rock, they saw two deer again. Jim raised his rifle, but Nora put her hand on his arm.

"Wait. I don't know how it can be, but look at that great boy's antlers."

"It's the same one all right. Look at the gouge on the one point."

Later, before the small blaze in the rough fireplace, Jim released the ribbon fastening Nora's braid, loosening the three bright plaits one by one. Then he spread the undone hair over her shoulders. He bent to kiss her. They moved into long-familiar rituals of an old love, understanding each other in passion as in all necessary things.

■ ■ ■ ■

In a year, Nora proved up her claim. Without Michael and Dawn she lacked the joy she'd anticipated holding the deed would bring, but Jim and she acknowledged it as the culmination of all their efforts. Jim went with her to Kalispell, but refused to enter the church. She said her confession, rejoining him afterward with a troubled expression. "Oh," she said in answer to Jim's question, "the priest believes you should be a practicing Catholic, you know."

"He may keep his belief," was the response. "Let's buy the supplies we need and go home."

"Let's go home," Nora agreed.

At Evening Star, Nora tried to stop herself from looking to the river several times every day to see whether Michael and Dawn might not be riding over the bank toward home. "Evening Star is your home," she whispered to her absent children. "It's where you belong. Jim and I are keeping it for you. Forgive us for the mistakes of the past and come home."

But as the pale light of late summer rested on the quiet mountains only deer moved toward her from the river except for the occasional hunters or settlers. There was talk of a national park to be established on the east side of the North Fork. Nora and Jim heard with relief that the west side would not be included in the government's plans.

"Everything has to stay as it is," Nora fretted. "Michael and Dawn will come back to us one day. They must be homesick for Evening Star by now."

She began to lose weight, looking thin and strained. As they lay in bed one night, Jim tried to comfort her. "They are young. We moved across the world when we were young. Alone and much farther than they are from home."

"Ah, yes. I was younger when I sailed from Ireland than Dawn is now. Just fourteen I was, even younger than Michael when he showed up here. What a day that was when he walked back into our lives. You were right. I should have told him the truth that night. I only wanted to keep him here with us. What would he have done, then, I wonder?"

They had switched sides of the bed after Jim's shoulder wound. It felt backward to Nora to be on the outside. She burrowed against him. He stroked her hair.

"You weren't ready to tell him, so we'll

never know if Michael would have been ready to hear the truth. All we know is that there is sadness now. Let's hope that from it will come a day of joy. I believe they will forgive us and return." He winced. The shoulder still hurt after a day's strenuous work.

Nora waited until he slept, then slipped away to the kitchen. She sat at the table over a cup of coffee, recalling the past. She'd sat like this at her kitchen table in Butte, waiting for Bat to return. Now she waited for Michael. She shook her head in annoyance, stood and rinsed her cup before setting it on the counter.

As she sometimes did, she touched her framed copy of the deed to Evening Star, hung on the wall next to a map of the world Jim had used to teach Dawn. A memory of their two dark heads bent over books at the table pierced her. In many ways she missed Dawn more often than Michael, especially inside where they'd cleaned, prepared meals, and sewed together. Nora felt short of breath, closed within the silent rooms.

She stepped outside. The full moon illuminated the earth near and far. Their work shone before her, cabin, outbuildings, fences, gardens, and meadows. The cattle and horses moved a little, restless at the sound of her steps on the porch, then as she walked toward the river. Nora turned and surveyed Jim's and her accomplishments. The sight comforted her. Whatever else changed, she and Jim had their life here, the buildings and animals on the ranch something she could grasp in her hands.

The mountains weren't human; therefore weren't subject to all the skittering dramas creatures like Nora and those she'd encountered seemed destined to engender. The glacial peace never failed to calm her. "Well," she whispered to the range to the east. "You'll not be going anywhere. Remote as you are, you've always brought me the peace of my insignificance. Still, I miss Michael and Dawn."

She walked on toward the river's soft gushing. Another constant. The land had settled into its steady, dark, indifferent nocturne of forest stillness, broken only by the twig snaps and brushings of little night creatures. The permanence comforted her. As moonset began, Nora felt hope, then certainty. All her immigrant life she'd experienced gains and losses in waves. Some buoyed her, some threatened to pull her under, but she'd held her dreams above any rising tide.

Michael would come back and Dawn with

him. She couldn't see them now, but this place, her and Jim's land, would draw them back. It waited for them, what she and Jim had created to bequeath. And what if those were right who said we can't ever truly own land? Well, here she stood, her own ranch behind her . . . a pretty good illusion of landowning, for certain. But in the end it wouldn't really matter. She belonged here as the creatures around her did. Her children as well. It owned them and they owned it, by virtue of belonging. They'd made themselves part of the permanence.

Nora kept watch through moonset until first light peered over the peaks. She tipped her head back as the first light of morning rose over the timeless peaks. She heard the cabin door open and footsteps approach. Jim Li came to be with her.

In time, their children would do the same.

ABOUT THE AUTHOR

Karen Wills lives with her husband just a few miles from her beloved Glacier National Park in northwest Montana. Their children are grown. She loves to write, hike, read, and visit with family and friends. She is also an active volunteer for social justice. Karen has practiced law, including representing plaintiffs in civil rights cases. She also taught English and writing at the college and secondary public school levels, including at the Cheyenne River Sioux Reservation in South Dakota, and in the Inupiaq Eskimo village of Wales, Alaska. She's encountered bears, both grizzly and polar, and still believes passionately in the value of wild creatures and country.